Advance Praise for Read by Strangers

"Philip Dean Walker's *Read by Strangers* is a nightmare wrapped in a riddle dipped in epiphany. His attention to detail, especially in his characters, makes living, breathing, complicated people heft themselves out of the page, fully-formed creatures from his madcap lagoon. Particularly the way he sees inside women and their often secret, darkest views on motherhood, on aging, on desire, on the aging of their once desirable husbands…he embodies the night-vines of our own admissions, those that sneak up our chests and wind around our throats."
—Julia Whelan, author of *My Oxford Year*

"The stories that comprise Philip Dean Walker's *Read by Strangers* are sexually frank, intriguingly open-ended, and nuanced in their depictions of flawed human nature. Walker is a talented and observant storyteller whose plots and characterizations engage and unnerve in equal measures."
—Wally Lamb, author of *I Know This Much Is True*

"Vividly and bitingly rendered, these stories often made me morally and even politically uncomfortable, which might well be the point. Highly reminiscent of John Cheever, Richard Yates, Bret Easton Ellis and others who excelled at writing people, especially women, at their lowest, *Read by Strangers* seems confident in its sometimes surreal cruelties, perhaps to try to shake us out of our own worst instincts."
—Tim Murphy, author of *Christodora*

"Philip Dean Walker's writing in *Read by Strangers* is precise as a tuning fork, full of sentences whose beauty left me trembling and characters at the edge of unraveling who pulled me to precipices. These stories vibrate in the spaces of absence and desire, in what lurks in legend, in the uncertain waters of the fringe. Walker has a knack for knowing what's just out of reach, what humans risk slipping into, and in these pages he brings us to the recesses of unlit hallways from which a person, a reader, a character, return absolutely changed. A moving, gripping collection to stay up late with."

—Angela Palm, author of *Riverine: A Memoir from Anywhere but Here*

"Walker's sophomore effort is as sharply written and rich with character detail as his debut collection, though these stories feel a bit more personal, a bit more complex and grounded with a subtle and profound beauty."

—Scott Hess, author of *Skyscraper*

"As much as it is a collection of stories, Philip Dean Walker's *Read by Strangers* is a collection of characters. He documents the basic human struggle against the inertia of everyday life. He confronts loss and the possibility of loss. Hopes and the impossibility of hope. Most importantly, he celebrates small moments and locates humanness in corners of the world most other authors don't even think to look."

—Zach Powers, author of *Gravity Changes*

Read by
Strangers

ALSO BY PHILIP DEAN WALKER:

At Danceteria and Other Stories

Read by Strangers

❀ PHILIP DEAN WALKER ❀

❀ LETHE PRESS ❀
Amherst, Massachusetts

Read by Strangers

Published in 2018 by Lethe Press, Inc.
6 University Drive • Suite 206 / PMB #223 • Amherst, MA 01002 USA
www.lethepressbooks.com • lethepress@aol.com
ISBN: 978-1-59021-678-1 / 1-59021-678-4

The stories in this volume are works of fiction. Names, characters, places, and incidents are products of the author's imagination or are used fictiously.

The following stories first appeared in these magazines/anthologies:
"Unicorn": *Big Lucks*, Volume 4 (Summer 2011)
"Caravan": *Collective Fallout*, Volume 4 Nos. 1 & 2 (September 2012)
"Brad's Head Revisited, '94": *Glitterwolf Magazine*, Volume 3 (March 2013)
"Three-Sink Sink": *Pay for Play*, ed. R. Talent, Bold Strokes Books (May 2013)
"Women of a Certain Age": *theNewerYork, The Electric Encyclopedia of Experimental Literature* (August 2013)
"A Cup of Fur": *Anak Sastra*, Volume 17 (October 2014)
"A Goddess Lying Breathless in Carnage": *Driftwood Press*, Volume 2.2 (April 2015)
"Why Burden a Baby With a Body?": *Carbon Culture Review* (October 2015)
"Ten Seconds": *Lunch Review* (November 2015)

Set in Minion, Myriad, Bookman Old Style, and Didot.
Interior design: Alex Jeffers.
Cover design: Inkspiral Design.
Cover photo: Philip Dean Walker.
Author photo: Robert C. Walker.

LIBRARY OF CONGRESS CATALOGING-IN-PUBLICATION DATA
Names: Walker, Philip Dean, author.
Title: Read by strangers / Philip Dean Walker.
Description: Amherst, Massachusetts : Lethe Press, 2018.
Identifiers: LCCN 2018005664 | ISBN 9781590216781 (pbk. : alk. paper)
Classification: LCC PS3623.A4383 A6 2018 | DDC 813/.6--dc23
LC record available at https://lccn.loc.gov/2018005664

To my grandmother, SUE POWELL CARR (1926-2009), for her love and support and for being the strongest woman I've ever known.

Contents

"It is as though upon a face carved by a savage caricaturist a monstrous burlesque of all bereavement flowed."

—William Faulkner, *As I Lay Dying* (1930)

Unicorn

THE HOUSE IS MOSTLY HIDDEN by trees. The neighbors are happy for this fact, the ramshackle eyesore the place has become. But if it's a sunny day, and you look to your left right after passing the old campaign signs for the school board, you can just barely see it—a shadowy glimpse through the leaves.

Four acres of farmland flank it on both sides, but our town is so well past those days that no one has any idea what might've once grown there. The folks in the new development across the street loathe the house, even though you practically have to strain your neck to really see the place. The old mailbox with the cover dangling off its hinge, an overgrown slope of lawn in front of it filled with weeds and garbage, the things they've heard that go on there now—people turn their heads. No one can do anything about it, though. Apparently, the house is still owned.

We hear the story from our parents, a cautionary tale. It's told alongside other local legends such as the mother who locked her children in the basement then burned her house down. "She taught a bridge class once a week and served the most delicious macaroons and homemade strawberry wine," our own mothers are quick to add in her defense. And then there were the four teenagers who careened off Bob-o-link Road in a homecoming convertible and smashed into an oak tree, their bodies flung about in impossible, Gumby-like positions. There are clear lessons to be learned from each of these stories: Don't piss off your mother—it might be that one bad day too many, and she could have matches. Don't drink and drive. It's parenting through storytelling, and for the most part, it works.

But we don't know what to do with this house's tale, even though we've heard it many times and it grows more alive each time. The family's name is never mentioned. They had a horse and a daughter who wished more than anything to ride it. The mother worked in the cafeteria at our elementary school a few years before we started going there. They say she always dressed up for holidays (a mermaid for Halloween serving up orange pudding with blackberries on top, an Indian squaw for Thanksgiving mixing the corn gravy). From what we've heard, the father didn't do much of anything. He might've been perpetually looking for work or just taking care of that horse, a palomino a rich uncle had left him, his most treasured possession. The daughter wanted to ride the horse, but her father wouldn't permit it. She was too young, he said, and besides, they didn't own a proper saddle. We may not know her name, but we know what she did next.

One night she snuck down to the barn where they kept the horse. She brought a small footstool from the bathroom and attempted to climb onto the horse from behind, pulling herself up with the frightened thing's tail. The palomino didn't know her from a raccoon, as her father had never let her get near it, and when he felt someone come up from behind, he got nervous and kicked that girl in the head. She died with the half-round imprint of a horseshoe on her forehead that, we can only presume, had to be covered with makeup, if the family even had a viewing. We picture the little girl in a white dress with flowers by her side at her funeral. The barn later burned to the ground with the horse trapped inside. Then the parents disappeared.

WE CLIMB IN THROUGH A window on the back porch, careful not to scratch ourselves on the sharp edges of the frame. We find ourselves in the laundry room. The linoleum has curled in places, lifting itself away from the floor, and the middle of the floor is damp, sunken, quickly on its way to meet the basement. A stale pile of towels sits between the Maytag washer and dryer, with a few crusty socks sticking out like worms. A pink training bra is visible next to a black drain in the floor. Boxes of Tide are set up along a plank of white-painted wood, the labels discolored by the sun. The design of the insignia is different from the liquid detergent our mothers use. The lettering is bubbly and ecstatic, reminding us of Coke cans in '80s movies. Someone suggests we move on; there's nothing worth seeing here. A Mason jar shut tight with a lid and filled with loose change tips over as we leave. It rolls to the center of the room, then stops, letting the coins rest against the glass. It is mutually acknowledged that the house must hold a larger boon.

A narrow hallway leads to a living room, which one of us is quick to rename "the dying room," as a musty smell of abandonment lies in each dark corner. The girl's mother must've favored brown, orange, and all the hideous hues in between that now anxiously stand out in checks and circles on the couch and lazy-printed love seat. We sit down and sink into the cushions. They've become more decrepit with age, the stuffing inside eaten through by summer bugs that long ago must have claimed a free reign over the place. Yellowed newspapers litter the floor, hot-brown shag carpeting peeking through in patches like fresh mulch. We pick up copies of the *The Washington Post*, which all seem to span a four-month period in 1981.

A creased *TV Guide* on the coffee table that chronicles the week of May seventeenth of the same year confirms something we've heard before: the house died with the girl. This seems to have occurred at some point in the year that we turned three. *The Goodbye Girl*, a Saturday-afternoon matinee feature on Channel 20, is circled in red ink then crossed out in checklist fashion.

We break open a filing cabinet and take out papers typed in outdated fonts on stiff paper. There are bank statements, property deeds, report cards. We find out their last name, Innsbruck; her name, Jeannette. She got straight A's (a B once in gym), was well liked by her teachers, and was absent only one day during the 1978–79 school year. After we've pored over the papers for more clues, we toss them to the floor with the newspapers, adding more years to the pile.

Someone hauls over a stack of records documenting a bad taste in early folk music and Christian rock. We erupt into vicious hysterics, laughing at the shaggy togetherness of the singers on the jacket covers. They're draped over one another in long knitted shawls and bellbottoms appliquéd with floral garlands that snake up their legs. We hurl a couple of the records against the wood-paneled walls like Frisbees. They break into pieces of sharp black pie wedges and fall behind the couch to join layers of dust and the jagged curls of discarded fingernails. We glean a sense of mock ownership of the place from our ability to destroy the things inside it. We discuss the idea of heading upstairs. There's got to be something more up there, some tragic token of the family's demise.

Many of the steps are broken through. Someone scratches a bare ankle on a splintered piece of wood. It's our first sign that others have been here before us. We grab the crooked banister for balance to negotiate the warped, wobbling steps, and the entire banister falls to the ground, landing on the hideous couch and catapulting to the floor dead horseflies upon which we'd been unknowingly sitting.

We see rectangular squares of discolored wallpaper where pictures once hung, holes that once held nails staggered along at eye level. When we reach the top of the stairs, we see the only picture that still remains and it's perfectly aligned. The photograph shows the exterior of the house in a much earlier time, long before the Innsbrucks. A picnic table is populated with summer foods, a round glass pitcher filled with a dark, sustaining liquid. The porch is level and intact, with a row of old women sitting in rocking chairs, women whose eyes are darkened by the shadows of the trees before them, trees that haven't yet taken over the front yard. They're tamed and cut and seem to understand their primary purpose of providing cool blankets of shade. A new Model-T Ford is parked askew, half out of the picture's frame. A young blond man has one boot propped on the thin bumper, smiling as if he's the proud, lucky owner. A girl in a fringed dress with short-cut, sheer, flowing sleeves stands half hidden behind one of the Ionic columns. She's smoking a cigarette. The profile of her nose is so well captured against the piece of late-afternoon sun that peeks behind her that it looks like a steep ski jump and is so distinct that it's almost freakish. She also appears to be the only person unaware that a photograph is being taken.

The first bedroom is to the left of the staircase. A queen-size bed takes up most of the floor space. Old books thickened with dampness are interspersed with broken hairbrushes and the cord of an ancient electric heater in the middle of the mattress. The headboard is cracked in places and, like the rest of the house, threatens collapse. We pick through the heap of junk on the floor and find the first thing we'll take with us—an unused leather diary from 1975 still in its plastic wrapping, warped underneath despite.

The closet is filled with old clothes, nothing worth taking, all of it cataloging a utilitarian sense of fashion, unadorned and unaffected by changing styles. Animals have been here before us, which we can see from the droppings they've left inside shoes and crumbling into the floor in places we've just stepped. The bureau is empty, everything already on the floor. We pull out the drawers anyway and throw one against a long mirror that hangs precariously on the wall above the bed. It shatters into pieces, but the frame stays hung on the wall. Something has fallen loose from behind it, and we dig it out from the shards of reflective glass. It's a Polaroid of a young, thin girl with long brown hair and dark circles under her eyes. She's naked and standing in what we immediately recognize is the laundry room. It doesn't look much better than it does now, although cheap lace curtains cover the window we've just climbed through. In the picture we also see a patch of lawn through the window and try to envision it extending through the jungle it's now become. One of us pockets the photo, but we save our discussion of it for when we'll light the joint one of us has stolen from an older brother. Right now there's much more to see.

A bathroom separating the bedrooms is predictably foul. More dead flies line the windowsill. A yellowish stain covers the bottom of the old-fashioned bathtub, and black-and-dark-orange mildew spreads in the grout between the tiles and the curved mouth of the faucet. Someone opens the mirror and finds a box of Band-Aids with a bloody fingerprint on the paper lid. The toilet seat is up, and coarse, curly hairs are stuck to the brim. We notice a long needle on the edge but are afraid to pick it up and inspect it more closely. A Big Bird nightlight is plugged into a socket beneath the sink. Someone kicks it in a destructive reflex. Something about it resists the vandalism, though—Big Bird's head bends back slightly, but his smile stays round and glowing even without the light.

The door to the other bedroom is closed, but sunlight peers out from the slit at the bottom and through a keyhole. We wonder who would've closed it and why, and we almost knock. We open the door despite a collective, unspoken feeling that directs us otherwise. It is, by far, the brightest room in the house and not nearly as cluttered. It's the same size as the other rooms, but there seems to be more space to walk around, fewer dead things lying on the floor. This room has surfaces. A desk in the corner sits next to a window with a chair that looks like ones we've seen in storage at school. A collection of sun-faded stickers is grouped along the desk's edge. Unicorns. Some have been scratched off,

then reapplied. One is an oily sticker, with green and blue irides-
cent streaks that mix together when we press down on it. Another sticker shows a unicorn in mid-flight; a young maiden holds
on to the fabled horn with one eye fixed on a terrible danger behind them. The wallpaper is also unicorns, so faded in fact that
at first we think they're only horses.

We move to the other side of the room, where a mattress with
a brown stain in the middle lies half in, half out of the closet.
We see a light-blue blanket, soft with edges of tattered faux satin. It's twisted and curled around itself, as if it's afraid to touch
the brown spot underneath. We pull it off to reveal a child's riding horse, except, of course, it's not a horse but another unicorn.
The horn is slightly bent, but its mane is still precious, the twisted threads of white yarn mixed with longer strands of crimped,
sparkled silver. The painted wooden stick is stained at the middle, having been lovingly gripped. We prop it against the closet's
edge. The unicorn's black beaded eyes are scratched, giving them
the milky film of a silent, weathered observer.

In the closet next to the head of the mattress, we find plastic
sheaths that look to us, at first, like children's balloons long ago
blown into the shapes of a giraffe, a brontosaurus, or some other
impossible, long-necked creature. Small white globules of liquid
sit in pouches at the end like dollops of spoiled cream. Someone
says his brother has one under his bed next to a box of Kleenex
and a pink tube of clear gel. It's for sex, someone says harshly,
the word's finality leaving nothing left to speculation. We've never seen one of them like these, though—used. Unlike the needle in the bathroom, we have no problem picking up the slack
skins, the *condoms*, which we pronounce with a quivery rever-
ence, amazed that we now have an occasion to use the word. We
also jump to the likely conclusion that someone has had sex in
the dead girl's bed, possibly the same person who pushes off in
the bathroom. Except we don't call her "the dead girl" anymore.

We call her "Jeanette" and will continue to do so if we decide to pass the story along ourselves.

We light the joint. It's our first one, and we don't know what we're doing. We cough, and our faces turn red and puffy. The smoke hangs in the air, dancing in the shafts of sunlight that have managed to break through the defensive line of trees. Rather than taking the edge off things, the pot singles out the cool, harsh reality here. The naked picture from the other room is out. It's lying in the middle of the mattress on top of the blue blanket that covers the patch of brown. We pick it up, pretend to study it more closely, then place it back on the mattress. No one truly needs to see it again.

The story of the house needs revision. We've gone deeper into it than anyone else we know has, and it scares us. The responsibility is suffocating, but it also gives us a strange sense of power. No one we know has looked at the house, inside and out, and seen what we've seen. They treat it as a shell, a crack house, a fuck den. They don't care what happened here.

We don't discuss whom we should tell or whether anyone would care what we have to say. That poor family with the no-good father and the mother who went around town smelling of kitchen grease with her fake smiles and ghostly pale daughter. Weren't they better off left on the floor with the newspapers anyway? Either that's where they wanted to be left or where they wanted to be found. No one has the answers. Instead of deciding which, we talk about the barn, the horse, a brisk kick in the head.

We picture Jeanette creeping past her parents' bedroom, grabbing the banister in the dissipating glow of the nightlight and feeling the rest of the way by memory. We see her take the long route to the barn to avoid the open window of her parents' bedroom upstairs. She opens the barn door and sets down the stool. Or maybe the stool is already there, hidden by her the day before. It could've been planned. We wonder whether it's a hot night, whether she can see her way by the light of the half moon through cracks in the barn's wood. She stands, the stool's legs wobbling beneath her. As she takes hold of the long, bristly tail, we have to ask: Does she think the horse will really fly?

Revolution

ANNA STARES AT HANK AS they wait for Gloria and Billie to arrive for dinner. She stands behind him in the kitchen as he excavates the dark space underneath the sink. He's bent down on his knees, his wide butt peeking out from the boxers she gave him for Valentine's Day and a pair of khakis she just washed. *Say no to crack* is all she can think of—the sight gag of a plumber you laugh at who doesn't know that his ass crack is out there for everyone to see, a blubbery clown with a wrench and a tattered white V-neck with pit stains, just clueless. Anna, however, isn't laughing like she might have been if she had received a similar photo in an e-mail from one of her sons. They often send her inappropriate jokes and pictures, knowing their mom will chide them later, feigning shock at the obscenity of it, only to then share a giggle with them on the phone. Sometimes it seems like she's a school-girl, in love with her own children.

The beginning of Hank's ass crack—announced by a tuft of gingery hair that begins to blossom from his third-to-last vertebra long since buried in flesh—stands out like the opening of an oceanic fissure, something inviting Anna to peer closer. She cringes slightly at the sight of this man she used to lust over. When Hank was on the wrestling team back in college, he meticulously counted calories, maintaining a svelte 157 for all four years. Anna would help weigh him, taking off his clothes one piece at a time until he was naked before her, standing in the small bathroom of the apartment they shared during their junior year at the University of Vermont. She'd knead his muscled hamstring as she pulled the last article of clothing off him. She'd slide down his jockstrap and place each of his feet on the rubberized landing of the scale. And they'd both watch the needle bounce, stuttering indecipherably between 150 and 160 until, finally, it would land on his target number, which, eventually became *their* target number. They were a team.

She'd grab his ankles. How knobby they were with the hair from his legs ending just above them like a pair of furry pants he never took off. She'd bring her hands up the meaty thighs she loved so much until she cupped that wrestler's butt, the one she'd watch from the stands, all snug in his red satin singlet.

He's now on his knees in front of her, trying to retrieve her wedding ring that fell down the disposal. She somehow dislodged it from her finger while she was doing the dishes. Hank grunts, his neck twisting so he can inspect further underneath the sink, deep into the maze of piping.

"I think I've juuust got it," he says, panting. He draws out the word *just* as if the retrieval of the ring hinges on his holding the vowel as steadily as the hand that holds the wrench that grips the faucet pipe. Sweat drips from his brow onto the brown linoleum floor—a floor that wouldn't have even registered the small spatters had Anna not washed it to a fine sheen that morning.

"Hank, don't kill yourself," Anna says, fingering the grooves in a salt shaker, the one that looks like a doorknob, the one she always keeps on the wooden island in the center of the kitchen. These are the artifacts of her life, the things she touches. Through touching them, she knows who she is. She is Anna, wife of Hank, daughter of Gloria, and now sister of Billie.

It isn't that there's nothing left to say between the two of them. They actually speak quite a bit. "Oh, c'mon, Hank. Can't you please at least make an *effort* to clean out the gutters, or do you not live in this dorm?" and "Anna, there isn't anything I wouldn't do for you, but picking up your IBS prescription isn't currently part of my course load." Since they met in college back in the '70s, they often default to this kind of collegiate vocabulary and speak to each other as if they're both somehow still there—in their twenties, still in love.

But three boys and years of drifting away from each other, sexually at least, have transformed them back, almost without their knowing, into the platonic roommates they'd started out as back in school when they'd pooled their resources to share an apartment off campus. If not for her boys—Ben married, Ian at Middlebury, and Wade, still at home—Anna wouldn't know what to do with herself. She has an intense desire to feel needed.

"When are Gloria and Billie coming over for dinner?" asks Hank. The hollowness of the dark space underneath the sink almost swallows up his voice.

"What?" Anna asks.

"Gloria and Billie!" he yells.

"We're here!" says Billie's voice from the foyer.

"I always loved being announced." Gloria follows closely behind her into the kitchen.

Gloria, Anna's mother, was living alone in Washington, D.C., when she fell and broke an already weak hip. What began as a temporary convalescence in Montpelier to help heal her bones became, at some point, something much more permanent. First, at Hank's urging, she leased a small apartment across town. Then she began to amass a bevy of friends, whom she regaled with dramatic tales of modeling at Garfinkel's in downtown Washington and going on dinner dates with the likes of Tab Hunter. "I had him before he became a gay," she'd state resolutely. These were old, sheltered Vermont women, many of whom had never set foot out of the state. They seemed to regard Gloria as if she were a minor celebrity, and Gloria, of course, loved it.

Admittedly Anna and Gloria had never had the best relationship. For years it was just the two of them. The man Anna had considered and loved as her father, a man whose last name was Fe-renbach, had been driven out of the house by Gloria when Anna was only thirteen. Her mother complained that he had bored her, that he had been incapable of taking her seriously as an actress, an occupation she'd adopted based solely on one screen test she'd done in Hollywood at the suggestion of a producer whom Anna could now assume had used the promise of fame to sleep with her. Too much make-believe involved. Too much pretend.

Billie is a product of pretending. People pretended she didn't exist. Billie is Anna's half-sister. Two years ago, Anna had been at her mother's apartment while Gloria was recovering from hip surgery. She was there to collect some of Gloria's personal belongings to have with her in the hospital. From as far back as Anna could remember, Gloria had claimed she was terrified of doctors and hospitals. She told Anna she wanted to have her things with her in case she didn't wake up. "People go to sleep in hospitals, and they don't wake up," she said. Anna was putting an old photo album in a bag when Gloria's phone rang. The woman on the other end, quite bluntly, claimed to be Gloria's daughter.

At first Anna didn't know what to think. In a way, it wasn't surprising at all: Gloria, like a tornado, funneling through town after town, taking out small houses and farms along her path, leaving behind unwanted children and discarded lovers along the jet stream. There had been so much crisscrossing the country that Anna never had time to make any true friends. Gloria was the only person who could know whether Billie's claim possibly could be true, whether her existence, always a distant fact to Glo-ria, one that might never even surface, had in fact done just that. Anna's first instinct was to find something to give the woman—medical records, old pictures, money—anything so she might go away. It was too late to tell Billie that Gloria was dead; that was an awful thought and an even worse plan.

She had to tell Gloria about this woman. She was Anna's sister.

"Mother, I have to talk to you," she'd said several days later, dropping off a couple of things she'd picked up for Gloria at the Grand Union as she recovered.

"Okay, well, talk then," Gloria said, pushing her glasses down and looking up from her crossword.

Anna stared briefly at a drawing of an elderly black woman in an intricate maple frame that had always donned the walls of whatever apartment or house or rented room they'd occupied at the time. Gloria had it set up on the table next to her hospital bed. She claimed to have been this old black woman in another life, a former slave who still had a hump on her back from when she was beaten as a young girl. Some of Anna's earliest memories were of rubbing her mother's supposed hump for luck.

"I know about the baby you had before I was born. She's found you, Mother."

The color drained from Gloria's face, and her milky white eyes went blank. She began to sob. "I didn't want to do it. Mother and Daddy made me! Oh, God, I want to die!" They cried together for hours, and Gloria went into fits of rage alternating with hysterical crying about how much her life was a lie and everyone was now in on it.

A half-sister. No one had seen fit to inform Anna that Billie had existed at all. So it turned out that Anna was *not* the only child she once so completely self-identified as. Gloria had gotten knocked up at sixteen and was immediately sent to a home for wayward girls located in upper Georgetown, Washington, D.C. The identity of the father is another of Gloria's mysteries. Anna has reason to believe it was a young man named Dash Sinclair whom Gloria used to speak of in almost exclusively transcendental terms, a high school beau Anna could believe had been quickly distanced from Gloria's "situation" and probably at the behest of well-to-do parents. He saw what the future held and decided Gloria and a baby were not in it. These kinds of things happened back then in a quiet, antiseptic way. You popped out an illegitimate child, and you moved on.

Anna only gets the story in bits and pieces from Gloria and never in a coherent, plotted fashion. The whole ordeal is so painfully clichéd that she finds it difficult to imagine she can now actually claim it as family history. Suddenly there's a reason that Gloria has cried every Christmas (Billie was born on December 24). Or made such a fuss about women's reproductive health in the seventies (she'd been firmly pro-choice before it was ever in fashion to say so). Or went out of her way to avoid shopping in Georgetown when she and Anna had lived in D.C. She'd turned down an invitation to go to a cocktail party at JFK's townhouse once when he was a U.S. senator and speaks about it now as if she'd turned down an invitation to watch the signing of the Declaration of Independence.

Everything that Anna has ever wanted to be, Billie seems to have happened upon effortlessly. Billie grew up in California, the place where Anna has always dreamed of living—sunglasses and Hollywood. Billie was a stewardess back when it was still something of a status symbol of beauty. Anna always loved the uniforms they wore with the perfectly matched silk scarves and the cute little tri-peak caps. She secretly wished she was part of their cozy warren, traveling in the handsome wake of a gorgeous pilot. But it's Billie's current occupation that really plagues Anna, almost to the point of rage. She writes books for young adults. That is Anna's secret dream! The one that no one knows about, not even Hank. Billie's books are stories about young girls abandoned by the world and saved by the love of dolphins and horses. The latest one features a chimp, Anna seems to recall, after looking up customer reviews on Amazon.

She feels a tinge of jealousy at the lifestyle Billie seems to lead: flitting from here to there, switching careers on a whim, and being successful at absolutely everything she does.

The first time Anna met Billie, in a café with Gloria, she'd been wary from the start. In had walked this reddish-haired beauty, tall and statuesque, like a Chanel model. She was older than Anna but had the kind of milky skin that appears ageless.

"My God, you look just like my Great-Aunt Faye," Gloria said when Billie sat down. Faye, a woman Anna had never even heard of. Of course, Billie's features had to have been plucked from some distant, goddess-like branch of the family tree Anna had never known about. "I can't believe I'm actually standing here in front of you both," Billie had said with a smile that revealed a slight dimple on her left cheek. "It's a little overwhelming."

"Honey, let's take it all one step at a time," Gloria said. Anna had smarted from Gloria's use of the word *honey*. That was what her mother always had called *her*. Anna already sensed Gloria falling in love with Billie.

Anna told the boys at Christmas that year that she now had a sister.

"What do you mean you have a sister?" her oldest, Ben, had asked.

"Your grandmother gave birth to a baby when she was a teenager and didn't tell anyone. Believe me, this is as much of a shock to your dad and me as it is to you," she'd stated. Diplomatically, she thought.

"Does she look like you?" Ian had asked.

"Well, no, she doesn't really, no."

"What does she do?" Wade asked.

"She writes children's books. Young adult novels, I suppose. Just make her feel welcome when she's around, for your grandmother's sake."

"HANK, WHAT ARE YOU DOING down there?" Billie asks, directing her question lower, toward the cabinet, where Hank's head is.

"He's attempting to retrieve my wedding ring. It fell down the drain," Anna answers.

"You take it off?" asks Billie. "Why? If I had one, I'd *never* take it off." She smiles.

"It came off while I was cleaning a skillet."

"Cleaning a skillet." Billie turns her head in profile, directing herself to Gloria. "You know, how does one even *clean* a skillet? I can write about doing it, but I've never actually cooked in a skillet, let alone cleaned one. Isn't that funny, Mother?"

"It's hilarious, dear," Gloria says, smiling back at Billie.

"I found it!" Hank leans back on his left heel and rocks back a bit, his pants and boxers bunching back up to cover the crack. He anchors himself to the floor with his left palm face-down on the linoleum, then slowly begins to rise, bringing the slimy wedding band up to Anna's face like a Chaplin flower.

"Will you marry me?" he asks. "Again?"

"Once you wash that thing off," Anna says.

"What happened to 'for better or for worse'?" Billie asks.

"For better or worse or indisposed," says Hank.

"Or in disposal," Billie says.

"Ha! You're right," says Hank, laughing at her. Not only can Anna see them laughing with each other, but also their eyes are laughing with each other, which is so much worse. "Anna, I'm not going to Montreal with you tomorrow to chaperone Wade's school trip. It's decided," states Gloria.

"Mother!" Anna exclaims.

"I'm tired and don't feel like going on an overnight, especially at my age."

"But Mother, you promised you'd do this with me. And now I don't have a partner." Anna nearly pouts.

"That's why *I'm* going with you," says Billie, affecting a curtsy, as if she's suddenly in a royal court. It is bizarre.

Anna glances at her mother, who looks at her with pitiful, watery eyes. Her Stanislavski acting eyes.

"It'll be a good bonding trip for you girls," she says. Anna winces at the way Gloria uses the term *girls*, at the way the word suggests that Anna ever knew Billie as a girl. As if to suggest they have anything in common at all.

At dinner, Billie sits to Gloria's right, across from Wade and to the left of Hank, who sits at the head of the table opposite Anna, who is at the other end. Anna and Hank have always arranged themselves like this, across from each other at either ends of the table. They share knowing looks, nonverbal cues during dinner when all the boys surround them at the table.

What's so surprising for Anna to think about now is that this is the same kind of thing she did with Gloria as a child. Even when they were at one of Gloria's all-night dinner parties that inevitably arose out of an earlier cocktail party and then gave way to a boozy game of poker with cigars, there was Anna up way past her bedtime, mixing it up with the adults—always the only child. Gloria would stop flirting or drinking or accepting a cigarette from whichever male suitor had been beckoned to her side to give Anna their secret look—an exaggerated rolling of her eyes as if to say, "Isn't this all ridiculous, babe?" topped off with a wink.

"Are you working on a new book?" Hank asks Billie, pouring her a little more wine.

"As a matter of fact, I am," Billie answers, picking up the glass to take a sip.

"What's this one about?" he continues. Anna looks at Hank, hoping to catch a wink or a knowing nod. He read one of Billie's books once and didn't think it was very good. He called it "trite," if she recalls correctly, yet he now appears to be intrigued by her new one. He fails to return Anna's look.

"It's a novel about a group of children who escape from an abusive foster home, then become exposed to a chemical agent that allows them to see people's thoughts. They use their new skill to make the most private desires of the people around them come true. Or, in some cases, redirect those people whose unsavory desires might lead them down a bad path."

"It sounds kind of like *The Boxcar Children* series. Anna, I used to read that to you when you were little," Gloria says. She looks at Billie, and Billie nods.

"So it's science fiction?" Hank prods.

"It is, yes. Kind of. I'm thinking of doing a trilogy."

"What kind of 'unsavory desires'?" Wade asks. Wade, who is rarely checked into what is happening at the dinner table outside of eating, is unusually attentive to Billie. He is *involved* in the conversation. During a normal dinner, Anna might be able to get three or four sentences from him before he inhales his meal, then rushes off to hang out with friends or play basketball.

"Well, it's a young adult novel, so there's nothing too obscene in it. I have a bit of leeway with my editors, though. Listen, I think everyone has a stray bad thought in the course of a single day. It doesn't mean you're an awful person; it just means you're a human. What makes the children in my novel special, I think, is that they've tapped into their intuitive powers to 'read' people. It comes off as telekinesis or something supernatural, but I think it's something we all can do to a certain extent."

"Are there animals in this book, like the others?" Anna asks. She chooses a moment in which Hank, Wade, and Gloria all seem to be totally enraptured by what Billie is saying. Private desires and secret thoughts. This isn't groundbreaking territory, Anna thinks, and has to stop herself from saying it out loud.

"That's kind of my trademark, so yes, there's one animal."

"What kind?" asks Anna.

"There's a golden retriever the children save from being abused by their foster father. They take her with them when they escape. I'm thinking of naming the dog Gloria after Mother, of course," she says, turning toward Gloria.

"I'd be so honored!" says Gloria.

"Can I get anyone a second helping of chicken?" Anna asks as Hank passes her the casserole.

"Who's your father?" Wade asks Billie.

"Wade!" shouts Anna, letting the serving spoon on the chicken casserole clank off the side and spill to the table. A stunned silence takes over the room that lasts three seconds but feels much longer. Wade sits back in his chair with a confused expression. "Don't be rude," Anna says, placing the spoon to the side on her napkin.

"He's not being rude, Anna," Billie says. "He's just curious." Gloria begins to nod to agree with Billie but stops to sneak a glance at Anna. "I suspect that's more of a question for you, though, Mother. Don't you think?" Billie asks Gloria.

Gloria looks back at Billie, who, for the first time that night, appears as if she might not entirely trust Gloria. The chummy togetherness of the two of them seems broken for a moment. But put on the spot, Gloria is always at her best. She is, of course, an actress and has, presumably, been rehearsing these lines for decades.

"His name was Dash. Dash Sinclair."

Anna just knew it and feels temporarily vindicated at Gloria's confirmation. Gloria tosses her brown mane with the white shoots at either side above her ears and kind of stares off into the distance at the movie of her life playing on the opposite wall.

There's a sly way Gloria has of parsing out this information, telling it to the assembled table as if they're at a reading in a coffee shop, waiting to be entertained. Or at a one-night-only Broadway event. "An Evening With…" type of thing. By this point, it's not some painful memory she's reliving; it's been sculpted into a dramatic monologue, the facts of the story doled out in careful beats. "Dash was—well, it goes without saying—utterly dashing. He was the captain of the football team *and* the debate team. I wore his varsity jacket."

"What did he look like? You've never really said," Billie asks, her eyes hopeful.

"He had strawberry-blond hair, which is where you got yours, I suppose, dear."

"What about his family? Whatever happened to him?" Wade asks. Billie appears ravenous at this opening.

"Mother and Daddy told me never to speak of him again. By the time I came home, he had graduated and gone off to school. I'm not sure where." Gloria pauses for a moment, as if forgetting her lines. Then, as if she's just remembered what she wanted to say, she asks Anna, "Can you refill my sherry?"

In this moment, Anna feels a certain kinship to Billie. She feels bad that Billie must rely on Gloria's erratic whims in order to gain such basic information as the fate of her father, his appearance, his age—questions a fifty-something-year-old woman never should have to ask anyone.

Anna recalls asking Gloria the same questions in her childhood about her own father and being continually redirected in a way only her mother could do. Relying on crumbs of information to toss over and over inside her head like clothes in a dryer in the Laundromat downtown.

Anna remembers meeting her real father at a Senators game when she was about ten years old. She wasn't told the man was her father until she was returned home. He bought her a hot dog and a Coke while he drank large gulps from a wide plastic cup of pilsner. He smoked Marlboros down to the filter, then shoved the butts off the steps next to a woman in front of them who seemed to become more agitated as the innings progressed and he got louder and drunker. Anna never saw him again.

"Dash Sinclair. Sounds like someone out of a novel from the turn of the century," Billie says, a faint smile on her face.

"What about your adopted dad? Where's he?" Wade asks.

Billie becomes very still. She picks up her glass to take a sip but holds it in midair. "He's dead. And so is my adoptive mother."

Gloria looks away from the table, as if she's just heard a doorbell or suddenly remembered something she had tried to recall weeks before. Billie looks over at Gloria.

"I have a younger sister—Alicia. My…" Billie stumbles a bit before saying, "…*adoptive* parents had a baby after I came to live with them." She finally takes a sip of her wine after the glass has been hanging in the air.

Hank stares at Anna. He finally gives her a look. But she doesn't know what this one means. She's never seen it before. He could be asking her to do something, but she's not sure.

"Cheers to Billie," Hank says, raising his glass. "Welcome home."

THAT NIGHT, AFTER GLORIA AND Billie go home, Anna gets into bed with Hank, who's already half asleep. She pulls the covers over and lies on her side, bringing her hand up to her face, bending it so that her cheek rests upon her knuckles. She feels Hank's hand begin to encircle her waist.

"That was nice, you agreeing to take Billie on Wade's field trip," he says. "I think she was touched. And Gloria seemed delighted."

"I don't know why it's so important to cultivate this relationship with her. She's a stranger. To both of us. I don't have the time for this."

"Shh…Billie's good." He brings his hand down around her waist and pulls her close to him in a spooning position. He pushes up her nightgown from the back and pulls down her underpants with the other hand, so quickly that she can barely register what's happening. They're having sex for the first time in what must be over six months. He presses up inside her from behind and she loses her breath for a second, letting her body relax with his as he settles into her. Hank is always such a careful lover. They made three boys this way, there's something still beautiful about that, isn't there, she asks herself.

But she also wonders if he was turned on by the sight of her half-sister whose beauty is more traditional, less squinty than hers. More regal, less domestic. Is he making love to *her*, she wants to know? He doesn't often take her from behind like this, so she has to ask. But she doesn't. She goes along with the rhythm he's established, like a good warm body, riding beneath the wave of him as he washes over her, up inside her. He's asleep almost as soon as he pulls out, as if it were only a dream.

A SIGN AT THE FRONT of La Ronde, the amusement park in Montreal, informs patrons that the staff of the park is currently on strike. The park—the sign announces with small insignias of construction hats and crossed pick axes and smiley faces—is being run by "independently contracted operators." *Scabs,* Anna thinks to call them in her head.

"Well, isn't *that* reassuring," Billie says, winking at Wade and two of his friends as they make their way past the sign. The group walks past the welcome cottages and ventures onto a tree-lined path, surrounded by blindingly white three-picket fencing and globular bushes in fresh red chips of fertilizer. Anna walks a few paces behind, watching as Billie shoots her arm through the hook in Wade's windbreaker. Wade looks at her and smiles.

The Ferris wheel at La Ronde dwarfs everything around it. Even the nearby arch, which is admittedly taller and resembles the one in St. Louis, seems to be bowing to it, dipping its apex in deference, quivering on its spindly iron legs. There's something almost prehistoric about the Ferris wheel—its massiveness, as if the thing has always been there, cemented to the ground and moving perpetually in a calm, circular motion, the rest of the amusement park—the entire city of Montreal, in fact—only built around it, trying to reach the heights it so effortlessly inhabits.

Instead of the open-air compartments Anna had seen in the Ferris wheels of her youth—the ones where children's legs would dangle and swing with each revolution—this one is fixed at the spoke of the wheel with a rust-red car able to seat four passengers, two seats facing each other. So gigantic it is, the wheel needs to contain its passengers in order to keep them from flying out into the sky.

Anna isn't afraid of heights in the traditional sense. She once stood on the observation deck at Niagara Falls with Hank and the boys. They were driving Ben off to college. Holding the hand-rail with a firm grip, Anna hastened to look straight down. The swirling pistons of water, crashing into one another at the bottom of the great falls, lulled her into a sort of peaceful daze, drawing her away as if by hypnosis from the reality of just how far she was from the bottom. The sounds of the water pulled her closer to the misty whisper of the crashing jets. As if the whorls of water could envelop her like a claw, lift her straight off the deck, into the air and let her float deliriously above them.

But years later, after she had climbed a tree in their front yard to retrieve a kite for a sobbing Wade, who had begun to pitch a fit on the driveway, she temporarily had lost her footing as she descended the giant oak. After reacting quickly by grabbing the nearest thing, she found herself hanging from a thick bough of the old tree, clinging to it for her very survival. As she looks back, she realizes it was perhaps the most terrifying moment of her life. She could see the whites of her fingernails digging into the bark as she felt something slip out of her—a sense of the most basic security. By some miracle, she was able to shimmy down the long bough back to the trunk and make her way to the ground, thick chips of bark scraping her knees and elbows. Wade, who only minutes before had been hysterically weeping about his kite, was shocked into catatonic silence as he watched his mother climb down to the foot of the tree. When Anna had scooped him off the ground, her knees skinned and arms rattling on their own accord, as if the blood flowing through her were now some kind of hydroponic fuel, he awoke from his trance and burst into tears again. Too stunned to cry herself, she had held him tighter. From that moment on, she'd been afraid of anything higher than her second-story window.

As they stand in line to get onto the Ferris wheel, the kids quickly assemble themselves into groups of four. Wade, always so popular with his classmates, soon has a gaggle of teens of both sexes on either side of him. Anna and Billie, like two kids left over from choosing teams, climb together into a car by themselves.

"Is there a safety bar? What's keeping me from falling out of this thing?" Anna asks the teenage girl helping them into the car.

"There are seatbelts inside. This door latch is controlled by those levers over there. No need to worry, ma'am. Enjoy the beautiful view!"

As the wheel lifts them higher into the air, Anna can see the other amusement rides become less focused in the distance. The roller coaster off to the far left looks like a Fisher-Price set she got one of the boys for a birthday years ago. The tiny cart zips along the tracks, fitting into tiny grooves, holding the tiny people with their tiny arms raised into the air. If she looks far enough, she can see the tall steel buildings of the business center of Montreal rising up out of the trees that surround the park. It would be easy, she thinks, to love the world from way up here. The way the air is crisp and clean and the silence is not threatening, but calming, organic. The wheel stops as they reach the top. Anna feels the same quiet take over yet now wishes they'd keep moving.

"I'm glad we have a chance to talk, Anna, because I wanted to bring something up with you," Billie says.

"Oh? What is it?"

"Well, Mother's birthday is coming up in February, as you know, and I thought how great would it be if you and I took her on a cruise." Excitedly, Billie looks out the grated window of the wheel car, looking, to Anna, as if she already can picture the three of them off in the distance, embarking on a mammoth white ocean liner.

"I don't think that would be such a good idea," Anna says.

"Why is that?" asks Billie.

"She was uncomfortable with the idea of going on this simple overnight trip. What makes you think she'd suddenly sign on for a vacation where she's on the water for days on end? No, it's not her at all. Not now at least."

"That's certainly not the impression I've gotten." The Ferris wheel jerks back to life and starts to move again, waking their car on its descent to the ground. "Gloria seems to have traveled more than most people have in a lifetime. I'd think a cruise would be tame for her, considering the miles she's logged throughout her life."

"It's so like her to exaggerate. If you went back into those stories—I mean, really delved into them—you'd probably find a lot less based on actual fact," Anna states. She notices that Billie has pursed her lips a bit. "Besides, she has restless leg syndrome. She'd have to pace up and down the ship's deck like a ghost every night. That alone would drive us both crazy enough to want to kill her." Anna knows this, but Billie, of course, couldn't possibly.

"What an awful thing to say," Billie proclaims.

"Listen, Billie, you might think you know her, but you really don't." Anna pauses suddenly, almost breathless. The Ferris wheel has stopped at the top again after another revolution so that they're at the wheel's apex, above the clouds even, it feels like.

"No, I don't know her like you do. How could I? What do you think I'm trying to do here but get to know her better? To get to know *you* better."

"I meant that you don't know her like I do. She'd actually find a way to think less of you for coming up with a trip like that—not more. Believe me."

"What is this, Anna? What's this really about?"

Anna looks to the floor of the compartment and sees dead leaves that have been tracked inside.

"I don't know what that question means. What is *what* about?" Anna says.

"I'm trying to connect with you two, and you're—you're making it so impossible. You're so cold."

"I'm not cold! This is just who I am."

"Then why can't you let me in? Mother has."

"Mother isn't even thinking about you. She's thinking about herself. This whole chapter in her book—the book in *her* mind—this chapter isn't about you. This chapter, like all the others, is about her." Anna's voice has escalated into a kind of growl. She notices her teeth have temporarily gritted together. Billie pauses for a second to take this in. A quick snap of wind passes through their car.

"Tell me, Anna. Would you have rather I died in the orphanage where I lived until I was three? Or at birth, even? Would that have been better for you? More convenient?"

"That's ridiculous," Anna says.

"What do you want from me?"

"Nothing! I don't want anything from you. I don't even know you!" Anna screams. "None of us do."

Billie stops looking at Anna in the eye. She's staring right past her, out the grating of the wheel car. At first Anna thinks she's simply angry at her. She had meant the things she said, but she hadn't intended to say them.

Then Billie says, "My God, look at that."

Anna turns around. Off in the distance, she sees a large black cloud that seems to be leaching out the sunlight and the airy brightness they had experienced when they first got onto the Ferris wheel, sucking it out of the air and making everything dark, like a black nylon over a nightstand lamp. The accompanying winds whistle around them so hard that they shake the car, a car that suddenly feels much more like a cage.

"We're finally going down again. That must mean they're going to start letting people off because of the weather," says Billie.

Anna can only nod as they begin their descent. She hears Wade and the others hollering in the car behind them. What an adventure this must be for them. She only has to look down once to get that feeling again. They always say that people walking around on the ground look like ants from a distance. To Anna they look like earwigs, those little brown sticks that pick themselves up off the ground and announce to the world that they're animated. If she had a shotgun, she thinks, she might take aim at one of them, just to see if she could hit the target.

"Wait, they're not letting us off. Why aren't they letting us off?" Anna can see one of the scabs working the controls of the Ferris wheel with a dull, blank expression. She's wearing a yellow T-shirt with a Mountain Dew logo and white Keds. To Anna, she looks very eighties and very stupid. "You need to stop this thing so we can get off! Right now!" she screams in the girl's direction. The girl only vaguely looks at them as she grabs a gray hooded sweatshirt to shield herself from the sudden onslaught of cold. Anna feels a few drops of rain blow through the grating. They have completed another revolution and are making their way straight back up to the top.

"Settle down. I've been up in a hot air balloon that blew out half of its heat source, and I made it out fine," Billie says.

"Well, it seems you always land on your feet."

As they get closer to the top, Anna senses a small swinging motion in the car, as if it's trying to tip her out. Some of the high school girls below scream. It's unmistakable.

"Anna, hold on to the handrail on the side here. Steady yourself. Everything is going to be fine."

She suddenly can see how good a flight attendant Billie must have been back in the day, soothing nervous passengers, bundling up children with blankets.

Anna looks out the grated window, a compartment that feels smaller than when she first got in. The entire sky has turned a grayish black, and the rain comes down in cross-cut sheets across the sky, erupting like a furious curtain of water. The wheel car rocks with more regularity. Billie looks out from the grating behind them then quickly looks back, searching for Anna's eyes so she can hold them steady. The Ferris wheel isn't moving. They're frozen at the top.

"You just saw something. What was it?" Anna asks.

"People are climbing out of their cars," she delivers calmly.

"What?! How?" Anna says, starting to peer out the window grating herself.

"Don't look down. Their door must've become unlatched or something."

"Wade! Wade, it's me! Can you see Wade? Is he one of them?" Anna screams.

"Wade is fine, Anna. He's fine."

Anna feels herself cave into a panic. The screaming around her has become even more manic and frightened (and not exclusively female, which scares her even more). She can't hear Wade's voice over the shouting and the creaking of the wheel car as they rock back and forth, not like she could hear it before. She prays they'll get out of this alive. Then, almost immediately after that, she prays she'll be struck by lightning before falling out of the car and landing on the cement near the base of the wheel.

"Everything's going to be okay," Billie says. "I saw some sort of maintenance crew on the ground. I'm sure they're trying to fix the problem."

"What's happening?" Anna asks. "What's happening?" But the question suddenly isn't just about the Ferris wheel and whether they'll get off. Billie leaves the seat facing Anna and moves to sit next to her.

"I'm not lucky, Anna. I know it's probably easier for you to think that about me. To look at me and my life in comparison to yours and think how fabulous and fun everything is. But I'm not lucky. You're the lucky one."

"How am I lucky?" Anna asks, looking at her more closely.

"You've had our mother your whole life. You have Hank and those wonderful boys and—"

"Yes, I can see how much you like Hank," Anna interrupts her.

"Oh, Anna. No. Really? Listen, I don't want your husband. You're all new family to me. I'm just trying to make the best impression I can." Billie sits back in the cushioned seat and places her hands on either side, palms facing down. Anna does the same so that, for a moment, they're mirroring each other side by side, like together on a swing, except Anna is leaning forward, not back. "Do you know what I would've given to be able to wake up in your house every morning the last however many years? To spend the holidays with you and Mother? To even *have* a mother? Do you?"

"I don't know what you're expecting to get out of this with her. Whatever it is, you're going to be disappointed. Gloria is selfish to her very core."

"Is that where you get it from?" Billie looks away, out through the grating toward the clouds. "I'm sorry for that. Why don't you just let me find out for myself?"

"She didn't look for you, Billie. She never even looked for you."

Billie tells Anna about when her adoptive mother became pregnant almost immediately after she and her husband took Billie in. From then on, she was like an extra child around the house. Never allowed to forget that she wasn't their biological daughter. "Do you know what that does to a person? To feel like a stranger in your own home? It's devastating. When they died," she said, "they left me almost nothing. My sister Alicia got it all."

Anna grabs hold of Billie's hand. Something feels right to her about doing it. The bones of her knuckles are very pronounced, but her hand is warm and silky. It has the feel of an artist's hands or what Anna imagines an artist's hand might feel like. Together they stare into the blackness of the cloud that hovers over the Ferris wheel, shaking their car. There's no way to stop the cloud from moving closer, and Anna feels a sense of calm from finally being able to recognize that.

There Is a Light
That Never Goes Out

SHEILA'S HAIR WAS BLONDE BUT whitish and thin, as if she'd been frightened into it overnight. Her cleft chin gave her a cartoon-ish profile. Her nose was fine, but her dull brown eyes crowded above it, too close together in a predatory descent. Three small moles sat under her left eye, but other than that, her face was entirely without blemish, not even the vestiges of acne. Her forehead had a slightly Neanderthal look, though, the way it jutted out beyond reasonable facial standards. If she were a straight man, she honestly wouldn't have looked at herself twice.

She drove a 1984 Toyota Celica with vanity plates that read "YO ADRIAN." No one could drive it but her. This was the only rule she enforced, the one pillar against which she stood firmly planted.

"That car is the one thing that has never let me down," she told Scott in the kitchen as he dug through a drawer, searching for chopsticks.

Sheila had struck its occasional lapses in motion from a near spotless record. How could she possibly fault a car for breaking down when it had been the thing that had brought her to Scott? "What can you say that about in *your* life?" she asked him in an unusually defiant tone. Tonight was a night she wasn't backing down on anything.

"Well, you, I guess," he answered.

"Take me out tonight," she said, grabbing his shoulder and pulling the white carton of General Tso's chicken out of his hand. Some of his friends were hosting a party, and she wanted to go. He claimed an almost rhythmic ignorance about it, so for proof, she went and got the invitation that lay on the foyer table.

"I want to stay in tonight," Scott said.

"You don't want to be seen with me. That's the real reason you don't want to go to the party."

"Don't be ridiculous."

"How am I the one being ridiculous?" Sheila said. "We've been dating each other for well over eight months, and the only time I've ever spent more than a passing moment with someone you know was when your friend Zack ran into us at Safeway and practically chained you down to the produce section so you'd introduce me. It was embarrassing." Her forehead was sweaty, and she stole quick gulps of air rather than appear winded.

"You met Ron and Augusta, didn't you?" he asked.

"If you call meeting two people staring at them through a windshield trying not to look like a complete idiot then, yes, I've met them."

She and Scott had been walking up to her car in the parking lot of the Target when he'd spotted the couple circling around in search of a space.

"I'll just be a second," he'd told her.

She'd watched him flag them over to where her car was parked as she climbed into her driver's seat. He leaned on the driver's-side door of Ron's BMW and crossed his feet, casually resting the toe of his left foot on the pavement in a haughty way, as if he were a raconteur entertaining several adoring fans. The couple nodded along at what he was saying, seemingly enraptured. He beamed. Sheila had remembered sitting with him in a restaurant in Carmel and seeing that same look of adoration on the eyes of fellow patrons, the quick, enthusiastic replies of the waitress as she openly blushed at his questions about the menu. He had that way about him that she so clearly lacked—an ease with people, a confidence.

The woman, Augusta, a name Sheila found pretentious and undeservingly royal, had darted several glances her way while Scott spoke to them. She saw Sheila watch them, then quickly gestured her way to alert Ron of the soon-to-be-vacant space. Somehow it had failed to enter the woman's mind that Sheila was actually *with* Scott (a man Augusta once had tried to make a move on herself, Sheila later learned). When Scott followed Augusta's pointed finger, Sheila saw a cold stare looking back at her, a glare he might've given her had she not been his girlfriend or, even worse, had she been a perfectly benign stranger, vacating their parking space at the Target. For a second, it had knocked the wind out of her.

Now she went into her closet and sifted through thin plastic bags from the dry cleaners.

"How about a movie?" Scott suggested brightly.

"No, we're going to this party." She chose a cranberry cocktail dress she'd bought impulsively but had never worn, intimidated by the spaghetti straps and sheer tulle rectangle that hinted dramatically toward her small breasts.

"You're going to wear that?" he asked.

"Yes. And I'm driving too."

She made him change out of the T-shirt and jeans he was wearing into a tight, ribbed turtleneck that accentuated his torso and pinstriped pants she'd found in a high-end vintage shop downtown off U Street. She remembered finding an old caramel in the pocket of the pants on her way home, then eating it without much thought, surprised at the enduring flavor of its chalky crème center.

As they approached the exit on the interstate, Scott rolled down the window. He lit one of Sheila's cigarettes with the burning stub she'd left in the ashtray. As he smoked, he leaned against the limp shoulder strap of the broken seatbelt. He thrust his hips against the frayed strap that hugged his middle and pulled absent-mindedly at a loose panel on the door. Sheila looked over at him. She enjoyed him this way—tied down for the evening or at least appearing under the illusion of bondage.

The driveway of the house was lined with candles placed in brown paper sacks, symmetrical designs Rorschached on both sides. It was just the kind of festive suburban touch Sheila wished she could think of herself. She recognized the danger in fooling herself that she was one of these women but felt a cool taste of glory being this close to the places they lived.

The entire house was lit up and filled with people and noise. It looked like one of those Thomas Kinkade paintings that respond to changes in light. Sheila had bought one during their trip to Carmel. The man in the gallery had told her they were fashionable to have in the dining room. When they had returned from their trip, she hung it up at Scott's, then spent the whole dinner that night jumping out of her seat to dim the lights, changing the little country cottage in the painting from daytime to night, candles alit in the upstairs windows like the house was just waiting for someone to come home. She had caught her reflection in a silver water pitcher and stared back at it triumphantly.

Pulling into the driveway, Sheila ran one hand down the side of her dress, checking for creases (momentarily forgetting the dress never had been worn) and gripped the steering wheel with the other. She spotted an empty space in the turnaround but hesitated before taking it—they'd most likely be blocked in. She heard noises from the house—the sounds of people and laughter. There were shadows cast against the walls. She maneuvered her car into the empty space.

Scott took her coat out of the backseat and helped her into it. Her high heels made muffled clinks on the brick walkway, grinding atop the remains of late-winter sandings. When she pressed the doorbell, Scott's hand quickly clasped hers.

"Scott! Welcome, welcome! I see you've brought Sheila. Please, both of you, come inside." The voice was so gracious, so hospitable that it took Sheila a moment to register that it belonged to Augusta. She was the hostess of this party—Augusta, whose small hands she now felt around her side, already taking an arm out of her coat like Sheila was at a fancy restaurant. Augusta led her toward the living room with such steady briskness—the smile on her face never changing from a perfect, balanced fullness—that Sheila could only faintly register Scott's sudden absence from her side.

Someone handed Sheila a drink, a man (Augusta's Ron perhaps, although, she'd forgotten what he looked like entirely). She latched on to it with a spidery grip. She could see from the dark, flat amber and soda that it must be whiskey, although there didn't seem to be enough soda mixed in; the pieces of ice bobbed up and down like chips of plastic that would never melt. She held the red cocktail napkin to the bottom of the glass and took a quick gulp; the liquor burning her throat on its way down.

She pulled her lips into a half grimace but then quickly produced a look that was almost satisfaction. That delirious sense of abandon she had felt when she'd wriggled herself into the cranberry dress at home had mysteriously disappeared on their way to the party. Now, surveying the other women, she wished she had stuck with something a bit more low-key. A little black dress maybe. Something ingratiating that would've allowed her to blend into the crowd, the unobtrusive color of typing ink.

The couch was occupied. Sheila took another long sip, groped for the cushioned edge, and sat down, crossing her legs. *This is going to be okay,* she told herself. Already she felt things were moving along swimmingly.

The group on the couch was seated boy-girl-boy-girl, yet no one seemed to be romantically linked. They were just a group of friends—early-to-mid-thirties professionals. Sheila felt she easily could blend in.

They were discussing a current film she had not seen. It was one of those art-house movies that always seemed to be playing in a small theater stuffed between a used record store and an Indian restaurant in a part of the city Sheila was not accustomed to visiting.

Sheila was utterly resistant to buzz of any kind. She heard about movies years after they'd come out, in outdated film guides in waiting rooms and on late-night showings on television. Turned off by the dreary subject matter, she mostly avoided art films altogether, preferring more traditional fare—comedies with irascible yet endearing old people; mysteries set in small, backward towns where the detective always learned something new about himself, eclipsing the predictably melodramatic conclusion of the case in importance.

She once had thought of her own life as a movie, especially when she'd been in the hospital. *One Flew over the Cuckoo's Nest* by way of *My Fair Lady*—a movie you couldn't help but watch over and over because the lead character was just so endearing. Of course, she wouldn't have played herself. Even the plain girl in the movies had something to tweak, some raw potential for a possible mid-plot makeover.

When Scott had entered her life so serendipitously—pulling over that day to help her on the Beltway when she'd stupidly run out of gas, driving her to safety, then doing the sweetest thing of allowing her to take him out for a thank-you lunch, this gorgeous Good Samaritan—it had all only heightened what she always had privately viewed as the cinematic quality of her life.

After the beginning months of their relationship, however, she began to feel as if she were perpetually ensconced in a grand mix-up. As if only having been asked to run lines with a gorgeous actor, she had suddenly found herself pushed under the stage lights, playing out a scene for which she hadn't rehearsed. A character far, far out of her range. As the movie played on, she watched Scott's character change. He became someone different from the person he'd been in their first scenes. He had transformed into someone she didn't recognize: an antagonist. Someone she had started not to like yet felt very eager to please. Even their conversations felt scripted now, with her own lines veering toward the role of the fool, the fall guy. Their love scenes were stale, undeserving of her steep, one-sided climaxes.

"What did you think about the ending?"

"Excuse me?" Sheila answered, clutching her drink closer.

"The ending of the movie. Was it a suicide or an accident?" the man asked, leaning toward her, his eyebrows hatefully arched.

"An accident," she said. "Most definitely an accident," she added for emphasis.

"What was your name?" he asked. The others had stopped their side discussions of the film and positioned themselves in her direction in sharp, targeted angles, like snipers.

"Sheila," she said.

"Sheila. Why do you think it was an accident, *Sheila*?"

She looked down into her glass. Perhaps the answer was somewhere at the bottom. She thought of suicides that had been ruled as accidents in the past. Marilyn Monroe, for example, although she'd always agreed with conspiracy theorists that it had been neither an accident nor a suicide but something more along the lines of a murder and cover-up. Her uncle, whose hushed overdose as a young man she'd only recently begun to suspect might have been intentional.

"Accidents can happen to anyone. Suicide takes a special breed."

She thought the statement was just elliptical enough to pass for profound. But the others looked at one another, unsure where to place her comment within the context of the conversation. It offered no possible segues and, like her, sat there, dead, in the middle of the room.

Sheila took another long sip of whiskey. When she looked up from the group, she saw Scott approaching her. She couldn't decide whether to be angry at him for leaving her alone or grateful that he had trusted her enough to hold her own with the people at this party. Either way, she felt relieved. It looked like the alcohol had loosened him up a little, unhinged him from that petulant mood he'd adopted at home and in her car.

If it were possible, he looked even more attractive to her than usual. She felt the fleeting inclination to end the night right there, take him home and seduce him, seize control of things in a way she'd been too timid to attempt before. *She* wanted to be the one to fall asleep first with Scott curled up next to her for a change, desperate for more. She wanted him to come multiple times, deep inside her, pornographically. She wanted to give him a proper fuck.

She had entertained the idea of giving fate a little nudge, sticking a pin through the silver-wrapped condom he kept in a black dish next to the bed. While his extreme attention to the business of contraception should've made her feel safe, sometimes she didn't see it that way. Was it so horrific a thought that she might conceive his child? Was a baby born to a mother who looked like her the worst possible scenario, a situation to be avoided at any cost? In all honesty, she wanted to know what he'd do. The mere probing of it made her feel ashamed, but it was nice to know there were ways a woman like her could keep a man like him around.

Scott picked her up from the waist from the edge of the couch so swiftly that she forgot about the discussion she'd been stuck in. The relief on her face was visible to anyone. Her drink spilled, so he fetched her another, this one stronger than before, darker; it seemed thick with syrup.

"Youhavingfun?" He said it all together, like it was her name. She realized he was becoming drunk.

"I am, now that you're here with me." She pulled close to him and hugged his middle, careful not to slosh her drink down the side of her dress. Her cheek brushed his chest. She kept it there.

"Ron, Augusta, over here," he called to them. Sheila withdrew and stood beside him.

"Sheila, let me introduce you to a couple of people over here," said Augusta, her fingers gripping Sheila's shoulders with more pressure than was entirely necessary.

"I'd like to stay with Scott," she said.

"No. Go with Augusta. It'll be good for you." He moved away from her and shared a quick, chummy look with Ron.

The women stood in a semicircle next to the fireplace. Two of them were actually wearing shoulder pads, a throwback to an '80s sense of empowerment. Sheila wondered whether the things had come back in style while she'd been in the hospital. She didn't know what was "in" anymore, and looking down at her own frock, she saw it now for the desperate attempt at glamour it was. Her coat seemed hopelessly buried underneath mountains of others at the back of the closet, so far away, in fact, she felt she'd never see it again.

"This, girls, is Sheila. *Scott's* Sheila."

The women perused her with museum-like dissection. They each picked a different part of her to inspect. One examined the dress, her eyes widening as they drew down to the tulle window. Another woman, blonde—like Sheila's hair but wonderfully alive with body, the perfect color of butter—smiled and looked into her eyes. Sheila always had thought her own eyes were too close together, so close that people looked at her as if she had just the one, then quickly turned away from its dreary focus.

"How did you meet Scott exactly?" one of them asked her.

"I ran out of gas on the Beltway."

She'd lost it right after the exit for the George Washington Parkway. The car had putt-putted to the side of the road for a few meters then stopped, slanted toward the guardrail, where its wheels had frozen in place. She'd flashed her hazards, looked behind her on both sides, and produced a tissue that she waved furiously from a cracked window. She imagined Scott must have seen a person for whom decency often needed to be coaxed, if not forcibly extracted, from passersby.

"Well, that's original. Does that happen to you a lot?" Augusta asked. "Running out of gas?"

"No, it doesn't actually."

The others issued murmured acceptances before exchanging a look. Sheila's tone had taken a sharp, icy dip that she could tell no one seemed to appreciate.

"It beats the way he met his last girlfriend," Augusta said. "She worked at his dealership. Their first date was in the backseat of one of the Corollas, if I'm not mistaken. Corolla, girls, or Camry? Do you remember her?"

"Oh, yeah, I do. Her goal in life was to blow someone during a test drive."

"Smile!" someone said.

Sheila turned around to catch the last bit of a blinding flash.

"Get in here, Jacob. I want a picture with you and us girls. Sheila, could you?" asked Augusta.

Could she what? Be in the picture as one of "us girls"?

"I'll hold your drink," another one said, the churned-butter head.

Take it. They wanted her to *take* the picture. She suddenly felt ridiculous for having ever thought otherwise.

Jacob handed her the camera, and she stepped back until her heels hit the carpet. She pulled her hair behind her ear two times, an affectation left over from high school. The women grouped around the balding, beady-eyed Jacob, tugging at different parts of his suit, trying out wide party smiles, none of them genuine. Sheila looked through the camera's small window but couldn't get them all in the frame.

"Zoom's on the side," Jacob said.

She felt a powerful rush at her left temple, as if someone had hit her in the head with an aluminum baseball bat and she had yet to experience the full blast of pain. The heel of her shoe gave out and her ankle collapsed outwardly at the sudden knock on the inside of her head. There was a flash. The camera hit the floor before she realized she'd just taken a picture of her own foot.

Her heel came completely off as she bent down to pick up the pieces. She went for the brown roll of film first, as if a quick snatch from the light of the room might save the film from exposure. The wooden floor pressed down savagely against her knees, and she felt one of the spaghetti straps fall down, almost on cue. She could see herself quite clearly, even through the drunken fog in her head: a woman in a too-tight dress, the color of a fresh period stain, crawling on all fours, trying to pick up the last pieces of something. No stunt doubles or stand-ins necessary. This was a scene she knew by heart.

Later she was informed by Jacob (who looked at her for the rest of the night as if she'd murdered his grandmother) that the now-ruined roll of film had contained pictures of him and Kim Basinger at a political function. The other women left Sheila by the fire. The crackling embers burned the backs of her legs, although she hardly could muster the resolve it took to move away.

Scott kept his distance. He stared at her from across the room with a look that seemed to repeat, "I told you so. You're the one who wanted to come."

She finished her drink and had another, still stronger. A game of charades had begun in another room. She heard shouts and malicious guffaws. Someone screamed "Fellini" to a riotous round of applause. She spoke briefly to a short Thai woman who hauled in huge sacks of ice to a now-empty bar. Sheila's questions caught the woman off guard, and she answered them in curt bites of broken English before snatching up crumpled cocktail napkins and leaving the room altogether.

At the end of the night, Scott found her behind the bar on the floor. She touched his face, and the heat of his flushed cheeks warmed her fingers. She grabbed hold of his offered hand and pulled herself up from the floor. Her dress was stuck uncomfortably around her waist, and when she tried to pull it down and attempted to catch her shallow, soused breath, she knocked over a drink she'd placed next to her. The laughter from the other room had grown louder. It had silenced for brief spurts but now teetered nervously toward a manic, agitated roar.

Scott found Sheila's coat and he put it on her. The dress underneath felt cold and even tighter around her, almost as if it had shrunk during the night and would now only come off if it were burned away from her skin in pieces. She felt for her keys in the pocket and made a motion to unlock the front door of Ron and Augusta's house. Scott moved to open it himself, ignoring her odd fumble. He pushed them both into the night, and Sheila wondered whether he'd bothered to say a single good-bye to anyone in her name.

As she'd predicted, her car was blocked in. There was a space just wide enough to pass heading straight into the lawn.

"Please go in and get someone in there to move so we can get out of here," she said, opening her car door.

"No. I can get us out," he said.

"You're drunk, Scott."

"So are you."

"Go get someone."

"Get in, Sheila." He pushed her to the side of the car. "I'm not going back in that house. Not tonight."

She remembered when he'd stopped to help her on the side of the road the day they'd first met. "I'm such an idiot," she'd said, but he was so breezy about it.

"I've got a little gas can in my car for emergencies. We'll fill you up then get you a full tank." She'd watched him from behind as he poured gas in her tank.

They had followed each other to the Crown station off the next exit. She leaned on the hood of her silver Celica while he pumped gas for her. He stared at her across the top of the car.

She smiled back, and for a second, the sun seemed to take away all his features until all she could see was his mouth, his tongue pushing through the white gate of his teeth like a pink fish.

She'd said one should never pass up a car wash attached to a gas station on sheer principle. "C'mon. Get in," she'd told him.

He got into the passenger side of her car, almost clipping his head on the door's sharp, angular frame. A man motioned for her to go into neutral and roll up her windows, then waved her forward. Her car was very clean inside except for a layer of dust in the creases of the gearshift's black apron. Sheila pushed in a tape, and the Smiths came on. Jet streams of multicolored soap covered the windshield, bleeding into one another to create a mélange of purplish gray, like the color of a bruise. The darkness of the car made the music seem more important.

"Can I ask you a question?"

"Sure," she answered.

"Why do you drive such an old car? I noticed that your gas gauge is broken."

She gripped the steering wheel. She could dance around this or she be upfront. "Do you want the whole story?"

"Of course," Scott replied.

"I was working for an advertising firm," she began. "Doing administrative work. I'd just completed a two-year certificate program after taking a few years off after high school. And I was so looking forward to starting a new job. A new life. All that."

There had been a woman in her office named Brenda. Brenda was a junior executive *and* head copywriter. She and Sheila, somehow, became fast friends. They would go to lunch and would sometimes get a drink together after work. It was wonderful. She was so beautiful with her black Snow White hair and the voice of an old movie star. And everything she said was brilliant. It was like Brenda was coasting through life on an escalator while everyone else was hurrying up the stairs, desperately trying to keep up with her. She'd never had a friend like Brenda. She'd never had many friends, period, let alone someone so captivating, so accomplished.

When Brenda was going away for a week on vacation, she asked Sheila to take care of her dog, Darien.

"Feel free to hang out at my place if you want. *Mi casa es su casa*. And Darien mostly will keep to herself." She gave Sheila a spare key on a Pizza Hut keychain.

Brenda's condo was, predictably, stunning. So sleek and modern with exposed ductwork and steel railings along a loft passageway, as well as thatched latticework like Sheila had seen in a spread in *House Beautiful*. Darien thankfully proved to be aloof and very low maintenance. One night, three days into her dog-sit Sheila came over late to take her for a walk. As they made their way back up the elevator after the walk, the horrid realization struck her: she'd left Brenda's spare key inside the condo and the door had locked behind her.

She begged at the main desk for a master key, but it was after hours, and the man at the desk was a contract security guard. He knew nothing about any master key.

"Don't they have to come in to change her air-conditioning filter or get in if she went missing or something?"

"Like I said, lady, I don't have a key. And I don't know where a key is. You'll have to wait until morning."

Pets were not allowed in Sheila's building. She couldn't take Darien back with her. She dialed information from a courtesy phone in Brenda's lobby and found a locksmith who was open twenty-four hours in Southeast D.C.

"Is this the first time this has happened to you?" asked a woman with an Eastern European accent and Slavic features. She had arrived with a man in a red sweatshirt and a hat who carried a toolbox.

"Yes, in my whole life. And this is hopefully the last time."

"This is a nice lock. Expensive," the woman said as she examined it. Darien jumped up to be let in. "You can't pick it. They usually put this kind of lock in office buildings. It's very secure."

"So what does that mean?" Sheila had asked. A nervous twitch had developed in her left arm, which she cradled with worry in her right hand, holding onto Darien's leash.

"It means we'll have to drill through the current lock and put in a new one."

It was going to cost $269 to get through the door then replace the lock.

"You're sure it's going to be the same quality lock?"

"It'll be better, because it'll be a locksmith's lock," the woman said.

"The new lock will come with two keys, right?" Sheila asked.

"Yes."

"And you have the lock with you?" Sheila asked.

"Yes. I just have to get it down from my truck."

The man in the red sweatshirt drilled the door while the woman went to retrieve the new lock. They made a lot of noise as they fit the new lock in the hole in the door. An older woman down the hall stuck her head out to see what was happening.

"This doesn't look remotely like the old lock. Look," Sheila said, pointing at the one on the door across the hall after they had finished installing it.

"I don't understand. This lock is perfectly acceptable," the woman said, shrugging at Sheila as if she were simply over the debate.

"That's just it—it's 'acceptable,' not high-end. This is an inferior lock. And the key is lightweight and doesn't even look like the old one. This isn't my apartment. I can't leave her with this lock."

"What choice do you have?" the woman asked.

In an envelope, with the two new keys, one of them slipped back onto the keychain, Sheila left Brenda a note explaining what had happened. She hoped for the best but she was worried.

"The next day at work," she'd told Scott, "I swung by her office to apologize about the lock and to see if I could take her to lunch to make it up to her. Well, I knocked on the door and then opened it when I didn't hear anything. She looked up at me like she had no idea who I was. It was unsettling. Then there was this flicker in her eyes like, 'Oh, yes—you. Can I help you?' I had no idea what to say, what to do. I was struck dumb. I sort of slunk out of her office back to my cubicle like a dazed prisoner. The whole episode was so disturbing. The next day, I asked one of the other admins about it. She informed me that Brenda had been telling people that I was obsessed with her. That I had changed the lock to her apartment so I could spy on her. She said I was creepy and weird, and she didn't find any of it flattering.

"I went home that night in shock. I was so heartbroken and depressed and embarrassed. I thought about suicide. I really did. I broke a mirror and picked up one of the slivers in the bathroom and I caught my eyes in it. Something in that look scared me. I could not trust the person in the mirror who was giving that look. I got into this car, drove straight to Charlottesville, and checked myself into the psychiatric wing of the hospital at the University of Virginia. It's where my grandmother stayed for several months in the seventies. It was the only place I could think of to go. I knew that if I didn't go right at that second, I would harm myself. This car saved my life."

Inside the car wash, the silence in the Celica stood out in sharp contrast to the muted rumblings on the outside. Labeled cylinders sprayed rust inhibitor on the car, then sealant wax, as Sheila and Scott moved through the wash, coasting in neutral. The last light rinse misted over them, and the sound of an air vacuum loomed ahead. Scott leaned over and placed the palm of his hand on Sheila's cheek. When he kissed her, it surprised them both. He looked at her in the approaching light at the end of the tunnel. Her eyes were wide open, as if it were the only way she could have believed that yes, absolutely, it was her this was happening to.

Back in Ron and Augusta's driveway, she heard the car door slam. He'd never even sat in the driver's seat. Her seat. No one had. No one had but her. The wind ripped through her. She started to open the door but stopped when she spotted her reflection in the misted glass. Her white-blonde hair stood up at the sides in thin straws, and the foundation she'd applied so carefully had hardened her face into a mask. She knew he wasn't hers, but if she didn't relent now, hand over to him her one precious thing, the vast meaning of it, the inseparable piece of her it was, he'd be gone.

She opened the passenger door and hit her head on the dulled edge, not used to the car from this angle. The lap belt tugged uncomfortably around her waist, making the dress seem tighter, if that were even possible. She could see the mark the belt would leave on her like the split of a chainsaw, Caesarean—thick and jagged; a woman cut in half yet somehow still alive. She took off the belt.

Scott said nothing as they made their way home. His head moved in and out of a zone that Sheila, at first, mistook for silent concentration but quickly identified as a kind of barely focused drunkenness. An AM station played jazz. She wanted to say it was Sarah Vaughn, but it sounded older, a scratchy relic, something that might've been played on a creaky Victrola. The lights from the other side of the Beltway bore down on them like a search party. She placed her hand on Scott's thigh.

An eighteen-wheeler began to spastically jerk in front of them. Scott tapped the brakes quickly. His head swayed, and one of his eyes blinked rapidly in his struggle to check in. Sheila wanted to say, "Pass it. Go around the thing. Pull over. Take this exit. Let's go back to that car wash. You know the one."

He was too close to the truck, riding its tail as retaliation for the driver having pulled out in front of him so quickly. The truck's brake lights flickered at them, warning, flashing. Sheila heard a desperate, preening moan enter the slow tune on the radio, a woman whose soft wailing was her sadness. Scott muttered a curse, and the car veered sharply to the left to avoid the rear of the truck. They were aimed to hit a solitary stone divider disconnected from the others, metal rods curling out of its center.

Scott slammed on the brakes and swerved the car out of the path of the divider with one hand. His other arm pressed against her tightly. They ground to a halt on the side of the road. He turned to her, breathing heavily and sweating, his tongue hanging out of his mouth, his arm still barred across her. She looked into his eyes; they seemed thankful that she was alive. His arm went slack, and then his hand fell into her lap. She placed her own hand inside it, curled up like a mouse.

Sheila imagined flying with the thrust of the impact through the windshield, an object in motion. The moment would seem to last forever. She'd feel her hand leaving Scott's thigh, and she'd know she wouldn't feel anything ever again. And in some ways, that was a good thing. She'd never again feel shame. She'd never curse that little voice inside, the one that alerted her to other people's hushed whispers. That panic would be squashed, the terror of people gone.

But she'd also never feel Scott's body pressed against hers in that way that told her she was desired even if it was just for that moment. She'd never feel that sense of joy at dinner when she'd look across the table at him and he'd smile at her and she'd know that, as long as the light in the painting burned in the small window, he could always find his way back to her.

Brad's Head Revisited, '94

I. CRISPIN

I FUCK FOR MONEY, AND I like it. The studio tells me how good I am, how much money I bring in, how I look even hotter on film, like a god. Just like a fucking Adonis. I lap it up, obviously. Who wouldn't?

On average I shoot eight movies a year—thirteen two years ago (kind of a peak year for me). I'm the star of the studio, and doesn't everyone know it. The best dressing room on the lot with my name on the door in gold, lowercase letters, fat and round like Bloomingdale's. It's not my given name, of course. No one even knows what that is. Sometimes I forget it myself.

I go by Crispin Mandrake. My second director picked it out after taking one look at me. I like to think I emanated that name, that it shot out of my eyes. My come-fuck-me eyes. I'm happy the word *man* is in there somewhere, because that's what I am, that's what I fuck, and that's what I like. And men are what make it all worth it, right? Hey, if things don't work out on this end, with a name like Crispin Mandrake I should be able to make the easy transition to soap operas. What's the difference between soaps and porn anyway? Same amount of sex, a couple more lines here and there, the same ridiculous storylines. It's all just people getting screwed, isn't it? I like Bo Brady on *Days of Our Lives*. He's got that daddy beard, drives a motorcycle. He's a cop. What a fucking stud he is. Every time I see him on TV, I imagine him as one of the bears power-driving me from behind in *Goldicocks and the Three Bears*, '91, a video I did for Chi Chi LaRue as part of her Naughty Fairy Tales series—the one where we used lube that looked like porridge.

I've got a look that never goes out of style. A shaved head with an eighth of an inch of platinum-blond hair on top, all-natural color (and no, I'm not balding; I'm only twenty-four). I go to tanning beds, since that's the big thing now, but I practically live on the beach, so I could get sun that way if I wanted to. I'm very tall—about six foot five. I've got muscles that give my body definition but don't hulk me out. And a boy-next-door face. I'm the neighbor who mows your lawn on those hot summer days, shirtless, chugging from the water pitcher, the streams running down my chiseled chest (*John Deere's Johnson*, '92). I'm the lifeguard at the country club who doesn't belong but certainly uses the members-only showers when everyone else has left (*The Caddy*, '92). I belong all right. Come on in after your nine holes or your eighteen holes or whatever, towel yourself off, step right in, and see how much I belong (and how much you belong inside me).

These are the "characters" I play. See how good I am at selling that shit? I'm the seemingly innocent young buck who doesn't think he wants it until it's wagging in his face, and then he's like a pro, taking it like he was born with it up there.

Yeah, I bottom on camera. Everyone seems surprised by this at first. They think because I'm the star of the studio, still such a marquee name, I'll be the one fucking the world, bending those twinky fags over the hood of a race car and shoving it in (*Grand Pricks*, '90). A tall bottom is somewhat rare, like a diamond, but I maintain more control in this position. You may not think so, but the bottoms establish the tone of the sex. We clamp down and tighten. We set the rhythm the top thinks he's made happen. It's more erotic for me like this, and I don't use up all my stiffness for hours and hours of shooting. I meant that pun too.

No one follows me around gawking or tepidly approaches me for autographs. I'm just not that kind of star. The guys who do recognize me aren't likely to admit they've ever been in a position to see me in action. I remember standing in line for a coffee at that cruisy Starbucks in West Hollywood, the one on Santa Monica Boulevard on the corner. A cute guy and his girlfriend are in front of me—content, it seems—from the view I have. The guy glances around a little, taking in the atmosphere of the place, bored with waiting in line, I can tell. Bored of her, I imagine as well. She looks like a bit of a nag. Then, while he's surveying the landscape, he spots me, and I notice a look of shock and heat and maybe a little hunger in his eyes. He turns back around, and the girlfriend pushes him forward, almost knocking his straight-as-a-rod ass over. They're up next in line, and I just know it must have been *Arctic Survivor*, '93, the one where I'm holding on to a chin-up bar in an ice-fishing cabin getting pounded by an impossibly hot Eskimo—a classic, a mega hit, one all my fans have seen. The guy is so distracted that he orders a number two like it's McDonald's, and the girl is so dumb that she says she'll have one too.

Sure, there are times when a limp-wristed ogre rushes over to me on the Venice boardwalk, maybe with a coy, nervous buddy, equally heinous, ten paces back, biting his nails and grinning. I'll sign his napkin or the back of a sweaty receipt and flash the wide grin I make for the close-ups, the one I give when I'm first penetrated, all sheer joy and ecstasy. Let's be honest—I have a smile you can see from space.

I've got to keep these guys happy, even the ones I wouldn't look twice at if I were out on my own cruising. They're my fans. "You expect me to ignore my fans? They're life and death to me, baby!" JC said (that's Joan Crawford, my personal Christ). They're the pale night owls, shut up in their dark, locked basements turning me on, pausing me, rewinding me, inserting me into their impossible fantasies, bringing me straight into their lover's bed.

I wasn't always so proud of the work. In fact, at first I barely could get through a night without waking up every hour, shivering, desperate for air to breathe in, then breathe out to expel the shame of what I'd done, what I was going to do tomorrow—and if everything worked out, what I'd be doing until well into my mid to late thirties. At one point, I thought I might have had AIDS—all that night sweating and worry—but I always use condoms, and I look better than ever. It couldn't have been that; it was just a period of adjustment. When a star is born, it must erupt over some nights, burning fast and bright at first then settling into a simmering glow of longevity. It can be scary.

II. SAWYER

I WASN'T ALWAYS LIKE THIS. I was in the closet so deep that I was in someone else's closet.

Back then, in high school, I had such an unreasonable set of expectations to live up to. This "playing straight" thing. It was so demoralizing. Feeling terrified of being found out, I went out of my way to make sure my secret—the thing I knew so early on about myself that I couldn't change—stayed as hidden as possible.

There was a boy in my year named Jerry. "Jerry Hall" we used to call him, because he slunk down the hallway like a model on a catwalk. He was so tall, like Jerry herself, almost obscenely tall, but stick thin with knobby wrists and a gaunt look. "Affected," one might have called him, with the pursed lips and the walk with the knees lifting up in the air like he was walking over puddles of diamonds. So unaware—it's like he didn't care at all what people thought about him. Kids walked behind him, kicking his backpack, knocking him behind his knees so he'd collapse into a heap in the middle of the hallway. Even the girls laughed at him. But he'd get right back up and keep walking like we were so many small, insignificant obstacles he had to glide through on his way to class, which he, of course, just made more fabulous with his very presence.

He was pale, with whitish-blond hair and translucent skin under which you might see blue veins running through, at his temples and along his spindly arms. Kind of like an alien. Just like he was barely even there. He looked otherworldly enough from his appearance alone, but his fey walk and penchant for affixing sparkly stickers and rhinestones to his backpack (and for declaring to anyone who'd listen his great love for the recently wed Princess Diana) clearly aligned him with a faggy kind of sensibility that I was scared to shit of and couldn't be associated with. He laughed right along with everyone else, though. No matter what I felt when I went to bed at night and closed my eyes (and I don't think it was anything different from what Jerry saw when he closed his), at least I didn't *look* like a fag.

Brad Malone and his best friend, Chip Sanders, were two of the most popular boys in my class. I went by Sawyer back then, although my full name is William Sawyer. We'd all grown up together, all the way up from grade school, and I'd always looked at Brad and Chip with a mixture of admiration and jealousy as the two of them took the basketball court—because, of course, they were always first string starters—or hunkered down together at the table in the cafeteria closest to the jukebox. No one sat at their table without being asked for fear of having the shit beat out of them. They always played Survivor's "Eye of the Tiger." They were really hot too.

I can't remember exactly how it happened, but somehow, against all known logic of the universe, I found myself in that chosen circle. Brad or Chip might've said hi to me one day, or one of the two of them might've asked me to sit at their table, although I can't imagine Chip would've done anything without Brad's approval, so he must have blessed it or been the one to ask himself. I can't recall the exact moment it happened, but soon enough I was hanging around with them at school, which made

it even more crucial to keep my "tendencies" hidden. It's funny
how I could tell that they weren't just having me on, that they
really had accepted me into their group. Brad's little brother, an
eighth-grade pipsqueak no bigger than a bicycle rack, started
saying hi to me in the hallway. Almost like a sign of respect, it
seemed. That was how I knew I was in.

How I managed to stay in the group was entirely up to me,
and don't think I didn't realize that. When someone gives you a
break in life you don't ask questions, and you sure as shit don't
go around biting the hand that feeds you. Like any big break,
you build on it. You don't undermine it by being Mr. Quizzical. I
knew my place in the high school pecking order had changed.

Brad always seemed to go after Jerry with a particular amount
of gusto. It wasn't a normal kind of taunting; there was something vicious about how he spoke about him. "Who does that
little faggot think he is, hopping around in those white jeans and
that fucking queer backpack? It's disgusting." Chip pushed Jerry
around in the hallways, but he didn't seem to outright hate him
as much as Brad did. "God, he can't just walk around like that,"
he'd tell me. "Someone needs to teach him a lesson."

One day after class, the three of us lingered in the locker room,
where Jerry was getting dressed. We all had lunch following gym,
so there wasn't as much of a need to hurry. All the other boys
from gym were gone; this wasn't going to end well for any of us. I
looked at Jerry while we all changed, and I tried to urge him with
my eyes to move quicker, faster—to run out of there in his sweaty
gym clothes, those short white shorts, how short they were back
then. Jerry's shorts seemed even shorter, perched as they were
on top of those huge ostrich legs, white and nearly hairless. He'd
worn a pair of white knee socks with pink stripes near the top.
"Just because I can," I'd heard him say to his gal pal Janelle, who'd
commented on them during class.

"Chip, go watch the door," Brad said.

Jerry had his shirt off and looked toward the exit. He dropped a deodorant stick on the tiled floor, from nerves it seemed, although he was still trying to act like nothing was out of the ordinary—that he'd just get dressed in his white jeans and flit away down the hall to lunch. The deodorant stick rolled under the bench toward the end, right where Brad was standing. Brad picked it up and brought it to him. "You looking for this, faggot?"

"Yes, please. Thank you," Jerry said, looking at the floor.

"Well, here you go." He offered the deodorant to him. Jerry cautiously lifted his head and made a movement to accept it, but Brad dropped it to the floor. "Aw, shit. I'm sorry. You'd better pick that up." That indefatigable light in Jerry leached out like a flashlight on its last scrap of battery. He didn't want to pick it up; I didn't want him to pick it up. But he had to. There was nothing else he could do.

When Jerry bent over, Brad jumped over the bench and pushed down hard on this back, so hard that I thought Jerry's spine might break in half. "Hold him down," he instructed me, as he took his own shorts off.

"What?" I asked.

"You heard me! Hold him the fuck down."

I barely needed to use both arms; he was so skinny. I straddled the bench and grabbed his shoulders, those pale shoulders with a smattering of freckles. He gazed up at me with a look of absolute resignation. Not any hatred toward me. I was his comrade, his fellow fag, and he didn't even know it. And I didn't help him.

Already hard, Brad hawked a loogie into his hand, rubbed it onto his dick with one hand, while pulling Jerry's shorts off with the other. When Brad first penetrated him, Jerry bit his lower lip and let out a grunt. He didn't fight much, only when it seemed he was in real pain, and then it was with a violent swish of his head, like we'd seen him do before in the hall, affecting the toss of a nonexistent ponytail. This thrashing was like he was trying to shake off a yoke that had been placed on him.

With gritted teeth, Brad rode Jerry from behind with the expertise of a seasoned top. He went from holding his hipbones to placing one hand on the small of Jerry's back to achieve maximum leverage. The gym bench turned out to be just the right height.

"When I'm done, Chip, come over here. You're taking him too."

I looked down at Jerry's face. That twinkle that was always in his eyes, even when he'd been knocked down on the floor near his locker, had disappeared. Something harder had replaced it. He looked wiped clean.

Brad climaxed with loud groans and then pulled out. He collapsed on top of Jerry and then kind of hugged him for a second, a bear hug around the boy's middle.

"Sawyer, take the door while Chip has a go," he told me.

Brad pulled up his shorts and took the position I'd held of holding Jerry down. I headed to the door to keep watch. Half the scene was hidden by a row of lockers, but I saw Chip taking a rough turn with Jerry; the two of them were laughing and high-fiving each other. I pretended we were all just roughhousing.

Jerry was as gay as me. *Part of him had to have liked it,* I kept thinking to myself like a mantra. Wasn't it all a dream?

III. CRISPIN

I WAS IN THE BACKROOM of a seedy bar on Abbot Kinney. This was before the neighborhood got cleaned up. I'd been watching one of the TVs at the end of the bar that was showing porn from the seventies. A guy in a red Mustang convertible had picked up a sailor hitchhiking on the side of the road. He was taking him back to this mansion in the Hollywood Hills. The sailor had blond curly hair like a statue and looked like he couldn't have been more than sixteen or seventeen. He was next to the fireplace on his back in no time, wearing big white knee socks with red stripes on the top, like I used to wear at soccer camp when I was a kid. No music. Just the boy moaning painfully as the older man of the house stuck himself inside of him. I thought it was pretty hot, and as I watched, I forgot I'd done the same thing earlier that day. Only I'd been straight down, flat on my stomach, legs spread-eagle, as a couple of football players warmed up for their game by taking turns on me in the locker room, the water boy complete with a pail and white towels they used for cum rags (*Touchdown Tag Team*, '93).

As I focused back on the TV in the bar, a man started to rub me through my jeans, an older guy. He was balding and, yeah, a little paunchy. Like an ex-boxer gone to seed. But very Ed Harris. Hot. I let him go further, undo my fly and take me in his mouth right as the rich guy was flipping the blond kid over on the screen, propping him up on the billiards table for a hard pounding from behind.

Ed Harris was damn good at giving head. He placed his hands on my thighs as his head bobbed back and forth, up and down. The shiny top of his scalp reflected the overhead amber lighting above us. I tossed my head back and relaxed. I could see where flies that had gotten too close to the light above had burned, their desiccated husks grouped together toward the center of the over-hanging fluorescent—mass-casualty style. A little death pit hanging over me as this guy worked me over.

When I glanced at another screen, I saw something I recognized immediately. I took my hand away from the base of Ed Harris's neck and leaned forward to get a better view. There it was, absolutely—a solo jack-off video I'd done three years before (*Solo Twink Boyz: Volume One*, '90), not something of which I was especially proud. It was my first picture.

I'd answered an ad in the back of *Manshots* magazine looking for "models." The man told me to show up at a studio loft in Hancock Park at six in the morning, which I found weird. But it was a job, and I had no money and was really close to joining the hustlers on the Boulevard because at least they were getting paid while they were getting laid. And I wouldn't be wasting the money on drugs like a lot of them, but food, so I could bulk up more. Drop this skinny, ravaged-bird look I had going on then.

When I got there, all I found was a mattress on the floor. A fat cameraman tossed me a squeezable tube of silicone lube and told me to get started. I said I didn't need anything like that. All I had to do was take off my clothes, tweak my nipple, and my dick would rise all on its own. He said I wasn't being paid four hundred fifty in cash to perform a fucking magic show. He said he wanted me to lube my cock up and polish it like it was serving the royal family. Well, I love the royal family. Like seriously, I'm obsessed with them. Princess Di and Fergie and Princess Anne. So it's not like he could've said anything more perfect to get me going.

But that didn't necessarily erase the smell of the place and the fact that I was choking a little on the dust and dried skin that lifted off the mattress when I got on and started working myself over. And the constant leer of the cameraman as he watched me, taking on not the passive role of the observer behind the lens but something more menacing—an instigator, beckoning me to climax with hushed commands. "Yeah, boy. Do it, boy." I tried to shut him out, look past him to a spot on the wall, but I couldn't seduce a brick. So I stared straight into the camera and stroked harder and harder, and the cameraman kept goading me on, knowing he could later cut out his jeers during editing.

Honestly, I almost felt the cameraman inside me, whispering in my ear like he was a lover and could inspire this level of passion from me. When I finally climaxed all over myself as he had ordered me, I arched my back so dramatically that I felt I might meet myself full circle, do a complete revolution on the mattress, stick my own dick up my ass, and fuck myself right out of this room, into another place entirely. Into the stratosphere with my name in lights. The slob threw me a towel and told me to clean up because someone else was coming to shoot after me. He'd probably be the next kid in the video.

I wiped myself, then tossed the towel over my bare shoulder like I was off to the beach and took from the cameraman's proffered hand an envelope, creased with black smudges but thick with cash. I left my bike on Sycamore and walked home. I felt as if I'd stepped over into something, and that piece of myself I'd left on that video would stare out at me through the eyes of any horny guy who'd ever seen me in it.

Later, the other guys, other performers, shared with me similar feelings of having crossed over into something dangerous, out of their control. It gets easier after that, they'd said—after I figured out what I was doing and certainly after I'd learned that the largest part of it *is* the acting and that it's the saving grace of it too. In the end, it wasn't really me. There was someone before Crispin Mandrake. And now there was Crispin Mandrake. That's who was doing all of this.

Ed Harris took me deep down his throat, deeper than I could remember getting from anyone in some time. When I was about to come, I grabbed the back of Ed's head and pumped my load down his throat, still watching myself perform in that video at the end of the bar. I'd seen that someone, that guy I'd been before. I'd just forgotten when exactly.

IV. SAWYER

THE THREE OF US NEVER talked about what we'd done to Jerry. In fact, the more time that passed—and the fact that Jerry disappeared from school soon after—granted us the illusion that it never had happened at all. When he'd first left, the other kids came up with a bunch of different theories. Several of the girls suffered a kind of buyer's remorse over their years of mistreatment of him. Since Janelle, his one true friend, began circulating the notion that he was too good for our pathetic Midwestern high school and finally had left for New York City, I felt a bit of relief. I started to think maybe this was true, that what had happened to him wasn't traumatic at all but just the push he needed to find his true self. "He said he could close his eyes and see his name in lights," she told a group of students in the hallway as Brad, Chip, and I walked past. "I mean, didn't he just *scream* Broadway to you?" she asked them. But there was a doubtful look in her eyes. The more confidence she gained in her voice, the greater the look of fear multiplied. She was afraid for him, but she had no idea why.

Brad picked me up from school one day not long afterward. He'd been suspended from school for skipping classes and nearly driving his truck into Rick, the old retard who guarded the front gate and reported kids who tried to leave. He said we should go out to an old shed he knew of to shoot at some panes of glass he'd found. They were supposed to be installed in a greenhouse that was undergoing construction across town and being stored there temporarily by the man who'd fired Brad from his contracting job the summer before. He said Brad didn't know what he was doing and was freaking out the customers with his rage (throwing a hammer at one of the Mexican guys he'd hired for daily work, for one). "That fuck doesn't know how to install shit. With me gone, he's probably got his thumb up his ass. And those spics aren't worth a can of beans." I stared straight ahead and kind of laughed a little. "Beaners!" he said.

When we got there, Brad opened a small cooler of beers and popped one open for me. I'd smelled his breath on the way over; he clearly had already started drinking before coming to get me. He was sloshing his words a little.

He set up the panes of glass along a broken fence near the woods. The glass made everything behind it look really clear and crystal, as if we were watching it all on a screen. A nature show. Brad took the first shot. He hit the pane right in the center, and it exploded in a cascade of glass, disappearing into the weedy dirt, like it had never even been there.

"You see that, bro? That's what I'm talking about! That's it, bitch!" he yelled at me, then took another swig of beer.

I took a shot, but it only clipped the corner of the large pane and sent a crack down the side.

Brad squeezed my shoulder. "Hey, that's okay. Try it again."

I took a second shot, and the whole pane burst like it had for Brad. He clapped and hollered and then grabbed his crotch.

I don't think I knew how badly I wanted him until he was in my mouth and holding the back of my head. He had total control over how much I took, how fast I went, everything. And I heard him moan, like he was really enjoying it. But as much as I was enthralled over actually doing this with him, with anyone, the moans made me think of the locker room and Jerry's face. I started to pull away, but Brad grabbed the back of my neck like a vise with both hands and finished himself off. He pulled his jeans up and said we should reload and hit the rest of the panes. It was like nothing had happened at all. Afterwards, I had a beer.

The next week at school, Brad returned from suspension. I ran into him and Chip in the hallway along with this new guy they were calling Maverick. I said hey, and they all sort of nodded. A fire drill went off during fifth period, and I found the three of them standing near the soccer goal in the athletic fields, set aside from the rest of the class. I can't remember how they said it, but (and here are the buzz words I recall), my "loyalty was under suspicion." I said something like, "My loyalty? What is this—the Mafia?" And that dumb-fuck Maverick, who I barely knew, looked at me with his no-neck and his maroon varsity letter jacket like, "Yeah, maybe it is the Mafia, which means you'd better shut the fuck up."

The trio conferred for several minutes. Then they turned around and hawked the largest, most viscous, lumpiest loogies.

Real phlegmglobbers, you could just tell by the sound. They all spat them in the same spot on the grass.

"Sit on that," Brad said.

"Are you serious?"

"Yeah. Sit it in, and then we'll see where we are after you do."

I think I was wearing Jams, those shorts we all wore in the '80s. Yellow Jams with little surfers on them. I squatted and, in the most delicate way, lightly touched the small puddle with my ass.

"Don't fucking Nancy around with it," Brad said. "Get in it. Squoosh your ass right down in that shit."

It was cold and slimy, and it soaked through the fabric of my shorts onto my underwear then finally touched my skin. They stood around me in a circle so no one else could see what was going on. After a couple of minutes, they spread away from me and regrouped at the other side of the goalpost. When the teachers announced the drill was over, they headed back to class. Chip was the only one who looked back, and he was shaking his head.

I didn't wash their spit off my shorts. I left it there, and it eventually dried, but for the next few hours, I felt it every time I sat down. A dewy shame on the back of my Jams and me just marinating in it.

V. CRISPIN

IT SHOULD BE SOMETHING I would've learned by now. I should have the formula down. The right amount of food to eat, when and what and what absolutely not. And I do, to some degree. I've learned the hard way about Mexican or Chinese, those foods that sit like dead carrion inside you, getting poked by a long rod but never brought back to life. I've coaxed my body into evacuating itself. Flushing out—to be that empty, suctioning vessel so totally desired. To be fucked but not filled. Like a really good foster home, I imagine sometimes. I take in the hard-luck cases, nurture and coddle them, only to dispatch them satisfied and assured. I know they'll be looking for my dark little house wherever they're living from then on out.

I'm not a regular grocery shopper and prefer going out to eat or ordering in over cooking. I left home before I'd really gotten the hang of that, although I can make a killer grilled cheese with tomato. When I was really training hard and bulking up, I'd go out and eat for days. Three-foot-long subs, a pint of ice cream, fistfuls of peanut butter—and I still needed more. It was like I'd been starved in the dark for years; I couldn't stop putting things in my mouth, lifting more iron. I even did steroids for a couple months, but I stopped when I felt they were changing my mood. Making me think of darker places I didn't feel like going. Besides that, I didn't want bitch tits.

I stand in the middle of the kitchen and survey the possibilities. There's still a nice collection of snacks to feast on, most of them in unopened packages. I take down a bag of Tostitos from the pantry and sit on the floor. I'm hungry. I didn't eat the day before, not because I couldn't handle the shoot. There was just barely any time to take a leak, let alone chow down on a Philly cheesesteak.

I was sure the new top in town was going to be in the studio that day—Brad Chambers—but he wasn't. I couldn't risk my first meeting with him taking place between mouthfuls of doughy bread and cheese melting down my chin. This could be the new super pairing of the decade in gay porn. If I play my cards right, I could solidify my place in the industry by luring that expensive dick over to me. If Chambers likes me enough, I could ride this thing out long past my prime, because Brad Chambers is a huge name in straight porn, and this is his first crossover. He chose to cross over with me. He's going to bring with him a totally different audience.

You'll laugh, but I've imagined scenarios where Chambers puts fucking me into his contract. A bottom clause. "I must fuck this guy in at least five movies a year." I'd had another actor demand as much a couple of years ago. I'm that good. Damn it if I'm not going to go all the way with this.

The chips are lightly salted. I take two or three at first in one hand, savoring the taste of the corn and the oil; my buds are salivating. Once my stomach gets that quick fix, I dig in my other hand, double-fisting them into my mouth, which I can open very wide. I crawl over to the fridge and find the salsa, meaty with thick chunks of onion and green peppers. I dip three fingers in and scoop it straight into my mouth, mixing it with the chips already in there. Then I pour the whole bottle right in the bag, close it at the top and shake it all up. You can learn a lot when you improvise.

When I get to the shoot, the lights are so bright. A couple of them are on dollies so the best boy or the grip or whoever (they're all just regular people in the background wearing black T-shirts, so really, who cares what the fuck they do?) is arranging them to light the set, a locker room. I see him almost immediately. Brad Chambers. Brad. It's like a name from a past life. He's huge, almost as tall as me but super muscular, which makes him seem that much bigger. I can read pretty muscular on camera, but this guy's body will make me look downright puny.

"We gonna do this?" he says, like he's asking for permission.

"Hell, yeah," I answer. "I've been waiting for this." And I have. All my life.

We've both already gotten the sides for the scene some days before, but there aren't that many lines, so I take the extra time before the shoot to do some push-ups and curls. Make sure my abs are popping out just right. I have this image of myself from before, when I was super skinny with a little twink belly shaking like a fanny pack as I was getting pounded. It's not cute. You can be a fat person caught in a thin person's body. It's true—look it up.

When we're finally ready to start shooting, Brad comes over and grabs my shoulder and gives it a little squeeze. "I'm big, okay? Just a warning."

All I do is smile. He has no idea what I can do with "big."

I start by blowing him, and he's right—he's fucking huge. I'm almost gagging on it, because, yeah, I still have that reflex. It's not exactly something I'm looking to get rid of.

Then in walk three other guys. I recognize one of them, Troy Majors. I did *Raising the Titandick*, '91, with him a couple of years ago, but the other two are new. I've never seen them before. Big meaty guys, all three of them. The director looks at me like, "Surprise!"

Troy and one of the other guys hold my arms back behind me while the third guy pushes my mouth down on Brad, and I really am gagging on it now and it's getting to be a little much. But the cameras are rolling, and I have to keep this up because the studio is expensive, and like they always say, in Hollywood, time is money. This girl Lois who's working one of the mikes gets in the shot a little, and the director yells, "Freeze" because he doesn't want to ruin the shot, just in case she can be edited out or wasn't too far into the frame. So I'm frozen with Brad's cock shoved down my throat. I look up, and Troy smiles at the other two guys like, "See how good this kid is? I told you."

Before I know it, I'm taking Troy from behind, and the other three are surrounding me. Troy's warming me up for Brad, his big gay premiere moment, although I'm sure he must've done this before. He certainly isn't acting like this is the first guy he's face-fucked. Then Troy switches with another one of the guys, a darker, more Latino guy. And then the third guy is taking a swing, but I don't notice until he's halfway through; I'm in a fugue state and still kind of hungry.

The lights shine down on me like the sun, and then I can tell it's Brad's turn because he's the biggest. The three other ones are either spreading my legs open or pushing down on my back so my butt pooches out. Brad holds on to my right forearm, which is twisted behind me. He pulls on it like it's a rope that's keeping him on a horse. There's music in the background, which I didn't hear before because I was trying to concentrate on what I was doing. But Brad's riding me hard, and it hurts a little, like when you try to go down a shoe size and it pinches your little toe inward. Just a pinch.

Still I keep on going. Because after Brad's done, the others might want a bit more. And it's the director's picture, not mine. We improvise that way out here. I can tell it's not really up to me this time. And I can take it. I'm a professional. I'm a star. Everyone knows it.

Hester Prynne
Got an A

WHEN JOAN SLEPT WITH HER daughter's English teacher for the third time, she asked him to give her a grade.

"Grade what?" Chad asked. He was ten years younger than her, with brown wavy hair and whorls of clipped chest hair that scratched her cheeks.

"My performance. In bed," she answered.

Chad grinned. "Is there a curve involved here?"

"Shut up!" Joan threw a pillow at him.

"You *were* a bit late today. I typically dock a student an entire letter grade for that."

Joan looked up at him from her berth at his chest. "I had to find a sitter for Coral."

"Bring her next time."

"That's ridiculous. She's just a baby."

"I'll accept your excuse…this time," he said.

"So the grade then?"

"Let's see. Considering effort, performance, enthusiasm—all of which were superb. And that bit in the beginning? With the—well…you know, extra credit."

"Yes," she said, dragging the "s" out like the hiss of exhaust through a hose.

"Mrs. Cashion, I give you an A+."

Joan leaned in for a kiss, so Chad pulled her on top of him, cradling her buttocks and combing her red hair with his fingers. She was only half kidding. She really needed that A.

THAT NIGHT, AFTER SHE HAD cooked dinner, Joan laid the place-mats on the table. Each placemat was about three inches from the one beside it, for a total of four around the dinner table. The distance from one placemat to the next turned out to be roughly the size of the distance from the base of her thumb to the base of her pinkie. She pressed her hand on the table, palm facing down, and kept it there for a moment as she leaned against it. She imagined Chad having backed her up too quickly against the counter so that she had to catch herself with her outstretched hand, forcefully taking control but still being coy and feminine about it. She came out of the pose and continued with the rest of the placemats.

The placemats were made of a rough oatmeal mesh. She and Russell had purchased them from a vendor outside of a pension they'd stayed in during a trip to Caracas years ago. It was 1994, she seemed to recall, the year fluttering into her field of view temporarily, like a butterfly just about to die.

Joan put the last placemat down and looked at the table, each chair in front of it empty. Charlie would be down first, always early to dinner. He'd sit to the right of Joan. He was a good boy: studious, considerate of others, an overachiever, something she'd never encouraged yet secretly delighted in. There was also a tenderness to him of which she'd always been proud. He cared for others in a way that felt authentic to her. There was little, if anything, put-upon about him. He and his best friend Dale constantly volunteered to help out at a soup kitchen or drove a van that picked up the inner-city homeless on cold nights. Honestly, he was exactly the kind of kid Joan would've hated in high school. She probably would have laughed at him, convinced that his do-goodery was an affected tool to get into a good college or something to lord over the godless heathens with whom she'd always aligned herself. But because Charlie was hers, she couldn't think of anyone she'd rather be like. She hadn't immediately ascribed a name to these traits, but they always made him seem other-worldly.

She heard his shuffle down the back kitchen stairs, coming down sideways like he always did, as if he were hopping over tiny wickets in the worn red-carpeted steps.

"Can I help you finish setting the table?" he asked, as he popped down into the kitchen.

"You always do."

He took hold of the top of the handles of the silverware from Joan's hand, and she felt the smooth graze of his fingers. He kept his nails so well manicured, much more than she did her own. She had a habit of allotting herself two that she was allowed to bite at will; Charlie never would have put one of his fingers into his mouth, let alone bitten a fingernail.

She held on to the end of the bunch of forks and knives for a second until Charlie playfully tugged them away from her and laid each utensil precisely on the placemats.

Charlie was Joan's; Dena, his twin sister, was Russell's. That was how it always had been, as if by contract. Coral, the baby, was a neutral party, a swing vote. She was too unformed—too pink and chubby and clueless—to throw her weight to one side.

"Mom, we have an away game tomorrow night, and I want to stay over at Kathy's afterward. Last week you said it was okay." Dena blew into the kitchen like a thunderstorm, with a duffel bag and several hair clips trailing behind her.

"Well, if I said yes once, I'm sure that was enough. Have you finished your paper on F. Scott?"

"Is the night tender?"

"Is that a yes?"

"It's finished."

Dena sat to Joan's left and Russell's right, although she always inched a bit closer to Russell during the course of a dinner. Daddy's little girl. Joan didn't mind because, after all, she had Charlie.

"Could you please pass the mashed potatoes, Dena?" Charlie asked, waiting patiently with his hands out, poised to accept the platter.

"Here. Will you be pocketing extra to feed the great unwashed masses later?"

"You're an absolute peach," Charlie said.

"Dena, doll, pass your brother the mashed potatoes. He can do whatever he wants with them," Russell said from the head of the table, uncharacteristically getting involved in the twins' business.

Not too smart, Dena was, and she seemed to be headed down the high-school-slut route, if Joan were being honest with herself. Dena did, however, possess a certain saber-toothed precision that she could apply to something she really wanted. Joan had seen it before in Dena's pursuit of a particular boy at school or in the way she'd work on Joan to get her to buy an expensive piece of clothing at the mall on one of their forced mother-daughter days (which always seemed to end in a slammed car door and at least forty-eight hours of mutual avoidance). It was true that Dena lacked the traditional ease of book smarts that allowed someone like Charlie to glide through life, but there was no way Joan could say Dena didn't go after and often succeed in getting what she wanted.

Russell didn't see Dena's faults. He was blinded by the uncultivated admiration he had for Dena that was based almost entirely on the fact that she resembled the girls he hadn't been able to sleep with in high school. This was Joan's theory, and she stood by it indefatigably.

Joan wasn't fooled, though—smoking pot, hanging out with those glassy-eyed wastoids who insisted on wearing black tank tops and plaid skirts. And the boys wearing eyeliner—when had *that* come back into fashion? So very the Cure of them, Joan seemed to recall from her own high school days. Even Dena's recent participation in cheerleading, which Joan had coveted as the beginning of something potentially encouraging, a path toward normalcy—was no more than a front to gain easier access to the better parties, an open ticket to harder liquor, hotter boys. Behind the cheerleading practices and away games lay secret dens of football players and drunk girls with pompoms that she could only envision as after-school specials. Quick, foggy rapes on beer-slicked linoleum.

She never could understand how different they could be from each other, Charlie and Dena. Dena and Charlie. Twins. Fraternal, but still. All that time inside her together, learning each other's rhythms, playing patty-cake, tickling the bottoms of each other's still-forming feet, making plans, one twin curled into a ball in the other's lap like a chrysalis. Then out they popped, more different from each other than if she'd found one of them on the street in a recently bombed Latvian village. It startled her. Even when she'd tried to dress them up alike as toddlers, Dena had always found some way to sabotage her outfit: deface the smiling baby in the puff-paint hot air balloon on her sweater, rip up her white tights so they resembled something left over after a serial killer had butchered a child.

Joan pulled Coral's high chair up to the table to her left so the baby would be positioned between Dena and herself. Dena angled her body away from Coral and more in Russell's direction.

"Dad, guess who made it to the top of the pyramid?" she asked.

"Is that supposed to be metaphorical?" said Joan.

Dena glanced over at her as if she'd only just realized another female was at the table.

"It's a cheerleading pyramid, Mother," she said, barely looking Joan in the eye. "The one we're doing is referred to as a 'teddy sit,'" she turned to say to Russell.

"Let me guess—her name starts with a 'D' and ends in an 'a' with an 'e' and an 'n' in between. What's that spell?" Russell said with a huge grin.

"Dad, you're such a dork!" Dena said, laughing.

In all the sudden laughter, Coral caught wind of a potential game and clapped her little hands in glee.

Coral was one of those accidental babies. Joan never wanted to push abortion off the table, but Russell was enthralled with the idea of their having another child. She knew he wanted a boy, some randy hellion who'd play little league and football and all the things Charlie had always shied away from. When Coral had finally popped out, a chubby baby with a salmon-pink hue (hence the name Joan had chosen on the spot), Joan felt Russell's disappointment, but it seemed eclipsed by her own. She'd somehow convinced herself that an additional child would be the staple on their marriage—a small, winking adhesive. But she wasn't.

"Babe, you make the best pot roast that's ever been created. Mother of the year, kids?" Russell said.

"The century," said Charlie, looking over at Joan with that side smile, the special one he reserved for her, with one dimple tucked under his glasses.

"The century's only ten years old. Can we aim a little higher, Charlie?" she said, grabbing his shoulder and smiling.

WHEN JOAN AND RUSSELL HAD gotten married she'd experienced (on her fabled wedding night no less) something akin to a death in the family: a localized yet still-yet-to-be-contained plague. It was the unfortunate—and bizarrely swift—death of her sexual attraction to the man with whom she'd put in almost a year preparing to spend a lifetime, which threw her into a state of absolute terror. It wasn't something she'd planned for, but as she looked back, she realized there had always been signs.

For starters, she had met Russell on the rebound. Her boyfriend before him had been in a heavy metal band called Nails on a Chalkboard. What initially had attracted her to Gage, Chalkboard's leonine front man, besides his golden mane and the smoky way his voice made the most terrible lyrics sound beautiful ("I hide/My love for you like genocide") was the fervent sexual chemistry they'd shared almost instantly.

Joan had met him at the Delta counter at Dulles Airport, where she worked part-time as a ticket agent; Gage had been traveling with his band to San Francisco. She didn't think much of him when she first saw him at the back of the long line that had started to curve out to merge with the line for American Airlines. He was sitting on his big Samsonite suitcase, as if it were a lawn chair, reading a book while his band mates stood in front of him. As they moved closer up the line, she noticed that it was a copy of Kurt Vonnegut's *Galápagos*. She'd seen it in a display case at the bookstore in the terminal and had picked it up one day during her lunch break.

"How do you like the book?" she asked, as she printed out his boarding pass.

"S'okay," Gage said.

"I like it when the schoolteacher is about to suffocate herself with the dry cleaner bag. But then she just…stops," she said, scanning the small computer in front of her for an upgrade option.

"You get to the brink, and then you yank yourself back. Right?"

"Exactly," she replied. "I've upgraded you and your companions to first class. You'll be at Gate B-4."

"Before," he said.

"Well, B-4, but yes." His band mates began to walk toward security.

"What I mean to say is *before* I take off, I want your number."

Joan nodded and quickly produced her number on the back of his baggage claim ticket.

"Just to let you know, I'm anything but a Yoko Ono," she said.

AT BACK TO SCHOOL NIGHT the fall before, Russell and Joan showed up in separate cars. Russell had been working on a case downtown, and she had an early-evening shift at the airport, so they'd decided to meet at the high school. When Joan entered the front door of the school, a wash of tension passed through her. The hallways seemed cramped and the ceiling low.

Other parents walked in pairs alongside them and were commenting on the displays set up at strategic points in the hallway, demonstrating some of the more superior work from the student body.

"How about I check in with Charlie's teachers, and you take Dena's? We should switch things up, yeah?" Russell had approached her and placed his hand on the small of her back as he led her through the small crowd.

"Seems fair," she said.

The twins had been in separate classes since they'd begun school. It had never really been up to Russell or Joan, but then again, they'd never objected to it. Joan easily could imagine Dena cheating off Charlie or manipulating him into doing her work.

She and Russell pulled out the twins' room assignments and traded.

"English with Mr. Chandler. Sounds thrilling," Joan murmured.

"Meet you in the cafeteria in about an hour," said Russell. He shuffled down the science wing to meet with Charlie's chemistry teacher.

When she finally located Mr. Chandler's classroom, he was finishing up with a squat woman in a black bun and her lanky husband. The teacher was smiling and nodding enthusiastically. Younger than she had expected. Thirty-three maybe. Very handsome. He noticed her through the black crisscrossed glass window in the door and waved her in.

"Come in, please. I've just finished up here with these folks, so please take a seat."

The other couple regarded her politely and headed out. The wife looked at her a second or two too long, but she didn't think much of it. The combination of Joan's sky-blue blouse and red hair was striking. She couldn't really fault people for taking a second look, male or female.

Mr. Chandler was leaning against a large metal stool that towered over the two student desks the woman in the bun and her husband had just vacated. When Joan sat down in one of them, she was forced to look up in order to meet his eyes. Otherwise her eye-level was in direct line with his groin. She had noticed a very visible penis line when she first sat down that brought an unexpected rush of heat to her face.

"So which one is yours?" Mr. Chandler asked.

"Joan. I mean, Dena. I'm Joan. Joan Cashion. Dena's mom." Joan held out her hand and Mr. Chandler grabbed it. His hands were soft, like they'd been sitting on top of a warm radiator.

"It's wonderful to meet you, Mrs. Cashion. Let's talk about Dena," Mr. Chandler said. He wore a dress shirt that looked like graph paper.

"Eek. Is it okay that that just made me a little nervous? Suddenly I feel like I'm in trouble, Mr. Chandler."

He laughed, and Joan noticed how white his teeth were.

"Oh, gosh no. Not at all. This won't be too painful. And please call me Chad. 'Mr. Chandler' makes me feel like I'm a hundred and five years old."

"Hardly," Joan said. She felt a flush in her cheeks. There was a slight pause, and Mr. Chandler—Chad—smiled.

"Dena has had kind of a rough start to the school year. She's a smart girl, and she participates when she actually shows up to class, but that's been a fifty-fifty situation since the first week."

"I'm completely embarrassed." Joan brought her hand up to her forehead as if to shield herself from the supposed embarrassment.

"We've read *The Scarlet Letter* and *The Awakening*, and we've just started *Tender Is the Night*."

Just the mention of those books, made her think of Gage. When they were together, they'd lie in bed and read just as much as they had sex. It had thrilled her to talk about all those books with him. She got such a kick out of the fact that Gage didn't look like the type who'd like Iris Murdoch (or even know who she was), with the long hair and the tattoos of scorpions and raven-haired biker chicks running up his arms like they were chasing each other across his body. But he spoke as passionately about novels as he did about his music, the lyrics of which Joan liked to think had gotten better since he'd started dating her.

"Dena had to write a paper on one of these books. I asked the students to provide an outline. It was due last week."

"Let me guess—she didn't turn it in," Joan said.

"No, no, that's not it at all. Not only did Dena turn her paper in early, but it also was one of the best student papers I've read on this material. I'm using it as a sample for next year."

"I'm…well…I'm shocked," Joan said.

"Dena has a ferocious quality that will serve her well in her studies. She acts like she doesn't care, but I've rarely seen this kind of dedication. It's inspiring."

Joan's cheeks flushed. She couldn't have seen it all laid out more clearly: her daughter had a crush at the very least.

"I'm inspired just by hearing about this," she said.

AS JOAN LEFT CHAD'S APARTMENT building and got into her car, she studied the surrounding street. People were generally rather quiet this early in the evening: folks coming home from work, or out on their lawns raking the fall leaves. She saw one couple having cocktails on their porch. She and Russell never shared a cocktail together. Only if they were at a party and they were offered would she even have one herself. She drank a glass of Cabernet once in a while with dinner, but that was rare. Russell's mother had been a raging alcoholic and, in one of her more lucid moments, had warned Russell that if he weren't careful, he'd be completely seduced by the sauce and go full-blown *The Lost Weekend*. Russell, so afraid of the prediction delivered to him from the gaunt, sallow-faced woman he barely recognized as his mother, stayed away from the stuff. Consequently so did Joan.

She always felt this way when she left Chad's place: overly cautious. In the first few minutes of being back alone in her car, she'd convince herself that she was being followed, watched from afar by a spy—although it was never, in her mind, actually Russell who was following her. He was somehow too far removed from the situation to be a possible interloper in her affair. The idea of Russell haunted her more than the actual, physical *person* of Russell. In her cruel imagination, it was always someone else, someone with Russell's best interests at heart, who would expose her.

As she inserted the keys in the ignition, she saw—parked two cars ahead—a blue Malibu with two young men inside. Charlie's friend Dale drove the same car. He was always picking Charlie up for school and sometimes on the weekends. As she looked closer, she realized it *was* Dale and that was Charlie next to him sitting in the front seat. *Those two are always together,* she thought, and of course she was happy for it. Charlie was entirely too attached to his studies. Never once went out on a Friday night, except with Dale this past year. It had pained her to see him without a group of friends, like Dena had. He stayed at the library all hours then went to the public library in town once the school's had closed. If it weren't for Dale, the poor thing never would have left the house at all for a non-library reason. She admired Dale for always being such a good friend to Charlie. Dale was much more in line with the kind of son she thought Russell might've always wanted: sportier, with an enthusiasm for weightlifting and football. You could tell a lot about your children's friends by how they spoke to you, and Dale always greeted Joan as if she were his own mother. So polite, wholesome, a wonderful young man. She'd found a T-shirt of his in Charlie's hamper once. She brought it up to her nose and inhaled deeply, finding the smell of it comforting, like the scent of possibility in a recently purchased book.

She looked closer at the two of them, still keeping herself hidden, slunk down low in the bucket seat of her Volvo two cars behind. The boys appeared to be fighting. Dale was yelling at Charlie, and gesturing with his hands and arms a lot, and Charlie—her poor Charlie—was shaking his head and twisting one of his hands around the strap of the seatbelt, tethering his hand tighter and tighter, as if he were hanging on to it, dangling over a steep cliff.

They're having a lovers' quarrel, she thought. It was unmistakable. She would've guessed it if she'd only been a random passerby.

Dale turned away from Charlie and peered out the window. His fingers traced some of the condensation that had collected near the edge. Charlie untethered himself from the strap and reached out to place his hand on Dale's shoulder. The storm between them appeared to have passed. Dale turned to him and stared. He took Charlie's glasses off and kissed him sweetly on the lips, just as Joan had done so many times before, saying good night to him when he was younger. But then Dale broke from the light kiss and began looking around furtively. Joan ducked down farther into her seat but could still see the two of them; the front seat of the car in front of her was reclined so that it gave her an unobstructed view. After scanning the area, Dale pulled Charlie toward him by the base of his neck and kissed him harder. So passionately it was almost startling. Charlie responded by grabbing on to Dale's shoulder and squeezing it, bringing him in closer. The close contact between the two boys seemed to jolt

Joan from being a voyeur to an active participant. She suddenly felt like an invader.

She glanced at a scrunched-up straw wrapper on the floor of her car. Then she turned on the radio. It was "Misty," a soft piano version. Charlie really was hers after all. There was very little doubt of that now. They were both transgressors in a way, keeping secrets from those closest to them. You love who you love even when the world makes that love impossible. Or you lust. Suddenly the fact that they both were partaking in something illicit made her feel even closer to him. It made her love him more than she already did, which was too much, she'd always told herself. More than Dena. Maybe even more than Russell.

No, definitely more than Russell.

JOAN FED CORAL THE CARROTS first. For some reason, Coral thought they were the best thing in the world. It must have been the bright color and the bit of extra sugar Joan mixed into the baby food. She inevitably turned everything into a dessert, thinking the baby would eat it faster that way. She grabbed the grocery list off the fridge with one hand while holding Coral in the other.

Dena watched her from the kitchen table. Her arms were crossed, and her brown eyes bore into Joan. "I don't know why you're trying to make this into a grocery trip for my benefit. You don't need to cover this up with another transparent excuse. Your lame fucking lies. I know where you're going," she said in a voice Joan never had heard before. Stern and unforgiving, like a distrustful parent, a tone neither she nor Russell ever had adopted in the rare instances they'd punished her. Joan always had felt as if she were acting whenever she'd tried to inject seriousness into her commands and knew Dena always saw right through it.

"Don't say 'fucking' to me, young lady."

"Fuck you! You knew I liked him, and you went and fucked him anyway. How many times, Mom? How many times did he fuck you?"

"Honey, I didn't realize you had a crush on him."

"Don't belittle it. And don't call me 'honey.' You're no more than a slut."

"Dena, I need to pick some things up. I'll be back soon. You can go meet your friends if you want. I don't want your father encountering *this* when he walks through the door." *This* meaning Dena, cold and blank, like a sociopath hooked up to a lie detector test.

"Don't tell me what to do. You don't get to tell me what to do ever again," Dena shot back.

Coral giggled and clapped her tiny hands together as if Dena had told an especially funny joke. Joan hugged her, unsure whether the pounding in her chest was hers or the baby's. She headed out the back door to the garage.

After fastening Coral in the car seat behind the driver's seat, she sat down, holding the keys. She reached into her purse and pulled out her cell phone. She texted Chad to tell him that she was coming over in thirty minutes. She didn't tell him why. By now Chad was used to getting last-minute texts from her like this one, alerting him to small snatches of time that had arisen in her schedule when she'd be able to meet him. She didn't want to risk calling him and have Dena come out the door to find her talking to him.

She pulled out of the driveway and headed toward the grocery store. She really did need to pick up some things. She gazed out the window at the houses that lined the street. It was early enough in December for people to have already put up Christmas lights. They seemed to get more aggressive as she looked from house to house. A simple string of white lights tastefully strewn over a couple bushes near the front door gave way to oversize colored lights that snaked their way through gutters and piping, wrapped around a Santa Claus on a roof as if he were Joan of Arc. It all felt vaguely threatening.

Joan glanced in her rearview mirror and saw Coral's hands grab at a hexagonal toy with a bell inside. It's tinkling rang through her.

She pulled into the Safeway parking lot and surveyed the other cars. With the engine off, the chill in the air felt disquieting and unsettling. After an Indian summer, then a hasty fall, their recent descent into winter seemed premature. No one should be forced to end a relationship in the winter. It was inhuman.

Joan got a cart and placed Coral in the front, facing her. Coral, always so easy to manage and amuse, was delighted with all the colors, the neat, ordered groupings of produce, the bright-colored packaging of the cereals. For a child, a grocery store is a place of endless possibility.

She looked at the wide smile on Coral's face, then recalled a moment that autumn when she'd considered the distinct possibility that Coral was retarded. She didn't have the Mongoloid features of a Down-syndrome baby, but there was something too happy about Coral. Too simple. She was easily fascinated by weird sounds and colors, not in the normal way of a child discovering the world. It was as if she were discovering them anew each time. Joan wanted to get her into a language or an instrument as early as possible.

She placed several items in her cart: eggs, heirloom tomatoes for the salad she knew Charlie liked, Tampax for Dena, Grape-Nuts for Russell. Alongside the vibrating hum of the fluorescent lights above her, she heard "What I Did for Love" from *A Chorus Line*. It sounded far away, as if it were playing on a fairground outside the store. She and Russell had played that record in his first apartment. They'd played it loudly to drown out the sounds of his roommate making love on the other side of the wall. The song was about what it meant to give up dancing, but she felt what it had to say about the uneasiness of having to say good-bye to anything. It hurt no matter what it was: dancing, singing, a lover, your own life, your child. Losing anything is patently hideous.

The woman at the checkout counter was in her late fifties and wore a red smock with a name tag affixed above the "S" in Safeway. Her name was "Deborah!" She scanned each of Joan's items, then placed them in a paper bag.

"What a sweet little girl. Your daughter is lovely," she offered with a smile as she handed the bag to Joan.

"Yes, she is. But she's not mine." Joan exited through the sliding glass doors.

She pulled up to the curb outside of Chad's house and turned off the car. In the early-evening dusk, an orange glow came from the front room where his couch cut the room into a diagonal. On the left-hand side, she saw the footstool he'd found in an alleyway that he'd fixed up and painted turquoise. A guitar was leaning up against a corner where the south and west walls met; he'd never played it, and she'd never asked about it. In many ways, he'd been the anti-Russell—manic with his interests, bookish to a fault, a heart-on-his-sleeve kind of guy. She could only imagine he would've eventually grown tired of their affair after too much longer. That was why she'd asked for the grade at its height. She could tell it would only have gone downhill from there. She got out of the car and crept down the flagstone walkway.

Chad answered the door shirtless, ready to take advantage of the unexpected visit.

"Dena knows. Everything. She knows everything," Joan said as she brushed past him into the house.

"Oh, my God. How? Why?" Chad said, pulling her around to face him.

Terror washed over his face: the potential layoff, the tarnished career, the now-worthless résumé.

"I mentioned your...smell. It was a slip up. I don't know why I said it. It just came out. People say things."

"I can't believe this. My smell?"

"You have one—like cinnamon mixed with fresh-cut grass. It's something a girl notices."

"Why would Dena have noticed?"

"She has a schoolgirl crush on you, Chad."

"This is insane."

"Look—she's not going to say anything to Russell or anyone as long as I break things off with you right now. Tonight."

"All things considered, this seems to be the best-case scenario, no?" He brushed up closer to her.

"I can handle Dena. I've done it for years. She talks big, but she's just a frightened girl looking for her father's approval. She'd never want to hurt him. She'd never tell."

"As soon as you leave here, it's over," Chad said.

He brought her down to the couch and cradled her head in his hand as the last bit of their affair slipped out of him into her. She hadn't climaxed like she had with Chad since before the twins. Before that, it had been with Gage, who'd made her come every time, without much effort. It was like certain men fit inside her perfectly, and others were just off. Like trying to put the rectangular peg in the circular slot.

He was getting closer; she felt it. He always ramped it up like this. So she grabbed his right buttock and moved him in faster. This was it. He looked at her—his wavy, thick hair hanging over his eyes, which were so bright. When they started to roll back in his head, she knew he was about to come, and she felt herself go too, and then they were rocking back and forth together like a horse pistoning up and down on a carousel, a child's ride and then…

"Oh, God, Coral!"

"What?"

Joan got out from underneath him and scrambled for her underwear. "Where are my shoes? Where are my goddamn fucking shoes?"

"Joan, what's happening?" Chad asked, still sweaty and naked.

"I left Coral in the car! She's—she's—oh, fuck, my shoes!" Wearing only a bra and underwear and holding her keys, she threw open the door and ran toward her car. The flagstone on her bare feet was ice cold, so she leapt onto the grass, which had become crinkled with ice. She approached the passenger side of the car and saw Coral on the other side with her face turned toward the window. Leaping over to the other side—the side of the car she only now realized she never should have had her daughter sitting on since it was directly behind her from the driver's seat—she could see Coral's eyes closed. She finally unlocked the door.

Her daughter was cold; she could feel that even through her clothes. She unlatched Coral from the baby seat and ran with her toward the house. After placing her on the couch, on top of the blankets upon which they'd had sex only minutes before, she rubbed the girl, the little angel, with her hands and the blankets. She didn't even notice where Chad was, if he was there at all. All she cared about was her daughter, the little girl with the big smiles and peachy cheeks.

And then it happened just like that. Coral opened her eyes and seemed to look at her like nothing had happened at all.

A Goddess Lying
Breathless in Carnage

WHOSOEVER COVETS THY NEIGHBOR'S WIFE, *he shall never stray.* Whosoever has woken up next to his wife but thought of his neighbor's instead; whosoever has cherished the fact that his wife's back often faces him when he wakes up in the morning, so that he can pretend, even for just that predawn moment, that she is someone else, that the long slope of her alabaster back dips unknowingly into regions he can only imagine; whosoever has never been to his neighbor's wife; whosoever has never been *in* his neighbor's wife; whosoever has volunteered to wheel the trash can and the recycling bin down to the end of the driveway just so he can look through the window above the sink of his neighbor's house down the hill at the base of their cul-de-sac where she always washes dishes after dinner while her husband walks around in the background just oblivious; whosoever has, on a whim once, driven into her carport and pretended that he lived there and even got out of his car to meet her at the front door and when she, of course, opened her own door to see who was standing there, came up with the excuse that he was missing some mail and wondered whether it might have been mixed up with hers and did he think she could check, and then while watching her pillage through her handbag thinks in just that moment that he'd make himself as small as possible to fit into a place she visited often: He'd live in the back of her mailbox anxious for her fingers to graze him as she reached for bills and catalogues; he'd

crouch into a ball at the bottom of her purse, sitting on the plank
of a nail file balanced precariously on the edge of her key ring
and a pack of tissues; he'd shrink into something so small that
he could live on one of her eyelashes, then move up and down
with each closing of her eyes, each impossible wink; whosoever
has imagined cradling her short-pixie-shorn head in the palm of
his hand, gently guiding her down to his cock from which she'd
enthusiastically receive whatever avalanche of gifts she'd be able
to coax out of him, grateful and ecstatic to receive his bodily flu-
ids as if they had curative, magical powers; whosoever has made
love to his own wife yet actively imagined she was someone else,
even going so far as to cover her face with his wide palms as she
tossed and whipped her large mane of brown hair against his
chest as she rode him with her knees pulled into a clench, like on
a ride in an amusement park too tightly secured; whosoever has
licked his lips at the sight of his neighbor's wife at a cocktail party, in that bombastic, eager way he has with that face he has that
reads "devoted," "stable," "safe" (his mother would say "a catch,"
but then whose mother doesn't say that?), who has fixed her a
drink at the makeshift bar set up in the living room, taking just
shy of too much time to clink one ice cube after another with silver clawed tongs into one of the gold-leafed crystal goblets someone thought were impressive enough for this crowd, who then
poured mostly gin with her tonic and squeezed her lime in such
a way that both of them were momentarily blinded by two escaped pistons of lime juice and who then laughed at the sitcom
hilarity of it all while watching each other through now-squinty
eyes (for, of course, whosoever covets thy neighbor's wife must
also imagine that she covets him, if only for that moment when
they both share a laugh and a lime-clouded look); whosoever has
treated every problem he has with his wife as a non-issue in the
alternate universe where he's fucking his neighbor's wife, who
looks at a sagging roof in a thirty-year-old house or the dramatic
slope of a broken gutter as things his wife has cooked up simply

to annoy him, to occupy his time, whose two children are pre-ternaturally astute and fluent in exotic languages that he cannot speak such as Mandarin Chinese or Latin, languages to which his exceptionally intelligent wife is already well attuned and can therefore carry on conversations with them so he can sometimes walk into his own kitchen in his own house in the United States of America and feel like he's stepped into a Chinese noodle shop off a noxious alleyway in Hong Kong, underage whores dispersing like rats from the screened-in backdoor, whose wife's propensity to forget to shave her legs, occasionally rubbing up against him in the middle of the night makes him want to vomit, reminding him of cheap vacations where he had to sleep in a bed with his father while his mother and sister slept in another bed across the motel room; whosoever has imagined choking his wife just so all the languages she knows might spill out of her mouth, word after unrecognizable word, like dead black eels found in waterlogged corpses at the bottoms of drained creeks and lakes; whosoever has followed his neighbor's wife down an aisle of the Safeway, his own cart temporarily parked out of sight, past the fresh produce section with the fine mists of the sprinklers dowsing the leafy cabbage and long, tan turnips like a vineyard at a winery he once visited in Sonoma with his wife after they were first married, who picks up a bottle of mangoes swimming in viscous syrup with which he can imagine himself poised above her, dripping juices off the edge of the flaccid mango slice, pooling in the crater of her belly button before he sucks it right out, who dreams of taking her into the chilly trough of cellophane-wrapped packages of ground beef and tenderloins and coiled turkey-sausage links and fuck-ing her in it, fucking her right in the meat bin so their thrashing limbs puncture the packages as the meat escapes, wrapping itself around her legs, stringy bits of ground turkey curling themselves around her ankles like sea creatures, a goddess lying breathless in carnage; whosoever cheats on his wife every day in his mind, as if she is a burden, a disappointment to him sexually, a serial boner-killer, who could very well be carrying on her own mental affair, with one of her students even—that boy she employs as a teaching assistant or that one girl in her class she refers to as "the Nadine Gordimer girl" (his wife described herself to him once as "sexually fluid" and has admitted to having had affairs with several women during graduate school before they met); whosoever secretly hopes that she feels these things for other people so he may justify his own silent, daily longings; whoever feeds on these silent, daily longings, who subsists on the fantasies like a prisoner subsists on his sweet, rationed bread, who is actually held at bay by his desires, propped up by them, able to be a good husband, to be a good father by the very existence of his secret interior life, whose wife is physically saved from domestic violence or marital rape by virtue of the fact that he imagines his neighbor's wife is *inside* his own wife and therefore cannot be beaten or violated; whosoever finds himself coming home from work and, seeing his neighbor's wife once again in the window of her den straightening a pile of magazines on a low glass coffee table, just as she might've done if the two of them had been preparing the house for a party, or getting it ready to bring home their baby or selling it and moving away together, leaving behind his professorial wife and his children; whosoever sees her and thinks, *What if she were mine?* He shall never stray.

Three-Sink Sink

FIRST, PICK A FAKE NAME. Something totally different from your own but one you'll remember to answer to. Nothing too porn-like. Buck, Ryder, Storm, Dick, Apollo: These are names to stay away from. Choose something simple and boyish. Like Jake or Chip or Hunter. Dylan is popular. The fake name will come in handy later on when you want to pretend it's not you who's doing this.

Use a fake e-mail address (preferably including your new fake name) to post an online ad. Use Craigslist or rentboys.com. Don't exaggerate, and don't oversell. You know your best assets. You have a great ass, for example. Take a picture of it, and put it in the ad. Don't get too specific. Give your vital statistics, then say that everything else is negotiable from there. You don't want to leave too much of an online footprint. Use phrases such as "looking for generous men" except replace the "s" in "generous" with a dollar sign. Be subtle, but make it clear from the start that you're looking to have sex for money. This isn't a dating site. Your willingness to be firm and in control of the situation will serve you well later on. Remember that.

Try to weed out the obvious flakes and weirdos. Learn to look out for them. Men who don't use proper capitalization or grammar are probably not for you. Ones who use ALL CAPS like they're shouting at you from across cyberspace—again, best to avoid them. Stay away from black men sleeping around on their girlfriends. They're on the down-low and more likely than not have AIDS. Statistics back this up. Men who are willing to send you a picture of themselves are rare but suspect (although not wholly discountable). Your best bet is to find someone with something to lose. For this reason, white married men are cash cows. They're hungry for sex; they haven't fucked something tight in a while; they have cash to burn; and they usually come quick so it's an in-and-out job.

Don't set age limits for yourself. You might have to fuck someone really old or someone really ugly. Good-looking, young men don't pay to have their dicks sucked by twinks barely out of high school. Expand your list of dos and shorten your list of don'ts. Start an online conversation with someone. Be coy. Ask him what he likes. If he brings up his wife, ask him what she doesn't let him do and say you'll let him do it to you. Let *him* bring up the wife—don't do it yourself. Talking about wives gets men nervous, then guilty, then scared, then gone. Learn to suss out whether wife or family talk is a turn-on or a conversation killer. Same with the "daddy-son" stuff. Again, follow his lead. If he gives you an opening, take it. Role-play. You're the son. Your dad wants to fuck you. Go from there. Whole subgenres of porn are devoted to this scenario. If need be, do research.

When you find a guy who's interested, learn what the job entails. Stress your adherence to safety. It's true, and it'll make your date feel more secure. Except this isn't *Pretty Woman*, and you're not Julia Roberts, so don't use the word *date*. You're a gay escort. Use the word *trick*.

Just so there aren't any surprises, negotiate your fee upfront. Don't kiss anyone on the lips. Get his address, and find a time that suits both of you. Make sure it doesn't conflict with anything you have going on in your real life. Write his address on a piece of paper that you can throw away later. Write down the name he gives you: Gene. It could be as fake as the name you're giving him, but who cares? You're not getting married. Describe what you'll be wearing. Tell him you'll be in jeans and a white T-shirt. A baseball cap is good, if you have one. It'll make you look boyish. They like boyish. Makes them think they're fucking that kid they had a crush on back in high school forty fucking years ago. Your job is to be that boy they had a crush on, the one they never could get.

Walk around to the front of the building. Light a cigarette, and pace up and down the sidewalk, occasionally pulling the slip of paper with the address out from your pocket to make sure you're in the right place (even though you know you are). This will get out your nerves. Your hands probably will dampen. Wipe them on the sides of your jeans. Stub out your cigarette, and finally enter the building. Don't look around to see whether people are watching you go in. No one's watching you go in, and it'll make you look suspicious. Act like you belong there. The elevator will go straight up to the penthouse, then open directly into the man's foyer. Oddly, this will remind you of the elevator in the movie *Three Men and a Baby*, which you saw in the theater multiple times in 1987.

Immediately you'll notice that Gene is much older than he claimed to be. He's not "forty-nine." He'll look like he could be in his mid-seventies, older than your own grandparents even. Suddenly you'll feel panicked, but you'll already have stepped out of the elevator and accepted his spindly handshake. Resist the urge to run away. Things will move quickly from here on out, yet certain moments will slow down in a dramatic fashion, like what it must have been like when the *Titanic* first struck that iceberg or how long it took Carter Cooper to hit the sidewalk after he leapt from Gloria Vanderbilt's fourteenth-floor window.

Gene's hands will be cold and oddly smooth, as if he has no fingerprints or palm prints. As if he's a vampire. When he's shaking your hand, he'll place his thumb on top of your hand and move it around in circles, as if he's already taking some kind of liberties with you, testing the waters. The penthouse will be spec-

tacularly decorated with large oil paintings and immense Orien-
tal vases sitting atop their own gilded pedestals. You'll see book-
shelves behind glass cabinet doors that go up to the ceiling. He'll
tell you he's a writer, and you'll see a couple of his books lined
up at eye level next to framed pictures of his kids and—judging
from how recent the photos are—grandchildren. You'll begin to
regret the fee you've already negotiated with him and think you
should've charged much more than eighty dollars. Remember
this for next time: Always aim high.

As you're eyeballing his apartment, you'll notice a woman in
a maid's costume. Don't ask Gene who she is. She's obviously the
maid. She won't speak much English, so don't speak to her. She'll
be on her way out. She's paid well to not speak of things like *you*.
Issues Mr. Gene has like *you*. When she catches your eye from
behind the glass-paned French doors that separate the living
room from the dining room, ignore the dumb, glazed look she
casts your way. Look at her like you're better than her. You are.

He'll chat with you a little. Stick to your story. Don't tell him
anything about you that's true. Use your fake name. Remember
to answer to it. If he asks you if it's fake, tell him it's your real
name. He'll know you're lying, but he won't press you. He'll ask
you to take off your clothes in front of him. Remove them slowly. Tease him a little; draw this part out. Get him excited. He's
old, so the idea of a nineteen-year-old undressing himself will
be enough to get him going. His dick will start to stiffen, and
you'll see its tumescent outline against his cream slacks. Once
you're down to your underwear, bend over so your bubble-butt
ass wags in his face. Wear briefs; they'll make you look more boyish. He'll stick a couple of those crypt-keeper fingers underneath
the elastic band of your underwear. Don't shudder when you feel
his cold skin press against yours. Act like you like it, like it's turning you on. Moan a little. Let him pull your underwear down
to your ankles. He'll finger you. His fingernails will be long and
might scratch you inside. Again, act like you think it's hot. Resist

the desire to kick him in the face when he's down there worshiping your tight asshole.

Gene won't be able to get hard enough to fuck you. He's old.

You'll feel high as you walk to your car with that cash in your pocket. Take it out and smell it. Put it in your back pocket and squirm on top of it while you're driving home. Pretend you're Demi Moore in *Indecent Proposal*. Take the cash out when you get to your place. Call your dealer and tell him you want a bag of his best crystal. Smoke it, and then don't leave your house for a couple days. When you need another bag, hit the Net again.

YOUR NEXT TRICK WILL BE in town on business. He'll say you can come to his hotel. It's a nice hotel, much nicer than any you've ever been in or stayed at. He'll tell you to wear khakis and a Polo shirt and to meet him in the lobby at seven o'clock. You don't even own a Polo shirt. You go to Ghetto Vintage downtown on U Street and find a used red Lacoste shirt. It has a hole in the bottom, but you can cover it up when you tuck it in. The Jamaican girl with the dreadlocks will charge you twenty dollars for it. "It's used. Can't you sell this to me for five bucks?" you'll ask. She won't even bother with your negotiating. "It's vintage, not used," she'll say. Smile on your way out. Look at her pathetic retail job and laugh to yourself.

You'll stroll into the hotel lobby and pick a spot on a pink-and-turquoise-striped satin sofa. This place will be fancy as shit. Hold your legs together, proper-like. Or cross one nonchalantly so the ankle of one leg rests on the knee of the other. This is the scene where Julia Roberts goes to the horse races in the brown polka-dot dress—your desperate attempt at fitting in. A man in a blue blazer with gold cufflinks will come off the elevator and beeline toward you. "Dylan?" he'll ask. He'll have an accent. Texas? "Yep, that's me," you'll answer. "Shall we, sir?" he'll ask. Oklahoma? You still can't place it. Don't ask him where he's from. Follow him toward the elevator. Your tan loafers will give your heel a blister.

The last time you wore them was to your high school graduation two years ago, and they hurt even then. You graduated a year early. Your teachers told your parents you were too smart. You were bored there.

You'll stand side by side in the elevator, but you'll be able to see him in the mirrored walls. He'll be handsome, early to mid-forties, with black wavy hair. His cologne will smell like one of your friend's dads.

When you get off on his floor, travel down the hall with him to his suite. Look on the wall where it says, ROOMS 901–925 ←, ROOMS 926–950 →. Think of movies set in hotels—*The Shining*, for instance. Think of all the different people who've had sex in the room you're about to enter. And other people who might have died there or been killed there. Or raped. The man will open the door and push it open for you to follow through it, as if he's holding open a carriage door. Suddenly you'll feel special and kind of rich. Almost immediately you'll realize this is the gold standard of tricks. The best they ever get. Quickly formulate a plan to give this man the best fuck of his life to ensure his calling you every time he's back in the city.

He'll ask you to undress in the bathroom and come out in the robe that's hanging on the door. The bathroom is about the size of your apartment. You'll see small samples of hair and skin-care products in wire-mesh dishes wrapped in cellophane and tied with hunter-green and white ribbons, which you'll realize, by the logo emblazoned across your robe, must be the official colors of the hotel. Slip off your loafers and incongruous tube socks and the stiff khakis you got from the dry cleaners and the Lacoste shirt with the hole. Leave them in a heap on the floor under the three-sink sink like sloughed-off skins. Take off your white briefs and stand naked in front of the mirror. You just got a haircut, short and kind of butch. It makes you look significantly younger than you already are. Reach in the pocket of your khakis for a quick bump. Take it out and hold that little one-hitter up to your nostril. See yourself in the mirror again, and put the bumper back in your pocket without taking a hit. Slip into the robe and go out to meet him.

He'll be in a robe too. His chest will be barrel-like and will stretch across the opening of his robe like Superman. Like it's bursting to get out. He'll have a clipped chest with small flecks of white swirling around like Van Gogh stars, and he'll open his arms up and take you in them. "I just want to hold ya for a minute before we go. That okay?" "Of course," you'll answer. He won't be wearing a wedding ring, but you'll be sure he must have taken it off beforehand out of respect for the wife he most surely still loves and the kids he most definitely has (he just exudes "dad at a football game"). He'll scoop you up in his strong arms and lay you down on the eight-hundred-thread-count sheets (you'll have read that on a fact card in the bathroom). He'll open your robe and rub your smooth chest with his large, rough hands. He's a workingman turned businessman. You can tell from the brawny shoulders that don't ever quite fit in the suit jackets he wears, his ropey forearms that seem thick and stocky from his having baled hay, his hard, callused hands. You'll realize you're kind of falling in love with this man, which will jolt you back to the business you have before you. You'll grab hold of his cock and knead it through his robe. Watch him throw his head back. Let him enjoy your warm hands, getting it ready for your mouth, then your ass. He'll take off his robe and jump on top of you, seemingly brought to life by the switch of the knob that is his dick. Break your rule and kiss him on the mouth, deeply. See if that's okay with him, and when he reciprocates, let his tongue swim inside you, peeking through new depths, into this new person. This Dylan person you've created. Watch him slip a Magnum on his thick cock, spread open your legs, and plunge deep inside you. Look at his eyes; watch how they don't avert from yours, like he's pretending he's someone else too.

Take a shower, and get back into your clothes. Feel the bumper in your back pocket and congratulate yourself for being sober for that experience. When you reenter the room, he'll be dressed and putting on wool socks and a new shirt. There'll be a wad of bills on the table next to the door. Pick it up, and shove it into your back pocket. Meet his eyes and shake his proffered hand. "Thanks, bud," he'll say. Leave his suite and walk out into the hallway. Note the pattern on the carpet and the crown molding where the walls meet the ceiling. In the elevator, take out the wad and see that he's paid you two hundred fifty dollars, a hundred more than you agreed upon. Walk out of the elevator, and head to the revolving doors that spill you out into the street. Accept the greeting of the doorman who thinks you're staying in the hotel. Turn around and smile at him, backing up as you walk away—like if you turn your back on it, you might forget it could ever happen this way.

PUT UP THE SAME AD, but sign it, "Love, Tina." When you hook a guy, tell him you'll take cash or crystal, whatever he's got. When you show up in the Perkins parking lot, walk over to the guy's car. He'll be parked in a dark blue Honda coupe near the green dumpster where the waitresses come out to smoke. Tell him you know a place where you can go. It'll be dark, so you won't be able to tell how old he is, but it won't matter. Get in the front seat. If he rubs you through your jeans, tell him to stop. He has to show the cash or the drugs, or this doesn't go any further. He'll pull out a plastic bag from the pocket of his jean jacket and ask if you want a taste. You'll say no, that's cool, and tell him to turn right at the road before the high school. Make him drive back to the end of the park road where there's a playground with a log cabin nearby. Tell him to park his car a little uphill, and then have him follow you into the cabin.

Walk through the door and lead him inside. Tell him you'll suck his dick and let him fuck you. He'll pull his pants down, and his dick will be thick and short, like a stump. Get your mouth around it. Work the thing. You'll be high in ten minutes, and then you won't care about this asshole. You'll still be a little high from this morning, but it's fine. Just make sure to keep your eyes on the goal here. For a minute, you'll remember having played in this little cabin as a child. Your baby-sitter took you here and played Madonna mixes on her boom box and let you organize her stickers—oilies and scratch-and-sniff. She gave you a scratch-and-sniff with an animated pizza man, and you thought the scent had worn off, so you painted it with tomato sauce to capture the smell again, but it didn't work.

When you come to, he'll have bent you over a plastic bench against the wall of the cabin near the plastic window. You'll feel around to make sure he's wearing a condom. He won't be because you'll have forgotten your golden rule of always being safe (you, more than likely, also forgot to insist upon this in your e-mail). You'll push him off you, but he'll have a reserve of strength that you will not have expected. Keep trying; keep fighting. Get out from under him. Your chances of catching something increase the closer he gets to ejaculating inside you. Scream. He'll put his hand over your mouth and bear down harder on you. Bite his fingers. You'll taste the metallic bit of a ring in your mouth, and it'll be the first indication to you that he's married. "Ouch, you goddamn fucker!" he'll say, and he'll punch you in the face while he's still fucking you. After he comes, he'll pull his pants back on and call you a faggot. Don't argue with him. Just ask for the bag. He'll say, "Fuck you," then leave you on the floor of the cabin. When you hear his car pull away, think about how you're going to get home. You can hitch a ride back to Perkins. Or walk. Use the water fountain outside the cabin to clean yourself up. Wash between your legs. Take a shower when you finally get back home. Grab the wooden box you keep your stash in and dump it out on the glass coffee table. Arrange the little white flakes into one manageable row and Hoover it up. Ignore the small bits of lead and dust. Light a cigarette and put some Blondie on. "Atomic." Go to bed.

TAKE A COUPLE OF WEEKS off. Find the old man you went to that first time. Gene. When his maid stares at you too long while he's in the bathroom, tell her "What the fuck are you looking at?" in Spanish, and then tell her to mind her own goddamn business. Ignore her when she utters "*Maricón*" under her breath. Tell Gene your services cost a hundred and twenty dollars now. He'll be nice enough about it, but there'll be a flash of distrust in his eyes, a whiff of unfamiliarity. He'll sodomize you with thick cigar containers greased up with Vaseline. At one point, he'll push one in too deep, poking your vital organs, it'll feel like. *Is this what the extra forty is for?* you'll wonder. When he can't get hard enough to fuck you, he'll slap it against your thigh until he comes—thin, but chunky like watery gruel and tofu. Consider swiping something on your way out. One of those crystal dishes or the Majolica plate or a green-painted egg. On your way out, hawk a loogie into his building's flower bed of white peonies. Say, "Fuck you" out loud. Light a cigarette. Call Marcus and get a bag. Shoot it up this time for kicks. Don't wake up until Tuesday.

PICK A NEW NAME. YOU don't feel like a Dylan anymore. How about Paul? Or Tommy? You look like you could be a Tommy.

Ten Seconds

THE ONLY WAY TO REALLY describe our film, *Ten Seconds*, is that it's a documentary/performance art/drama hybrid. It will be called "genre-bending" by some critics. A "snuff film" by others. But don't be fooled. This is pure art *of the moment*. It's spectacular anticipation valued over career longevity. Really, it's just ingenious.

WE'RE PLANNING TO APPROACH ZOSIA Mamet for the lead. She played the kooky, fast-talking, slightly rodent-like Shoshanna Shapiro on HBO's *Girls*. Her character smokes crack by accident at warehouse parties and gets de-virginized by homely men. She's the daughter of Pulitzer Prize-winning playwright David Mamet and Academy Award-nominated actress Lindsey Crouse. She once played a lesbian on *Mad Men*. Why Zosia? Well, she's clearly up for anything, which is exactly what we need for this role.

THE WHOLE THEORY BEHIND THE film is that after a person is beheaded, there's enough blood in their head to allow for a final ten seconds of consciousness. Ten seconds in which the eyes still function. Ten seconds in which the mind still comprehends. Ten seconds during which that little movie in the back of your head ("your whole life flashing before your eyes") plays out until the house lights dim. Forever.

WHEN WE CONTACT ZOSIA ABOUT this project, we'll be sure to tell her that there are several other actresses we have in mind, but that she's the first one we've actually approached (actresses love hearing that). We'll tell her that Lena Dunham was *never even considered for the part.* We'll make it sound like this is the most coveted film role of a generation. But she will only be cast if she agrees to do the film *outright.* She will know nothing about the film or the nature of her role until she agrees. In fact, she'll know nothing about the film until we actually begin shooting.

SHE'LL HAVE TEN SECONDS TO make it count. Only ten seconds. What will she see as her head rolls down the slight incline we'll erect for its final descent? How quickly can art be captured before it simply bleeds out of her?

A Cup of Fur

WHEN TETSUYA REACHED INTO THE top drawer of his desk at work, his hand brushed against a breast. It reminded him, with a surprising fondness, of his mother back in Tokyo. Shortly after his father died, when Tetsuya was a young teen, she had fallen down the stairs and broken her arm. The cast she wore was so big that it covered the middle of her left shoulder all the way down to her wrist and was held in place not only by its own plaster, hard as drywall, but also a metal rod that ran diagonally to support it.

Getting around the house was difficult at first, but she quickly picked up the twists and turns through doorways and negotiated the side tables populated by villages of ceramic figurines. She became agile, adopting a confident yet bulbous swagger while gliding through the house. With the recent crack in their family, it seemed fitting to Tetsuya that she should emerge from the battle of a marriage that had ended in suicide with such a magnificent wound.

On a lazy Sunday morning, Tetsuya had been sitting in the kitchen eating a grapefruit while his mother showered upstairs. Then he heard a loud crash of glass breaking, still falling, and he was up the flight of stairs as fast as she'd fallen down them. Concern taking over his usual sense of privacy, he opened the bathroom door. The sliding glass door of the shower displayed a hole the size of a mammoth fist; sharp slivers of glass dangled precariously then fell to meet the bits below. His mother stood there, naked and dripping, staring at her cast, amazed at its sheer, solid bulk. When she saw him, her hand fluttered in a panic, and with the choice of two places on which to land, it went down below to cover the dark patch, of which Tetsuya had caught only a brief, blurred glimpse.

The cast covered one of her breasts, but the other was prominently exposed. Before he had enough sense to leave with his mother's safety verified, he got a look at that breast, and his mind took a picture of it that would project onto the white screen at the back of his head at random moments for the rest of his adolescence. Until he finally had a breast of his own to gaze at without restriction, his mother's would be the only female nakedness he knew and, like some prototypes, the origin of his concept of perfection.

As Tetsuya's hand reached inside the desk, he at first mistook it for a hardened apple or a paperweight someone had left behind. He lifted the clay breast delicately, as if it might hatch. True to Mei Ling's Greek passion for detail, the aureole was slightly darker, glazed perhaps, with small bumps surrounding a finely shaped erect nipple that begged to be pressed like a button. The note attached to the bottom said simply, "A piece of me." She had never mentioned anything about doing sculptures of her own body. As he studied it, he saw only a dim resemblance to her breasts, those breasts he knew so well. He placed the clay piece back in the drawer.

TETSUYA WAS NEW TO SINGAPORE. His Tokyo office had transferred him there two months before, and as was customary to his nature, he didn't complain. Things in Tokyo had not been going well. He'd been living with his mother since graduation. At twenty-two, this had seemed a convenient choice for both parties. Rent anywhere in the city was ridiculous, and his mother was lonely. The food was overpriced and had become a bore. Tetsuya never would admit it to anyone, but he wasn't a fish person, which severely restricted his choices in most Tokyo restaurants. His mother, a housewife her entire adult life, doted on him. She loved to cook foreign dishes for him, particularly Mexican and Korean.

He'd always considered himself lucky to have such a reliable mother. They'd been on their own for years. In the beginning he'd resented her, secretly blamed her for having driven his father to suicide with her suffocating kind of love, her unreasonably high expectations. His father had lost his job when the asset bubble burst in 1991 and the next day stepped in front of the *Shinkansen* at Ueno station, as so many did that year.

Tetsuya's mother had been the one harmed most by his father's sudden exit and had handled the ordeal with a silent, admirable grace. If she'd been tormented, she dealt with it privately. She'd refused to exhibit any shame, which was what practically everyone—including her own parents—had thought was called for under the circumstances. She was the one upon whom Tetsuya always could lean.

The longer Tetsuya had stayed at home, however, the more intense his mother had become. She was suffocating. It was as though his time away at school had given her the necessary fuel to create new reasons he should stay at home, dire needs only he could meet. Who but Tetsuya, for instance, could possibly accompany her to the cinema? What about her shopping trips to Ginza? Was she expected to hold her own shopping bags? And with whom was she to take lunch? She longed for his company and held him prisoner; she hated for him to go out.

"Where is there to go? What is there to do?" she'd plead.

"Mother, I have friends outside of this *house*. I have to leave."

On the rare nights he left her, he'd return home to find her in his room sitting on the floor, waiting. At twenty-five, Tetsuya decided it was time to move out.

His friend Kazuo had asked him to move into an apartment with him in Tokyo's Shibuya district. It was an expensive area, but Kazuo's uncle owned the building and was prepared to offer them an apartment at a very reasonable rent, granted his nephew and Tetsuya occasionally cared for an infirm, childless woman who lived on the top floor. The woman had been something of a mentor to the man in his youth. She had taught him *ikebana*—Japanese flower arrangement—and conversational English. She'd opened her doors to him, keeping him out of the streets, and had shielded him from an almost certain troubled future. Tetsuya welcomed the change that the move to Shibuya might bring. He liked meeting new people.

His mother, of course, wasn't thrilled with the idea. She insisted he visit her three times a week and call with even more frequency. And of course, he complied. After all, he did owe her.

Keiko, the old woman on the top floor, was not a pleasant human being. Her apartment was rank and untidy, and two minutes into Tetsuya's first visit, he suddenly understood why Kazuo's uncle no longer had time to care for her. Although the agreement had been a joint one with Kazuo, the burden somehow had landed solely on Tetsuya's shoulders.

He visited with her in the mornings before work, did light shopping on the weekends, and even changed her linens when she had the occasional accident. He saw slight traces of the chipper woman she had been, happy to guide his friend's uncle as a boy. But what had possibly been eccentric and entertaining in her younger years had become cloying and irritating. What Keiko said and did disturbed him at times. She seemed to resent him for not being someone else (whom, Tetsuya could not say). Once, when he came through the door unnoticed, he found her muttering something about a cat of hers that had run away. Instead of feeling remorse, she appeared vengeful, as if the cat were now an enemy that must be sought out and destroyed.

When Tetsuya's company, a burgeoning chemical manufacturing outfit that specialized in women's fragrances, proposed a promotion and a transfer to their Singapore office, he quickly agreed. When he informed Keiko of his plans, the news instantly resurrected what he assumed was her former self. She advised him, endearingly, to stay off the streets at night. One time, she told him, on a vacation to Singapore, she and a friend were attacked on their way home from a restaurant. "They are jealous of Japanese people. Our freedom is very desirable to them," she warned. She told him to write to her and even jotted down her address, although the only difference from his own was her apartment number.

He told her he had to leave, so she kissed his cheek gently and said she had enjoyed his company and thought she'd probably miss him. Then she turned away, as if he were already gone, and stared out the window at the street below. Tetsuya showed himself out, clutching the slip of paper with her address.

AT FIRST, TETSUYA WAS CONVINCED he'd made the biggest mistake by moving to Singapore.

His mother called him every day in the beginning. She spoke about the most commonplace things. She said that she needed to be reminded to pick up eggs for the week because there was a special or that she'd found a stone shaped like a face in the park near Sugamo and what did he think that meant and should she send it to him? Her voice sounded far away, forced into unnaturally high tones he'd never heard her use before. Tetsuya imagined her excitement while she dialed his number and then the slow, steady letdown that came halfway through their conversation as she realized that her son no longer needed her, that he surely could get by without knowing the price of bread for the week or the hair appointment it had taken her weeks to book. Sure, he needed a mother like everyone else, but now she seemed to be just another thing to return to nostalgically from time to time in his mind. She was part of the same fading photograph, the details of his life receding into the background and becoming part of a great, white wash. He knew everything and everyone in his life eventually would find its way to that place.

Singapore smelled. Tokyo had been no great joy, but there at least had been a certain charm to its odor: old, wet flowers waiting to be tossed. The Singapore smell was decidedly different and made him think twice about going outside.

His first day at the new office was a welcome change from the time he'd spent in the surrounding environs. The building itself was brand new and located in a high-end business district—both gloriously smelling like nothing. If he had to package the scent as one of those dangly car trees, he would've called it "Corporate Chill," and the tree would've been a light gray, the color of fresh cigarette ash.

Tetsuya's office was at the end of a long hallway with the restrooms for the floor right around the corner in their own niche. The company had given him a secretary, Mei Ling, whom he shared with one other employee, a man named Ji Min. Tetsuya and Ji Min met only briefly upon his arrival.

Everyone used English in the office, and Tetsuya was comfortable with that. The years he'd studied with native-speaking tutors had given him a mastery over the language and a bit of a New Zealand accent, as his primary tutor had been from Wellington. He'd even managed to triumph over the unconquerable "r-l" confusion by making the word *licorice* part of his daily vocabulary.

Never having had a secretary in the past, he wasn't sure what to do with Mei Ling. Fragrance research and development wasn't something he necessarily needed assistance to perform. Having worked on the chemical-manufacturing side of the business in Tokyo, he had more than enough experience in carrying out market research and conducting fragrance field trials and whatever else needed to be done. That was why he'd been promoted to his position in the first place. Ji Min was an obsessive perfectionist and worked Mei Ling long, inconvenient hours. Tetsuya was happy to just let her proofread his reports and get the occasional coffee.

At first she seemed to have taken offense to the limited duties, as if he somehow didn't trust her to perform the simplest office tasks. However, she spent only a couple days around Tetsuya before this notion was dampened. His intentions and demeanor were too kind. He was spectacularly unjaded and without agenda. Most people found him refreshingly odd, almost like a tourist, withholding judgment until the end of the trip.

One day, with Ji Min out of town, Mei Ling came into Tetsuya's office earlier than usual. She wore a white carnation in her hair and brought two cups of coffee. She had begun to put more effort than necessary into making the perfect cup after finally coaxing out of him the way he took it.

"Thank you, Mei Ling," said Tetsuya, as she handed him his black mug. He invited her to sit down.

"Everyone is very pleased that you're here, Takeda-*san*. They wonder how the Tokyo office ever saw fit to let you go." She wore a white skirt and a black blouse that was unbuttoned to reveal the edges of a brassiere of the same color. The carnation nodded along with the movement of her head, as if in agreement.

"I needed a change. Honestly, Japan can be a bit monotonous, you know. Have you worked here long?" he asked.

"Only a year. This isn't where I really want to be, though. I consider myself an artist. Chemicals and fragrances are so predictable. They follow such a rigid formula."

"What's your medium? As an artist?"

"I sculpt in clay," Mei Ling said. "Small, abstract pieces mostly. Right now, though, I'm working on a study of my roommate. I've done her arms, neck, and four fingers of her left hand. But I'm having trouble getting the thumb right. It's such an odd shape. She works on the fifth floor of our building. That's how we met."

"Why your roommate? Only willing model?" he asked, his hands running through his coiffed, gelled hair, something he almost never did.

"She has body-image problems. I want to show her how beautiful she is."

Tetsuya watched as she rubbed the space below her neck, that hollow. So sexy. She noticed his eyes and brought her hand up to the carnation as if it had been disturbed.

He spoke next without much forethought, another uncharacteristic move. "Would you like to get out of here for a little while? Maybe get a cup of coffee?"

"I'd love to," she said almost immediately.

So caught up was he, in that moment and with Mei Ling, that he forgot, right on the spot, what he'd already been drinking.

MEI LING DIDN'T JUST SCULPT clay; she seemed to mold the lives around her. During that first date, although it really had been no more than an extended coffee break, Tetsuya had witnessed what kind of a woman Mei Ling was. As they sat across from each other, people in the café stared at her, somehow immobilized. He received a clear message of intent from each of them. The women weren't jealous, just curious, as if staring at her deeply enough eventually might yield all her secrets. The men all seemed to appreciate that someone was with her, even if it wasn't them. It was entirely possible that Tetsuya simply was projecting this onto people based on his own attraction to her, but he didn't think this was so.

When Tetsuya was with Mei Ling, he felt imbued with a calm, tranquil energy, almost as if he were in the presence of a great mystic. He seemed to be discovering firsthand the powerful satisfaction that comes from pursing a relationship. Immodestly he felt validated as being some supreme judge of character.

Walking back to the office after coffee, he tossed his cigarette to the ground. When Mei Ling noticed he was no longer smoking, she quickly doubled back, intent on finding the butt. When she finally did, she stubbed it out then tossed it into a nearby trash can. It was all done with such swiftness, the carnation in her hair never moving out of place, that Tetsuya would've forgotten the episode altogether had it not been for the words she uttered as she linked her arm back through his. "Please be careful," she said.

They spent their first night together at Tetsuya's apartment. Mei Ling told him she was embarrassed about the possibility of keeping her roommate awake and suggested they go to his place. Her roommate had enough issues as it was, she explained. There was no need to bring around a man she was seeing.

That first night they sat on the sofa drinking Malbec and talked into the early morning about everything. Tetsuya opened up to her about his father's sudden death and why his mother was especially attached to him now. They discussed art, and Mei Ling was impressed to hear that Tetsuya was familiar with many of her favorite artists, such as Kinji Akagawa and Madeleine Boschan, the latter of whom she commended for her use of found objects. She considered the *Winged Victory of Samothrace*, that great Hellenistic masterpiece, to be the most formidable image of woman ever created, made even more powerful by her lack of a head.

"With the absence of a head and therefore brain, it's almost like something else is propelling her toward us. The spirit of her body perhaps."

"Didn't the statue originally have a head, though?" Tetsuya asked.

"Possibly. But no one—that we know of—has ever seen it. She triumphs without it. She doesn't need to see us to know who she is."

As the dawn light peeked through the slats of the blinds, Mei Ling brought Tetsuya's head toward hers and kissed him lightly on the lips. His lips, she said, were the softest she'd felt on a man. She slowly removed his clothes and traced her fingers over each muscle. It felt to Tetsuya that she was reading his body, committing to memory the trails of veins that ran up and down his forearm. She told him to tense his abdomen so she could lick the lines of his muscles. Tetsuya watched her as he brushed her hair through his fingers. She treated his entire body with the same level of worship, investigating each piece of him with exquisite care and authority. When she slid his underwear down to his ankles, she stared at him in wonder. She whispered to him, almost a warning of what she was about to do. He caught the words *love* and *pieces*, but her voice was too soft for him to make out a full sentence. He didn't care. She kneaded him gently with her small hands, then took him in her mouth.

After they made love, she wriggled out from beneath him and reached for a clip, which she used to tie her hair back from her face, though a few stray hairs stuck to her forehead. She lit one of his cigarettes and went to stand on the balcony. She drew a blanket around her breasts, although she seemed confident enough in her own nakedness. The blast of heat from the open balcony door came to him instantly, and he pushed the duvet down to the edge of the bed with his feet, writhing into the mattress with a reserve of energy. The foam mattress was the kind that retained the shape of the body on top of it. Tetsuya imagined himself poised above, looking down at the outline their bodies had made on it, like lovers immortalized in chalk at a crime scene.

The street smells from outside didn't reach up this far. The only scents Tetsuya could make out were the hot air, cigarette smoke, and his own spilled sex, which all had combined to create an anxious odor—a forbidden flower recently plucked. He wouldn't mind that awful street smell if it came. He might lie back, breathe it in, and wait—perhaps only seconds—to become even dizzier.

AS FAR AS THEY WERE both aware, no one in the office knew about their affair. Tetsuya and Mei Ling had a discussion about it and considered it a good idea to be as discreet as possible. With Ji Min in town, Mei Ling went back to working almost full-time for him. Tetsuya felt crazy in her presence around the office and found it increasingly difficult to keep up their boss-and-secretary act. He kept imagining his office door closed and the glass fogging up and her screaming while he took her over his desk.

He'd argued with her after they'd been together two weeks. "I don't care what people think. I've never felt like this before," he said.

"We can't be like that here, Tetsuya. You can't flaunt your personal life and expect people to take you seriously." She leaned closer to him, her eyes darting around to make sure they were alone. "If we keep things between us, they'll be that much more ours. Don't you want that?"

She was right, of course; he just found himself incapable of acting professionally around her. They walked side by side to the lab to consult with the chemist on a new scent he was developing. All the while, he had to stare straight past her into the spaces around her, to the side, never head on, because he would have to sleep with her right there if he did. It was like a scene in a play he had to rehearse to perfection, convincing the audience night after night but never himself.

He decided to actively lie about Mei Ling. He went out to lunch with Ji Min and told him about a girlfriend back in Tokyo whom he was hoping to bring over as soon as he had established himself in Singapore. He said she was perfect, with a stunning body, but she wore expensive clothes she couldn't afford and shared an apartment with a friend in Shibuya that wasn't within her budget. When Ji Min asked her name, he said it was "Keiko," the name of the old woman he had befriended back home. It was the first time Tetsuya had even thought of her at all, and he was surprised how she'd finally turned out to be of use to him. It wasn't like him to lie, but he found it easy and gratifying. He rationalized the lie to himself with the knowledge that the imaginary girlfriend almost certainly did exist in Tokyo because there were thousands like her living there.

Mei Ling told him her roommate was asking so many questions about her whereabouts lately that it would be easier if Tetsuya just met her.

He showed up early with a bottle of Shiraz and white roses for both of them.

"What a wonderful gesture, Takeda-san. Just perfect," Mei Ling said, accepting the bottle and one of the bouquets. She wore an apron that was clearly not hers, as she was swimming in it. She kissed him and brought her arms up around his neck, as if she needed to mark him for the night. As she clung to him, Tetsuya spotted someone descending the stairs with careful deliberation; Mei Ling turned around and met her at the foot of the stairs.

"Tetsuya, this is Yan Fang," she said, taking on the new role of chaperone.

"It's nice to meet you." He brought the flowers to her in a gallant motion.

He saw where the body-image issues Mei Ling had mentioned came from. Yan Fang wasn't fat, but her big-boned heftiness made her seem larger than her weight. Standing next to Mei Ling, who was small and petite even in high heels and the roomy apron, Yan Fang seemed like her weathered, older sister, an exchange student who'd been improperly matched to her summer host. She had a round, globular face and lips she had hastily smeared with an unflattering shade of cherry-red lipstick. She was gussied up in a way that showed the infrequency with which she must've attended formal events. Her hands were beautiful, though: white and smooth, well cared for in a way the rest of her seemed not to be. Tetsuya imagined they must have inspired the most lifelike of Mei Ling's sculptures.

"I've heard a lot about you," Yan Fang said. "You sounded so perfect that I was beginning to think Mei Ling had made you up."

He heard the precision with which she chose her words and thought she might've had few chances to practice English in the past.

"Let's sit down," said Mei Ling. She opened the wine in the kitchen and returned with three glasses. She filled Yan Fang and Tetsuya's, then her own as an afterthought.

"I understand we all work in the same building, Yan Fang. What do you do?" asked Tetsuya, keeping to the comfortable basics.

"I'm in advertising," she said.

"Yan Fang is putting together the ad campaign for Jamais Vu, that new fall fragrance Ji Min is managing. She also headed the campaign for Chingta Biscuits you see all around the city," added Mei Ling.

"It was much better before it went to committee," Yan Fang said. "My sexy teens on the beach were turned into a bored housewife in minutes. They said young people have no interest in baking. Whatever."

Tetsuya thought she used the last word with a peculiar amount of gusto, seeming to imitate the way she might've heard it in a movie.

"They say she can sell anything," said Mei Ling, gravely.

Glass in hand, Tetsuya stood and wandered to the mantle. He fingered the ledge over the fireplace, digging his nail under a part where the cream lacquer had chipped. A small, rectangular mirror that was propped up at an angle surprised him when he met his reflection in it. It leaned against the wall on top of a red cube. Perched upon the cube was a silver cup with a small handle, like something that might've once held a child's first milk. He peered inside the cup and saw it was halfway full of dull brown wisps, some matted and clumped together. He stuck his finger inside. Fur.

"What is this?" he asked, looking at Yan Fang in the mirror.

"My cup of fur," said Yan Fang with a certain amount of pride.

"Her childhood cat wandered away and was caught in a hideous trap in the woods. She chewed her way out but never came back. The fur was all she left behind," Mei Ling explained, as if it were a story she'd heard so many times that she could now lay partial claim to it. "Isn't it morbid?"

"A bit, although people do keep ashes in the same place," he said. "How did you know it was your cat?" he asked Yan Fang.

"I just knew. I'll never forget the color of her fur. I loved her," she said, with a finality that ended the discussion.

Mei Ling's cooking skills weren't up to par with the rest of her winning attributes. She had attempted *char kway teow*, an ambitious dish for even an experienced cook—something Tetsuya's mother used to prepare on anniversary nights for his father. It was made with thick, flat noodles stir-fried in dark soy sauce with prawns, eggs, bean sprouts, fish cake, cockles, green leafy vegetables, and Chinese sausage. But she had burned the sausages at the end so that small, hardened black bits stuck to the vegetables and swam in the sauce like flecks of dirt.

The two roommates ate it heartily, so Tetsuya followed their lead, praising the food with each satisfied moan. He looked forward to the coffee, an area in which he knew she wouldn't disappoint.

Yan Fang followed the conversation with her eyes, occasionally offering a brief opinion or a question. At one point, she asked Tetsuya if he'd ever been married.

"Of course not, Yan Fang," Mei Ling answered for him. "Don't you think I would've told you?"

"I thought maybe you didn't know," she said, tossing back the rest of her wine.

Later, over coffee, Mei Ling related a story from work to them. Tetsuya watched her closely, a brief wave of amazement washing over him. He smiled to himself, childishly, as if momentarily discovering the delight of his relationship for the first time. He glanced at Yan Fang who, while nodding along at everything Mei

Ling said, seemed to be squinting at her. When she caught Tetsuya looking at her, she affected a wide-eyed concentration.

After dinner, Yan Fang was eager to do the dishes. She was up and into the kitchen before either of them could protest.

"Just let her," said Mei Ling. "She's acting strange tonight. This might not have been the best idea."

"She's just jealous. You could make a paper bag look sexy. And your bad cooking was adorable."

"You didn't like my cooking?" she asked coyly.

"I sat through it for my chance to be alone with the cook." Tetsuya moved her to the couch and kissed her, cradling her head in his hand, delicately manipulating its position with the grip of his fingers. Because he was kissing her, the sounds of the apartment had receded into the background. But he suddenly noticed the sink was no longer running, and the dishes, clinking and crashing before in a way that had almost sounded deliberate, were now silent. "Where's Yan Fang?" he asked.

"Gone to bed, probably. Should we do the same?" Her eyes were half closed, and she spoke with a smile that was just short of being self-satisfied.

"Where can I find the bathroom? I had a lot of wine."

"Upstairs. I'll be right here, waiting."

When he reached the top of the stairs, a long hallway of blond wood stretched out before him with five doors, two on each side and one at the end, all closed. He tried the first one on the right, but it was locked. He thought it must be Yan Fang's room. *Good,* he thought. *She must already be asleep.* The opposite door opened too fast, but he stopped it before it banged into the wall. It wasn't the bathroom but a multipurpose area devoted to Mei Ling's clay work. A table stood near the center of the room, covered in a white sheet; the tallest piece underneath held the brunt of the teepee structure. Tetsuya saw the pinkish clay of one piece exposed in the corner. He pulled the sheet back and picked up Yan Fang's hand.

It was an amazing likeness. Mei Ling had captured the long, slender fingers that were so at odds with the meaty girth of the rest of her body. The details were incredible—fingernails set in relief with cuticles and even a hangnail on the pinkie, giving credit to the whole piece by showing its willingness to record imperfection. The veins of the hand connected like roads on a map, visibly raised and alive. The hand looked as if it had been caught in a moment of pressure, perhaps dangling off a padded stool with a model's fatigue, the blood rushing to the fingertips. Mei Ling had been right about the thumb, though; it was too fat, exaggerated, out of proportion and set at an odd, impossible angle. It made its own evolutionary statement; it was so out of place that it seemed unnecessary.

Tetsuya shut the door carefully, summoned away from further investigation by the more immediate need to relieve his bladder. He pushed open the next door. At first the heap of clothes on the floor utterly confused him. Was this Yan Fang's bedroom? No, there were black-and-white tiles on the floor, a sink, a pink razor. He took it all in, seeing Yan Fang last, resisting an initial instinct to avert his eyes.

She was red faced and panting, her legs in a full straddle over the toilet seat. Her wide hips bucked, and three fingers of her left hand glided in and out of her vagina, lubed and glistening in the harsh overhead light.

A look of instant horror flashed in her eyes, her brain telling her hand to stop. But she was too close, and the damage had been done. She came in quick jolts, knocking her knees together, the caps as big as saucers. When the whites of her eyes settled back in their sockets and she was able to focus on him, he noticed an involuntary fluttering of her eyelids, something that often happened to him during his own climax or the moments just afterward. Her glazed look was desperate, and she stuttered indiscernibly between shame and enticement. She opened her legs back up as some sort of last-ditch invitation; they were shaking.

Suddenly she looked very cold. She opened her mouth as if to say something but then brought her hand up to her face, which was red and splotched with strain.

He quickly pulled the door shut and came down the stairs, staring straight ahead in a regal pose. His bladder still pushed up against his other organs. Then he felt a small click inside where he knew some urgency had been rerouted. He found Mei Ling in the same position on the couch, only she had removed her skirt and unbuttoned the top of her blouse.

"Relieved?" she asked.

"Yes," he croaked out, unprepared to speak.

Mei Ling reached for his belt buckle, but he pulled away from her and sank to his knees to pull off her underwear. There was something he would do for her, both hot and sweet like an unexpected favor. With their lovemaking of late so mapped out in its events, the novelty of the act completely jarred her. In the throes of a sudden panic, she clutched his shoulders, possibly urging him to stop, if only half-heartedly. Pillows flew off the couch. The coffee table moved inches, revealing ancient indentations in the carpet. He peered over her mound of hair and took a breath before going back down. He saw the mantle, the propped-up mirror, Yan Fang's cup filled with fur. Sounds were loud, vibrating somewhere, maybe all around him. He'd accessed a moan from Mei Ling so deep that even the mirror seemed to tilt away from them in avoidance of their reflection.

THE NEXT DAY, JI MIN came into Tetsuya's office. "We're going out tonight with a couple of the bosses. They're asking for you to come," he said.

"I was going to leave early today."

Ji Min stared him down.

"I guess I can change my plans," Tetsuya said.

They went to a Japanese hostess bar. He didn't choose it; he just got swept up along with the group, everyone clad in dark suits carrying their briefcases in one hand, cigarettes in the other. Tetsuya felt as if he were part a pack of marauding corporate raiders propelled by their own noxious fumes, subsisting on nicotine and alcohol—a trail mix of the wide-checkered-ties set. The drunker you got, the more your boss accepted you. That was how things had been in Tokyo as well; Tetsuya was well aware of this. Matching your boss drink for drink displayed more loyalty than good work or showing up on time.

Somehow he had managed to avoid this initiation in the past by ducking out the back of the building to meet Mei Ling for a taxi ride to his place. The route to his apartment through the packed roads was so familiar to them that Mei Ling would wait until they'd passed the noodle shop on the right to light her cigarette, knowing she would reach the filter just as the doorman opened her side of the taxi. They always talked on their way up the elevator and fondled each other casually, dancing around the idea of pushing that little red button and doing it right there like they'd seen in a movie once. It excited her; she became much more daring once they left the office. He'd take her straight to his bedroom and let it all out, the stress, those fleeting moments of panic that made up every day. And there was Mei Ling moving with the rhythm of this feeling like she knew what he was thinking even before he did. Like she knew him better than he knew himself.

From what Tetsuya had gathered, this was a special night, a departure from the normal routine. There were girls everywhere, and the place smelled like a hot mix of perfume and anxiousness. The hostesses swam around the tables of men, never staying in one place too long.

To Tetsuya, Ji Min seemed like a different person. He hung on every word of anyone who was even slightly his senior, kissing ass so blatantly that his mouth moved indiscernibly from glass to cigarette to butt cheek, making him look busier than he ever did in the office.

He sloshed his drink down the front of his suit, then ordered another round, urging everyone else to empty their glasses. Tetsuya tossed back the rest of his Scotch and loosened his tie. He felt a little sick, like he might throw up. So he calmly sat at the table for a moment, focusing on a spot behind the lit bar until his stomach settled.

Their glasses blended into the black, lacquered tables, and the dancing ends of cigarettes gave a fluctuating head count as men drifted in and out of private backrooms. Cerulean lamps lit from above made the entire place seem as if it were underwater. Everyone looked dead. A dull buzzing sound erupted from the speakers with just enough variance in rhythm to be passed off as music. The hostesses weaved through the tables, invisible to each other, just daring Tetsuya to touch one of them.

Ji Min whispered in his ear, "You're so busy, Tetsuya. You never come out with us." His breath was a horrid mix.

"Yes, well…" he stumbled. His tongue was loose, and he felt terribly unfocused.

"It's funny how I can never find Mei Ling either, after about seven thirty or so. I always think she's doing extra work for you, but you're usually gone as well," Ji Min said cryptically.

"We're both quite busy."

The discussion stopped, and everyone looked at one another. A couple of men glanced nervously at Tetsuya's boss.

They know, Tetsuya thought almost instantly. *They all know.*

As if on cue, the lights dimmed, and the room suddenly became unnavigable. A chill filled the air once Tetsuya lit a cigarette to give his hands something to do. For the first time, he noticed bars on the windows. The club was underground, but he didn't remember having walked down any stairs. He looked around the table at their half faces, indistinguishable from one another but all bluish in pallor. There was no one he could trust here. Not even someone who'd make apologies for him if he decided to go home and be sick, which, at this point, was all he wanted to do.

Suddenly a blue arm emerged from behind and encircled his neck. The polish on the fingernails looked deep purple in the light. The buzzing sound that was now unmistakably music was all around him now and not just inside his throbbing head. At some point, a horn slowly had snuck its way in sync with the other sounds. A jazz beat that had made his heart jump when it first entered the song gave the blue arm something to move to. The hostess picked him up from the waist like a toddler and placed his arms on her shoulders, leading him deeper toward the dark center of the room. He tried not to step on her toes, but she wouldn't let him look down, so he stopped trying to follow where they went. With one hand she grabbed his face; her nails felt sharp against his cheek. In a second's worth of light, he caught a cursory glimpse of her face. She was older, thirty-nine maybe. Or even forty. Her mouth appeared as a straight line painted in the same shade as her nail polish. Her eyes were wide, unnaturally so for an Asian woman. Bulging out of her face as they were, her eyelids were pulled tightly against the temples in a way that looked surgically assisted.

The lamps dimmed even further, and Tetsuya knocked into a chair. "Excuse me," he said to it. The woman laughed and pulled him closer to the center of the room, where the light converged into a hollow void. He sensed a sneeze coming on but lost it and felt extremely cheated by everything. The jazz beat was techno, having shifted again so seamlessly. He felt himself being watched by the dull-lidded, rheumy eyes of his colleagues all around the room, slightly goading him on. He was fearful, yet curious, of what the sad tune might turn into next.

TETSUYA REMEMBERED HIS FIRST EARTHQUAKE, a relatively large one for Tokyo at 5.4. He'd been getting ready for school, and his glass of water had slipped off the sink. Watching it skip its way off in a jittery journey to the edge, he'd felt no urge to save it from falling. He'd been too caught up in the drama of it all, the visible wreckage, however small, needed as proof that he'd actually been through this. As he stood in the doorframe as he'd always been taught, he tried to recall the list he'd once compiled of things to take from the house in case of an emergency. His coin collection; a love letter he'd written to his second-grade teacher but never sent; a framed picture of his family, the three of them caught in a moment of rare togetherness, standing next to a fountain in Yoyogi Park, his father's eyes the only ones looking away, focused on some offstage diversion he was soon to follow. He knew there'd been more he wanted to save—things he would later discover were so easily replaceable.

On Tetsuya's way to school that morning, his mother had turned up the radio when the announcer was reporting the news of the earthquake. No major damage or direct casualties. But he did report a strange side note—a story about the death of a man who apparently had tripped down the stairs and broken his neck minutes after assuring his wife over the phone that her antique set of Limoges had survived the quake. It was almost too absurd to be tragic, yet it struck Tetsuya as extremely unfair. Who had phoned in this ridiculous piece of news? Certainly not the wife. Would she ever look at that Limoges the same way or even dare use it again? Would she destroy it as a penance? Then there was the man himself. He'd gotten up that morning thinking it was just an ordinary day, and only hours later he was an amusing footnote to a disaster, a tidbit hurriedly crammed in between the weekend weather forecast and the baseball scores. News of the weird, fodder for the water cooler. It was then Tetsuya saw the honor in death by natural disaster, the way it saved you from personal fault, instantly enshrining your own history with that of the earth.

IT WAS A FEELING FELT, at some point, by everyone: the intense, immediate need to escape to the restroom. Had he paid more attention to his regularity the past couple of days, he'd have known he was more than overdue for such a boiling unleash. It was easier to think it was the lunch he'd eaten only twenty minutes before, probably stuffed with some raw mess of meat, or the three cups of Mei Ling's coffee he'd guzzled down that morning when he'd first gotten to the office than to admit that yes, indeed, a horrific bout of constipation was about to come to an end.

The indignity of such a base bodily function embarrassed him, like a child who gets up early to wash the sheets in order to keep his wet, nighttime accident a secret from his parents. Tetsuya didn't care why he was so desperately in need of a toilet or even who saw him creep toward the bathroom, his buttocks clenched and his face in a grimace. All he knew was that if he didn't find a toilet soon, he would have to leave the office with his jacket tied around his waist, then dispose of a very expensive suit—that, or jump out of the twenty-third story window, soiled but noble.

The men's room on his floor was quiet but not in the way he'd hoped. It was the forced silence of public defecation, the desire to stifle even the slightest break of wind. He'd done it himself, of course. Coughed when he knew there'd be noise, pulled the paper roll down to the floor before carefully tearing the serrated edge, dashing out with only the most cursory hand wash in order to avoid having anyone look him in the eye. He hated having to do this in a public restroom, always had, even at school where he'd wait until after the last bell, knowing full well he'd be late but who cared, just as long as he'd be alone. Some of the stalls hadn't even had doors on them, and that was its own separate nightmare. He'd take a side-by-side urinal buddy any day, even if they peeked, which some did naturally, or jiggled at the end like they were masturbating.

He squatted and swept the floor with his eyes, praying for an empty stall. What he saw were eight pairs of polished shoes and a newspaper's ripped edges; in addition, the physical position he was now in certainly was not helping matters. Without thinking much about it, he exited the men's room and hurried across the hall into the ladies' room. No one was in the hallway, which he counted as a minor blessing. The smell was different in this bathroom, lemony and sterile, as if an army of cleaning women recently had scoured it. He also inhaled a sweet smell of perfume he recognized but couldn't quite place. The lingering scent of Shalimar perhaps? All the stall doors were shut. He pushed in the one at the end and found that it was empty. With his buckle already undone, he sat down in a rush.

Tetsuya was relieved, and a cool, congratulatory sweat formed on his forehead as he felt a great block move out of him. He moaned over-dramatically and hoped to all gods that he was as alone as it had initially appeared. Barring the custodian's recent visit, as evidenced by the smell of lemon cleanser, the place did feel vacant.

He left the stall and was glad to see he was still alone, but as he passed the oblong wall mirror, he noticed an eye watching him through the crack of the first stall door. For one unmistakable moment, it looked at him, wide, full, and in a strange sense, trained to remember. Was it Keiko's cataract-riddled eye watching him? Was she there to alert him to danger? To spy on him? As soon as he noticed the eye, it was gone, and then he was out the door without even washing his hands.

He walked down the empty hall feeling a desperate need to be seen, to be noted as a person who could be found in many different parts of the office at any time of the day. A man to whom he'd never spoken more than two words stood at a desk, comparing figures on an Excel spreadsheet with a tall, focused-looking woman. Tetsuya passed by his office offering a smile, his hands in his pockets. He lingered a few moments too long, though, enough time for the man's face to change from conciliatory to suspicious. So he pressed on quickly around the corner and settled back into his office, forcing himself to answer e-mails. His hands were almost dripping with sweat.

Mei Ling came in with a stack of folders. She brushed her fingertip along Tetsuya's palm as she passed them to him. She stared at her wet index finger with a puzzled look, as if a stray dog had accidentally licked her.

"Yan Fang is on our floor today. She came to meet with Ji Min on the upcoming perfume launch. She's going to join me for lunch. Would you like to come?" Mei Ling moved some things around on his desk in a familiar manner. If she had looked at him right then, she would have seen a face confused, then scared, as if a dreadful question were being answered too quickly. If she'd been there later, when the local police arrived to take him away to be grilled in an interrogation room, she might've had to look away, embarrassed at the sight of the man she loved being so easily humbled into a boy.

Yan Fang appeared in the doorway dressed in an ill-fitting light-pink business suit. She pursed her lips defiantly and stated, "I am ready to eat."

～

IN SINGAPORE, AS TETSUYA LEARNED from the police, using the bathroom of the opposite sex was tantamount to a kind of visual sexual assault, public voyeurism with the intent to commit molestation. He found out that men in the past had been taken in for doing nothing more than stealing a roll of toilet paper from an empty ladies' room. They arrested men all the time as examples, inventing new definitions of lewdness along the way.

He cried when the police first entered his office, with expressions that suggested he was some sort of pervert. The tears erupted from a deep, hidden source within—the part of him that responded to irrevocable change. Nothing moved on his face, just the tears running in silent streams down both cheeks. He'd felt a conspicuous lack of surprise at their almost too prompt arrival, how they'd come so equipped to deal with him. Hadn't he known that the bathroom door he'd shut on Yan Fang at their apartment had cracks, certain ways of letting things through? And what had set her off exactly—the moaning he'd indulged in privately in the stall, or had it been Mei Ling's that night after the dinner? So inconsiderate; so grossly, sexually human.

The police ransacked Tetsuya's desk and produced the clay breast as further evidence of his sexual perversion. As he sat in the small room at the station looking at it, he finally was convinced it was based on Yan Fang. Mei Ling wouldn't have sculpted herself. He couldn't imagine her standing in front of the mirror with one eye on her chest, the other fixed to an unformed piece of clay. She might've been too afraid that the mirror would distort her perspective somehow, detracting elements of perfection from her body she wasn't ready to confront in order to produce an abstract lump with only the faintest resemblance to her own body. Maybe she'd simply confused the two of them. Roommates tended to meld into each other if they lived together long enough. It was possible that she'd sculpted so many pieces of Yan Fang that she really did think of them as pieces of herself too. Maybe Tetsuya had misread the meaning of the gift entirely and, more important, who had given it to him.

A slap on the wrist. A suspension without pay. Some corporate branding he'd take months to put behind him but eventually would, and he'd be stronger for it. These were the possible outcomes he allowed to play out in his head as he waited at home to learn his fate. He sincerely believed he could get out of it. They'd respect him again; they would. He could win them over. Still, it didn't look like any of this would come to pass.

The more time he waited at home by the phone after the arrest, the more likely a severe disciplinary action would be taken against him. It was the waiting that was really doing him in. The speculative scenarios running through his head and all ending up pretty much the same way: a flight back to Narita Airport in economy class and his mother waiting for him at the gate with a genuine smile because, despite the shame attached to the whole episode, he had come back to her, and she wouldn't be able to see it in any way other than how she might benefit. Then they'd take the express train together back to Ueno station. He felt a dull horror over the inevitability of the vision, like just imagining it had suddenly made it true.

He picked up the phone and checked the dial tone, letting it run until silence came and then a ringing to the operator. He hung up and glanced at a scrap of paper in a hodgepodge dish with the address and phone number of Keiko, the old woman in Tokyo. She was the one person he could think of who was least likely to be waiting by the phone for anyone. It was only the third time he'd thought of her since coming to Singapore. He knew she'd understand what had happened to him here, the cruel, draconian way Singapore had of making examples of outsiders. A person could be caned for throwing out a cigarette butt on the street. Now he could see the appeal of her sad apartment and empty life where no women patiently waited behind closed doors to ruin him.

He imagined it was people Keiko feared the most, not loneliness. Loneliness she could bear. She could mold it into whatever she wanted because, in the end, it was of her own making. People, though, they were uncontrollable. She had put her faith in them once before, and the returns were paltry, unrecognizably pathetic in their terrible morsels of almost kindness. She flung them back with spite, the only defense she had left.

Tetsuya walked up to his open window and peered at the street below. He ran his palm along the window's ledge, carefully, gently. It would be so easy to jump. He was high enough that there would be no question that his life would end. And wasn't that exactly what was expected of him? A Japanese man shamed into a somewhat obvious yet completely noble suicide? Wasn't that exactly how this was supposed to play out? He could avoid returning home to his mother. He could turn his life into the great tragic drama it deserved to be, sealing Mei Ling's love for him eternally. It was the quickest way out of the sticky trap in which he found himself ensnared.

What if his father had had second thoughts as he fell toward the approaching *Shinkansen*? What if, in that last moment, he'd seen a picture of his wife and son in his mind and realized that they would still love him without a job and that this—this man standing too close to the platform's edge—wasn't really him, that he shouldn't do this? What if it had all been too late?

Tetsuya couldn't do it. He couldn't turn his back on life. Gratifying as it might be in the moment or in theory, suicide was permanent. There was no changing your mind once you took that last step.

Poor Keiko's solitude was a defeat, he realized, not the triumph she pretended it to be. She acted the way she did because she had to. She hadn't lost the fight; she'd given it up years ago.

Tetsuya still had a choice. He could choose to turn his back on this place with its unrelenting heat and the rotten smells of cooked garbage and sweat dripping down the closed, locked thighs of women unfulfilled.

As he reveled in the finality of his decision, the phone rang at the moment that he could've least cared what the voice on the other end had to say about his future.

MEI LING OPENED THE DOOR wearing a Mickey Mouse T-shirt and faded jeans covered in damp streaks of clay.

"Ji Min told us all what happened."

"Is she here?" he asked flatly.

"No."

"May I come in?

"Yes." She closed the door. "Yan Fang said you tried to continue something that started the night you came here for dinner."

"And you believed her?"

"Well, no. But then Ji Min said you had sex with a girl one night in front of all these guys, and it sounded so unlike you, but it all added up to something, something I couldn't make any sense of." She sat on the couch, careful not to touch the fabric with her wet hands.

"We danced. I was very drunk that night at the bar, but I'm quite sure I didn't do *that*. I wouldn't do that."

"And Yan Fang?"

"I didn't start *anything* with her. Ever. You must know that."

"I know you didn't. I guess I knew it before."

"You were upstairs when I knocked. What were you working on?" he asked.

"Nothing, really. I was fooling around, trying to make a plate, but I got bored with it. Too functional," she replied.

"Show me," he said, already leading the way upstairs.

The door was open, and Tetsuya noticed that the large white sheet that previously had covered the table was gone. All kinds of body parts were spread out on the table, like the recent findings of a mass grave during an archeological dig: a varicose thigh severed at a sharp angle, almost where one might imagine a short tube skirt had tightened its way around the flesh in a tourniquet; a pair of calves, one leaning toward the other, modestly; a foot in a perfect ballerina flex; the top of a bare head, lobotomized; a finger bent at the first joint and pointing down; and at the far end of the table, a lone breast, full and familiar in shape.

He saw an ill-formed plate on a work stool. It was bumpy around the middle and curved, wobbly, at the edges—a Frisbee perhaps or a large ashtray, something into which any clay piece easily could devolve. Mei Ling was undoubtedly an artist who needed a model; anyone could see that much.

"What's the first part of me you noticed?" he asked quickly.

"Your arms," she said. "Your strong arms."

He took off his shirt slowly and encircled her hand around the peak of his biceps. "Do me," he said, motioning toward a lump of fresh clay that lay next to the stool.

Mei Ling pulled his biceps toward her and tossed the plate onto a stained blanket in the corner of the room. She moved her hand up and down his arm, getting the feel of it, gripping it in a pressure of points. After she'd made some sense of it, she dipped her hands into a bowl of water and went after the clay as if Tetsuya weren't there at all.

As he watched her work, he felt like he had, before this moment, only known a slight, unfocused, perhaps idealized, part of her. In the tapered light of the room, he finally saw something else beyond the shell he had worshiped. She seemed half caught in a searchlight, holding a rope and wanting to be tied to something—searching for an object to which she could devote her energy. Then she glanced up from the clay and stared at him discerningly, picking him apart with her eyes, separating the bones underneath the skin, from the muscle groups that connected in the fine maze that gave him shape. Baked and hardened to life, this was the piece of himself he'd leave behind.

The Gargoyles

THEY CAME UP WITH THE names as the plane began taxiing down the runway. Sherry named herself Allura, uttering the name with a brief, smoky rasp that made the other two women draw closer to hear her. She had a pitted face with the signs of teenage acne along her cheeks and she emanated a mentholated smell, especially her hair.

Karen pulled one of her thick, graying dreadlocks to her lips like a microphone cord and whispered into her clenched hand in the rich, velvety voice of a late-night radio jockey, "Pheramona. You may now refer to me, ladies, as Pheramona." Her laughter bubbled up from the pit of her stomach, then exploded with a vicious abandon. A flight attendant a couple rows ahead of them gripped a lap belt tightly as she modeled the use of its metal clasp, eyeing the women out of the corner of her eye. Another flight attendant, a handsome older man—a "steward" Karen might've been tempted to call him in another time—offered her a complimentary bottle of vodka. She felt like he might be treating her just a little better than the other passengers and she liked that. Certainly better than he did Sherry or even Lita whom men regularly followed around with a ravenous attention bordering on pathetic and rude, as if every other woman in the room were a potted plant or an extra-large traffic cone that was preventing access to her. "Here you go, sweetie," the steward said with a wink.

Oh, he was gay. Karen was sure of it. Gay men loved her. They seemed to consider large black women to be their spiritual soul sisters or something. Oh, honey, we've both been held down, haven't we, his eyes said to her. Here's a little extra hooch to lubricate the way. An older couple across the aisle peered at the three of them with disdain; the wife creased and re-creased an already questionably bound paperback copy of *The Thornbirds* while her nervous husband studied the safety card. Karen noticed a young man peering over at them from several rows behind with a kind of hungry grin.

"What about me?" Lita asked, the only unknighted vixen among them. Her light pink jumpsuit clung to her curvy frame; it was the perfect traveling outfit. Karen patted Lita's wheat-blonde bob and suggested some fairylike and rather unbecoming aliases: Pixetta, Pinky, Coybra, until finally settling, proudly, on Flirtatia. Lita repeated the name back to her, whispering it to herself at first like a giddy secret. *Flirtatia.* Then she said it louder, the name suddenly taking on a new sound, its own distinct meaning. *Flirtatia.* Sherry and Karen then chanted along with her until the new name had become a flotation device, lifting Lita out of her seat, knocking her inflight magazine and safety card to the lit aisle floor. The loose lap belt provided just enough give for her to arch her head forward, well over the row in front of her, and see the other passengers staring out windows and ready for takeoff, so that she might proudly proclaim herself.

"Flirtatia!" Lita screamed triumphantly while the other two women hollered and clapped from their seats, already buckled in. Karen poured herself another mini bottle of vodka on the rocks and then another for Lita, sloshing it on top of her watery orange juice.

A bald man seated in the row in front of them reached for the center console, searching for a button that might make all this stop.

THE THREE WOMEN WORKED TOGETHER at a public relations firm downtown. Sherry and Karen sat at desks across from each other that flanked the entrance door. They had developed the habit of looking at the door whenever it opened, no matter who walked through and no matter what time of day it was. Karen would wrench her head away from her computer screen like a serpent, distressed and annoyed in a most affected way as if she wanted the person to clearly understand that they had just interrupted her most important work. Sherry would tilt her head from her monitor with a robotic click to meet Karen head-on like someone had just plugged her in, then she would flip around to stare as well at the intruder, less coldly, but with an equally questioning demeanor, her stare imposing silently, "Well, what do *you* want?" People in the office referred to them behind their backs as "the gargoyles."

When Lita first walked into the office, the gargoyles had both thought she was maintenance or IT and treated her accordingly. She had, after all, done the impossibly stupid thing of dressing *down* for her first day of work. She wore baggy khaki slacks and some kind of a Payless boot, a cream waffle shirt that was too long in the arms and a silver balled chain like those used for displaying ID cards, yet there was nothing attached to it. She told Karen (who had looked up first as per their routine) that she was there to see Mr. Howell. They looked for a package, but she was only lugging around a purse with thick shoulder straps.

"And what business do you have with Mr. Howell?" asked Karen.

"I'm his new personal assistant."

"The hell you are," she muttered under her breath, but loud enough for Sherry to hear. The two women began staring her down, their eyes narrowing. "What are you wearing?"

"Clothes?" Lita said, the lilt in her voice turning the answer into a question.

"When were you supposed to start this morning?"

"Nine."

"Good. It's eight-thirty now. There's just enough time for you to get something else to wear. I know a great place." Karen wrote down the name of a salesgirl at a small boutique in their building. "Run along. Gigi will take good care of you." If Lita were allowed to get through her to Mr. Howell looking like a common delivery woman, Karen would never have heard the end of it.

The two women watched as Lita quickly turned around and scurried out of the office, her little butt somehow pert even through the baggy pants. "Fuck her," Karen spat.

"Yep," Sherry agreed. She chewed on the cap of her ballpoint pen, all cracked and creased with spittle, then looked back at her monitor, but not before sharing a knowing glance with Karen. Fuck her, indeed.

～

LITA HAD THE ONE THING the gargoyles envied above all else and they could tell she had it right away. It wasn't her youth or her apparent beauty they envied (although, looking back on it, Karen could've told Sherry that Lita had the kind of face that aged badly, a cute, perky cherub for a decade or so, if she was lucky, and then a slow descent into the face of a rabid chipmunk). No, it was nothing as obvious as that. What she had was a naïveté about her that seemed to almost guarantee upward mobility within their firm—an ingénue quality the two of them visibly lacked.

It wasn't the cutthroats who advanced at this firm at all. The gargoyles had both shown their fangs once and no one had ever forgotten it. It was as if someone had taken a picture of them at the worst moment of their lives and then frozen it in time for all to see in perpetuity—there was no changing public opinion. The silent acquiescents were the ones who needed to be watched—those women who didn't let you see the rungs on their ladders of ascension, those entrepreneurial acrobats, hurdling past Sherry and Karen, swinging with the greatest of ease into the positions that they deserved. They'd lost count of how many times they'd seen it happen: some entry-level pushpin walking into their office, flashing a little unassuming leg, bantering about with their quick, faultless wit and then plopping right down into the promotions that *they* deserved.

The last girl who'd come into the office, the reedy-legged and folksy Ramona, started out answering phones and coordinating meetings for the upper-level staff. Then one night two months into her new job, she stayed behind to take minutes during a brainstorming session in Mr. Howell's office, upon his request. According to now-legend, Ramona offered one brief, but brilliant unsolicited comment and was miraculously, and in near record-time (for the gargoyles kept a ledger of these kinds of events), promoted to account manager and proceeded to move into her own office catty-corner to the gargoyles' twin flanking desks. And if that were not enough to make them hate her, Karen was now forced to make her coffee, dousing it with the thick buttermilk she requested from the deli across the street. She winced daily at the glopping sound it made when it hit the surface and sank to the bottom of Ramona's "Jesus is Coming: Look Busy" mug, the cream cutting through the coffee like detergent, a gelatinous pool of fresh sick.

WHEN LITA RETURNED TO THE office twenty-five minutes later, she was wearing a navy blazer and a white silk skirt with a drawstring, red pumps and a floral handkerchief. "How quaint, how patriotic," Karen said as she rose from her desk to greet her. Sherry nodded and watched as Karen steered Lita down the hall toward Mr. Howell's office.

When she arrived at the empty desk outside of his door, she stopped in front of it, and laid her hands down on top of it, scratching her long talon-like nails across the lacquer before turning around.

"Mr. Howell is an extremely busy man and doesn't take to lots of frivolous questions. If you're unsure how to do something, ask me or Sherry. Don't take it upon yourself to guess."

Lita's smile, that same chipper grin she'd had when she first walked through the door, only slightly deflated. Karen thought it was possible she saw a hint of fear in her eyes. A woman could coast through life for decades with a look like that.

Karen gave a courtesy knock and then pulled Lita into the office to meet her new boss. He was on the phone, but waved them both in. "Conference call," he mouthed to the women.

"Your new personal assistant has arrived," she said quietly and closed the door behind them.

Turn her into stone and then we'll see how fast she can climb, Karen thought.

KAREN HADN'T ALWAYS BEEN A gargoyle. Far from it. She might have even considered herself a Lita at one time and the girls around her (and most certainly the men) had seen her that way, too. Her mama had always said that you don't get ahead in this world just watching things zip on by you. You have to go out and take it for yourself.

Everything was so easy and fun once. When she was feeling low now, like how she'd felt when they'd first seen Lita walk through the door all innocent and polite, so sweet until she moved right on up past them, all she had to do was look back. Looking back was her pastime, something she enjoyed like other people had an affection for crosswords or going to the movies. For Karen it was easy because she could pull anything back up to look at it in her mind, like a catalog card. Anything that had been good.

In high school, she'd been the sexiest thing walking down the hallway. Even the teachers looked at her like they wanted to screw her. That lesbian Mrs. Shane in biology wanted to do her, too; she could tell. That old dyke with the fuzzy sideburns had given her the easiest fetal pig to poke and cut up. Had it all laid out just for her, already pickled and easy to slice.

Karen had tall, smooth caramel legs back then that went all the way up to her neck it seemed; a high and tight ass that wagged behind her like a little dog she was always walking; shiny straight hair that she thought must've come from her daddy's side, whoever he was, because her mama's was kinky and spastic, all unruly tufts of scattered black sheep on her big head. Boys, even the few white ones in school, looked at her like all they could think about was splitting open her cotton panties, finding her wet spot, and poking it in the back of the football field, right in that old shed where the coaches kept the cracked football stanchions and Western High hurdles. And she did. It was good times for everyone, all around.

And Karen was smart, too. All she had to do was look at a textbook page once and she could remember it to the damn letter, like she had a little picture of it in her mind. So breezy, all that memorizing (which was really only just calling up that picture), and looking up the trigonometry formulas and the shapes and figures in Mr. Baird's geometry class and pi to the twenty-fifth decimal even when she never could figure out what pi was and why. The dates of Waterloo this and Emancipation Proclamation that. And she would recite for the football players—sitting on the bleachers in their scrimmage half-jerseys with the sweaty hair on their lower abdomens, slathered wet against their bellies, glistening in the late September sun—"The Worn Path" by Eudora Welty, her favorite story. Just by reading the pages in her mind. Not that the players cared what she said so long as she stood up there a few flights above them so they could maybe catch a peak up her skirt where her long legs ended and their happiness began. It was the easy life for Karen. It would never be that good again.

People who have fun in high school don't have fun any other time. It's sad, but true. Like a wonderful dream during a nap that someone shakes you out of and you hate them for it, the blissful-tight-and-hot, carefree Karen turned into someone else. She turned into the got-pregnant-after-high-school-from-someone-unimportant-to-her-and-got-rid-of-the-baby Karen. She still wanted to go to college. But then she got pregnant again and she was too far along with the baby (who would become Lulu) to get rid of it, so she gave birth. And then everything became about raising Lulu on her own and with just her paycheck. Everything became about getting Lulu whatever she needed and raising her right. She didn't want her to be a loose, trouble girl like her, opening up her legs to whoever felt like taking a gander.

So that led to the ugly truth—and this was ugly, so ugly that even Sherry didn't know and Karen didn't like to think about it too much. The ugly truth was that she had once cleaned Mr. Howell's toilet. And vacuumed up the little hole-punched holes littered around his desk. And she even had to wipe up on his fancy chair, getting all the bits of dandruff he left in there, in between the creases of the leather. She thought how could a man with so little hair leave so much dandruff? And there were no more boys looking at her in that way. In fact, the bigger she got and the rounder her belly, the more they looked away from her in disgust. And the women pitied her. She screamed to herself at night in her room, with Lulu and Lulu's baby down the hall, because like mother like daughter—she screamed, "Goddammit, don't you pity, me! I was on my way once! You don't even know who I am. Bastards."

It was in that office, past the two desks that flanked the door, where Mr. Howell found her cleaning one night and things got good again, maybe for the last time. They were instructed that it was rare to ever actually run into anyone in the office. The maid service she worked for had them clean after ten o'clock at night for a reason: they didn't want them mingling with the people in the office. It was considered unseemly. Karen certainly didn't care. She was tasked with cleaning the whole office and she sure took her time doing it. Mr. Howell's office was the biggest, almost as big as her whole apartment. He practically had an entire living room in there with a couple sofas and a liquor service, African art mingled together in a flat bowl. The kind of shit she noticed that white people hung up to make it appear like they had a worldly appreciation. They could have the mask of the God of Destruction of all Blond People hanging up on the wall and not even know it. She didn't like any of that crap anyway.

She picked up a picture on his desk of him and his wife and two college-aged children. It was one of those Olan Mills shots with a stuffy library in the back covered in hardbound classics, like the kind she used to read after school sometimes in the special collections section of the library. The ones she'd look at once, steal a glance at a couple pages in the time it took to wait for whoever it was (Bill or Hank or Drake or LeRon or whoever) to finish football practice so they could go hook up in the back of their car or behind the school. There was a brick wall that she'd hold onto while they did her, a wall with holes in it where bricks were missing or had just crumbled out over time. And sometimes she'd bring the page back up in her mind, the one from the library, and she'd read it right there.

As she wiped down the picture with a wet rag, she heard the door open.

"Not my best night," Mr. Howell said, the man in the picture, shorter than she would've imagined, but handsome.

"Oh, well, I'm—"

"The night we took that picture. At the country club in a room I've never been in more than twice before and we all had to act like it was our cozy little house."

"Your children are beautiful." She wanted to think she was still beautiful herself. Even with the weight and the dowdy uniform the service had her wear like she was the black Hazel or something. She wanted to still look good.

"Thank you very much. And you are?"

"Karen."

"Karen," he said like he'd invented the name himself.

THE LAYOVER IN MEMPHIS WAS only supposed to be an hour and a half. Sherry and Karen had both packed their entire belongings for the business trip in one suitcase. Black, efficient Samsonites, standard stuff. But Lita had checked an unwieldy suitcase and had carried the gigantic purse with the big straps on the first flight leg.

"She doesn't even know how to travel for business," Sherry whispered to Karen as the two of them trailed behind her en route down the terminal plank.

"We *have* to try the barbecue here. My guidebook said that Memphis is known for it," Lita looked back at them. Karen realized for the first time that day that Lita's lipstick was the same happy shade of pink as her jumpsuit.

"Are you telling me that you consulted a guidebook for a city we were going to be spending *an hour* in? And not even Memphis proper. The frickin' airport!"

"Always be prepared!" Lita answered with a wink. Karen looked at Sherry and the two rolled their eyes in unison.

"Ridiculous," said Karen. "Just utterly ridiculous." And she wasn't simply referring to the guidebook barbecue which was absolutely not in her diet plan.

In just three months at the firm, Lita had managed to make herself stand out in all sorts of hideous ways for which neither of the gargoyles could have foreseen nor planned. For one thing, she showed up for work impeccably dressed every morning, walking through the door like she was sashaying down a catwalk. It was like night and day from that raggedy outfit she'd come in wearing the first day. Karen had actually begun to suspect that it had all been an act coming in dressed up so sloppily, something to throw Karen off her game. Mr. Howell, so immoveable in his likes and dislikes, so hard to please (both of them had thought) took to her like she was some sort of siren, whispering incantations into his ear as she handed him his coffee and collated his presentations.

"She's so stealth," said Sherry, watching Lita pass by the two of them on her way into the office, with a careful, courteous nod Karen found steeped in condescension.

It wasn't just that she dressed better than the two of them, not an especially difficult feat these days (Karen felt her wardrobe options dipping ever closer to a large, printed tablecloth with a cloisonné belt fashioned out of her granddaughter's Playdoh and twisted paperclips.) No, it was more than just clothes. Clothes Karen could handle. It was the way Lita wore the clothes and what it meant for her in the office. It was that with each passing day, Lita's neckline seemed to plunge just a little bit further down, her skirt stopped just a smidge higher above her knees, her blonde bob took on just a little bit more of a sheen. Everything about her was *rising*. Karen knew what she was doing. She'd done it herself. And there was nothing stealth about it.

And what was that offensive scent she wore now? Karen would catch a whiff of it as she passed Lita's desk on her way to the kitchen to make Ramona's coffee and would feel the urge to pass out, vomit even. It was some type of flower-candy-vanilla crap as if the woman had dipped her face and neck in a milkshake before she left the house. What was it about that smell that made Karen hate her even more? It reminded her of young girls in malls, prowling around in packs, hungrily looking for boys. There was something almost feral in the way she flitted around the office so efficiently like her feet didn't even touch the ground. As if the simple laws of physics did not apply to her.

Sherry felt it, too, perhaps less keenly than Karen. (But wasn't that always the case with Sherry? Latching herself onto Karen like a tick, with never quite enough bite of her own?) Lita only rubbed her the wrong way, tangentially; her very existence didn't seem to be the direct affront it was to Karen. Sherry *had* provided the invaluable tidbit that Lita had a boyfriend though.

"He's possibly a fiancé. Have you noticed the ring that she wears?"

"I didn't really think much of it," Karen had answered, although she most certainly had noticed it. She just didn't want to allow for the possibility that Lita was engaged on top of everything else. Engaged, while Karen sat home with Lulu's daughter, her granddaughter Casey, never married, just knocked up and thrown on the refuse pile. She couldn't see her toes she'd gotten so fat over the years. "Well, what does Prince Charming look like?" she asked, through gritted teeth.

"Just like you'd imagine. Tall, young, handsome, kind of perfect, really. There's a picture on her desk. What else did you expect?" Sherry had answered with a certain amount of baiting to her voice Karen was loath to hear.

"He probably beats her," she'd said, and left Sherry alone in the break room.

The first time that Mr. Howell brought Lita along to Denver to meet with a client, the gargoyles knew something was slipping irretrievably out of their grasp.

"Have you ever heard of him taking a personal assistant with him to a client meeting? What can she do that I can't? I just don't get this," Karen barked at Sherry, who seemed to shrink behind her monitor for protection as if Karen might breathe fire.

"No, I definitely haven't heard that before," Sherry answered.

A UPS man walked through the door carrying a package. "Excuse me, ma'am."

"What?!" Karen yelled.

"I have a package for Lita Day."

"Oh, god," Karen said, shaking her head.

"I'll sign for it," Sherry said, looking over at Karen as she signed the man's electronic tablet.

"Wonderful. It's finally arrived," Mr. Howell said as he walked towards the gargoyles' desk.

"What's finally arrived?" Karen asked, as Mr. Howell began ripping the package open. He pulled out a leather briefcase with gold clasps and a big "L" monogrammed on the front.

"Lita's congratulatory briefcase. I've promoted her to head of accounts," he said.

~

ALTHOUGH TRAVELING FOR KAREN WAS somewhat of a novelty— she could probably count on one hand the number of times she'd even been in an airport—she did have a distinct feeling of non-existence in an airport terminal. They were almost like purgatories, all these people walking about aimlessly, waiting out their allotted sentences before being granted final passage through the pearly gates of heaven or across the River Styx into a new kind of hell. Anything seemed possible there and, at the same time, nothing seemed possible. Do I really need that pack of cards with Elvis's face emblazoned across the King of Spades? Why am I holding this foam beer cozy? Other passengers they passed as they walked down the halls of the terminal had a similar glazed, herded look as if they were only following the rest of the crowd, not really knowing where they were going or why, just that they must move, they must eat, they must wait in a long line outside of a bathroom they'd never seen before with strangers they'd never see again.

The gray cinderblock walls, low ceiling and dim fluorescent lighting made the Memphis airport feel as desolate as a rural middle school. The people were glumly filing down the hallways in rows. She saw a large black woman, not unlike herself, wearing a standard-issue smock. She was on her hands and knees cleaning up what looked like a pile of vomit outside of a bathroom. Her hair was ratty and hung in her face and she seemed to be gasping for breath at the stench of the mess in front of her, dousing it with a bottle of yellow ammonia that she then set on a large gray cart beside her stocked with toilet paper, paper towels, soap dispenser refills, and a wilted mop. She looked up at Karen and her eyes were moist around the edges, tears from the fumes of the cleaner.

Karen knocked into a motorized cart haphazardly parked in the middle of the concourse. "What the fuck?"

"Girls, let's try this place." Lita motioned them over to Sara Jane's BBQ Palace where a few huddled groups sat around a cascade of open containers of slaw and barbecue, shoveling it into their mouths in a kind of fugue-like ecstasy. "This looks delicious."

Then Karen saw the young man that had been on their flight. He was sitting alone at a table at Sarah Jane's. She'd noticed him catching glimpses at them through the half-closed first-class curtains. It had actually been what prompted her to come up with the little game of giving themselves sexy aliases for the trip. Him, and the pre-flight cocktails. It was her attempt to put all three of them on the same level again, shorten the distance that Lita's promotion had seemed to put between them. As she walked down the aisle of the plane on her way to the bathroom mid-way through the flight, she caught his eye and wanted to offer a smile. But she instantly got the impression that she was now *in his way*. In fact, he was staring right past her, through her it felt like, so that he could watch Lita who had occupied the aisle seat, her legs crossed and her knee bouncing up and down a little like she was laughing. And she could tell that Lita could feel his eyes, too. Arching her neck back as she laughed and bringing her hand up to the small hollow above her sternum in that faint, delicate— frankly *white*—way that made Karen just want to strangle her. It had taken all she could not to knock into the young man with her fat as she inched her way to the cramped bathroom at the back of the plane. That look on his face was unmistakable. A virile man, starving for a woman.

"I just got hungry," she announced to Lita. She pushed Sherry into Sarah Jane's with the weight of a guided hand.

"What?" Sherry gave her a puzzled look that Karen quickly met with a slight lift of her eyebrow. If nothing else, Karen was certain that Sherry could follow a lead when she saw one. What a dull crone she was. Karen could've gotten her to jump in front of a bus if she just asked her to.

Karen sat them down at the table right next to the young man and made sure that Lita was facing him. Doesn't she look delicious, sir? Like a pink powdered honeybun, she wanted to say.

"What can I get y'all?" asked a waitress. She had that disinterested, vacant look of someone who works in an airport, watching people come and go but never being able to leave herself. Her brown hair matched a swatch of gingham that she had pinned to the lapel of her shirt with a name tag that said "Ella." Karen could imagine "Ella" spitting in their food without a moment's hesitation if she didn't like them.

With glee, Lita said, "Oh, let me order for everyone!" She opened the laminated menu in front of her like a children's book, her melon-like breasts caressing the beverage and dessert sections separately. Karen looked over at the young man. He was quite handsome, but there was something she couldn't place about him that looked familiar. Maybe he reminded her of one of the boys from her high school. That one that was named Carl who she'd notice looking over at her from across the school cafeteria, eating pretzels and drinking fruit punch in a can. He'd wipe his lips with the sleeve of his shirt and he wouldn't look away when she met his stare head-on. He was blond with the pinkest, most perfect lips and who was she not to give him what she knew he wanted?

They did it at his place since it was just around the corner from school and his parents both worked. Carl laid out one of his mother's knit afghans on the couch in the living room and Karen would get on her back. He'd rip off his t-shirt and straddle her, his legs locking hers together so she would get all squirmy, wanting to open them up and get him inside her.

"You want this?" he'd say, one of his blond curls falling in his face so that he'd have to blow it away from the side of his mouth, just like he'd do when they'd smoke a cigarette afterwards.

Ella the waitress came back to their table with empty plastic cups emblazoned with the smiling face of Sarah Jane, a sister to Aunt Jemima, Karen thought, with her big smile and plates of hot, steaming barbecue surrounding her like she was cooking up right along with them.

"I'll fill these up at the beverage station." Lita rose from the table. "Sweet tea good with everyone?"

"I'll take mine with a splash of lemonade," Sherry said.

"Sweet tea sounds just fine to me," said Karen.

As Lita walked over to fill their drinks at the beverage station, Karen followed the young man's eyes to Lita. Her back looked curved and slender in that pink jumpsuit and she had it zipped down just low enough to reveal the color of her brassiere—a sort of dull egg-shell color, like some kind of special edition Victoria's Secret nonsense.

"She likes you, you know," Karen said to the young man. It took a second for him to realize that she was talking to him and it was still like he had to keep one eye on Lita while the other tried to focus on Karen and what she was saying. Lita was picking through a small dish of lemons with a pair of tongs like she was performing surgery.

"Oh yeah? How d'you know, huh?"

"She told me, that's how I know. In fact, she knew that you were watching her on the plane. And she loved it." The young man inched off his seat closer to her. "Go down the hall to the ladies' room past the jewelry kiosk. There should be one of those "Caution: Wet Floor" yellow signs next to it. Just wait for her. She'll be the wet floor." He scurried away, taking his backpack with him and leaving his tray behind.

"What are you doing? Are you crazy?" Sherry said.

"Do you want to go to this client meeting as one of her two office grunts?"

"No."

"Then just shut your mouth and let her do all the work. I can guarantee she's fucking Howell and that engagement ring on her finger doesn't mean shit. A little funny business in an airport bathroom is just the kind of thrill a girl like that loves, believe me. We'll sic security on them and she'll get dragged out of here like the little whore she is. Easy."

"What if he tries something with her? What if she gets hurt?"

"Him? He's as harmless as a schoolboy. We'll send security in there before anything gets out of hand."

"I'm back," said Lita, carrying the tray of iced teas and setting them in front of the two women. "They have the cutest stuffed lamb at the cash register. I might have to get one."

"Oh, shit," Karen said as she knocked over her drink into Lita's lap. "I am so sorry." Lita's tea had splashed down the front of her jumpsuit. Ice and a puddle of liquid was pooled in her lap. Sherry and Karen threw down whatever napkins were on the table.

"It's…fine. But I better go get cleaned up," she said.

"There's a ladies' room right down there on the left. Again, I'm so sorry, Lita."

"Accidents happen."

They both watched her as she walked down the concourse until she disappeared. Even if Mr. Howell wasn't sleeping with her, the minute he found out about the incident in the airport, he'd fire her. No one was going to believe she hadn't initiated it herself, the way she was carrying on in that tight, pink little jumpsuit, all zipped down with her tits hanging out. And probably drunk on top of everything. And that young man was obviously flirting with her from the second he saw her and she hadn't exactly been discouraging it.

Karen started to imagine something else though. What if Lita wasn't turned on by this young man at all? She might just like to parade herself around for the attention. It didn't necessarily mean she wanted to bend over, grab hold of a guardrail in a handicap bathroom and take a ride. Or what if he was a registered sex offender? She knew the ones in her neighborhood because she got e-mail alerts and then always, always looked at them. She had a granddaughter and had to be on top of these things. His curly blond hair, and his face that seemed too young for a man in his mid-thirties, that hungry grin she'd mistaken for virility, but could really be viciousness.

Karen got out of her chair and dashed for the exit. She had to push through a crowd of large people all wearing patriotic paraphernalia, large American flags stretched wide across their bulging bellies, and gigantic pins affixed to their shirts that said "America First!", a caricature of Donald Trump with a big head and tiny hands and extra orange face winking exaggeratedly with "You're Fired, Obama!" underneath. They were waiting to be seated and blocking the door. Karen, too big herself, could barely pass through. "Watch it, you black bitch," a skinny peroxide mother holding a mewling infant said as she accidentally knocked into her.

"Hey, you!" a man yelled out after her. But she ran. Down the concourse toward the restroom where she had seen the cleaning woman. Sweat poured down the nape of her neck and started to burn as it bubbled up on the palms of her hands, under her arms, in between her legs. It was like she couldn't quite move fast enough, as if she were running through a pan of cement, already hardening around her.

The Star

ON STAGE SHE BURNS LIKE a star. She's always seen herself like this—as a star. We've always known this about her, her tendency to shine so brightly, like a star, of course. For what else is there for an actress to be but a star? A star burns, then twinkles, then shines and shimmers, then burns even brighter. Then it burns out. Like a star, she is always burning.

IN LIFE—WHICH IS NOT ONSTAGE and is different—she burns as well. But it's a different kind of burning. It's a burning that's a kind of living, as she's living on the stage while she's burning. She can live and burn simultaneously onstage, just as the stars in the sky do so well. But stars don't live and burn at the same time. The star in the sky is burning as it is dying. For it to burn and twinkle and shine and shimmer and burn again so brightly, it must also give itself up to dying.

SO SHE'S DYING ONSTAGE. EVEN while she's living, she's dying. We're clapping because she's dying. She dies so brightly that she is burning to live.

Habitat

PEGGY FOUND OUT ABOUT IT from Jill on the phone. She then told the entire Potsdam crew: Ryan, Lucy, Jay, Chloe, Tandice, Lea, and myself in a group e-mail she started, which was then followed up by a conference call organized by Jay and Chloe, who'd gotten married after they'd met through Jill in Potsdam.

After Jill told Peggy how she met Mitch, Peggy added her own flourishes in the e-mail. I almost felt like I'd already heard the story even before I finished the e-mail because *it was just so Jill.* The whole thing. And Peggy always has this way of selecting the most potent details, peppering them throughout her recounting so we always have something to grab on to. She really has a knack for that.

Jill had moved to Alaska from Potsdam, Germany, where she had been doing some child psychology work for the Department of Defense while her boyfriend, Flap, performed grounds maintenance on the golf course at the American army base located there. After she left Potsdam for Alaska, she began work as a park ranger for the Tongass National Forest, which is the same kind of work she'd done in Oregon before Potsdam. Her coworkers in Alaska all liked her, but she had been complaining to Peggy on the phone that she wasn't really making friends.

"What do you do up there in your spare time?" Peggy had asked Jill before Jill had met Mitch.

"Besides drink?" Jill had answered.

Who could really blame her? People in Alaska seemed to have intense, often volatile relationships with alcohol. Jill was committed to having as much fun as possible, especially after having escaped Germany *and* Flap. For her that meant being able to go out for a couple of drinks to see where the night might take her. Flap was an ex-Navy SEAL who had emotionally and (from what we'd heard) physically abused Jill while they were living together in Potsdam. He had suffered brain damage years ago after getting hit in the head by a hammer in a bar fight that he himself had instigated, so there was also that.

"Jill *panic-leaves*. She panic-left Alabama for Oregon. Then she panic-left Oregon for Germany. Then she panic-left Germany for Alaska. She'll panic-leave Alaska too, I'm sure of it," said Lucy.

Lucy had coined the term *panic-leave* based on the various times that Jill would pack up and bolt practically overnight— breaking leases, leaving behind furniture, changing addresses like regular people change their sheets. It's no wonder anyone would have a problem taking Jill seriously when she kept saying that she wanted to settle down in Alaska. It wasn't in Jill's nature to settle down anywhere.

But no one could fault her for wanting to reinvent herself. And what better place to do that than in a state where no one knew who she was and the ones who did were too far away to remind her of who she was? This was Jill we were talking about, though. At the end of the day, no one ever really changes that much.

"Why Alaska? What is she *doing* there?" Ryan asked. We all wanted to know.

According to Peggy, Jill had met Mitch on Halloween night. She was wasted at one of the only bars in town, wearing a sheet with holes cut out for her eyes like she was a ghost.

"How inventive," Jay remarked.

"You know Jill," said Peggy.

Apparently, she had been drinking her cocktails that night through the sheet. Not lifting it up to pour drinks into her mouth but actually drinking them through the fabric, which made us all laugh. A woman covered in a sheet with holes cut through sucking down mai tais. Again, classic Jill.

"Well, at least she wasn't dressed as a slutty nurse or a slutty vampire. I hate that," Lea said.

Jill was coming up to strangers and standing there, completely still and silent, then howling like a crazy person, trying to scare them. Then she ran around outside in her costume, flapping around, trying to scare people from coming into the bar.

"Which is when she fell, right?" Jay asked on the conference call.

"Exactly," Peggy answered.

Jill fell down and split open her chin. Blood spurted through the sheet, which made the costume scarier. But she didn't even realize she was hurt. Folks thought she was just a bloody ghost. It was Halloween, after all.

So this guy named Mitch came up to her and asked if she was okay.

"'You're clearly bleeding' is what he said," Peggy reported to the group. Mitch was a sober recovering alcoholic and turned out to be the exact person Jill needed to run into. He drove her to the emergency room and stayed with her until one of the doctors on duty could examine her.

"Jill's health insurance is amazing," Tandice said.

Which is good because the cut on her chin required four stitches. And she was so wasted that the blood wasn't clotting properly.

"What was she wearing underneath the sheet?" asked Tandice.

"Thermal underwear and a black lace bra," reported Peggy.

"In Alaska? In October? Oh, Jill..." said Tandice.

"I know, right?" said Peggy.

After they got her stitched up, Jill somehow convinced Mitch to continue the night with her. They went to a different bar where, now that she had sobered up somewhat during the trip to the ER, Jill insisted on having a couple of nightcaps.

"No one has a 'couple of nightcaps,'" Jay said. "It's supposed to be the one nightcap. Otherwise it's not called a 'nightcap'; you're just drinking more and it's late."

But she did drink more, and then Mitch took her home and then, well, they got together after that.

"Of course they did," Lucy said.

BEFORE JILL PANIC-LEFT POTSDAM, SHE was doing quite well there. So well, in fact, that she'd become sort of the connective tissue between all of us wayward Americans, each trying to eke out a life abroad. As wild as she could be, Jill had a stable, nurturing side. She always took in strays—not pets but people. The only thing most of us had in common was that we knew Jill in one way or another. When Jay proposed to Chloe (after she had introduced the two of them more than a year before), Jill offered up her place to host an engagement party since Chloe's mom and sister were both so far away. Even her apartment felt almost like a home away from home. Who hadn't crashed at least once on her couch?

Her child psychology work, while challenging, also had been rewarding. She had a way with the more damaged kids, the problem children. She didn't give up on people, something that was clearly a valuable attribute in someone handling those types of kids. It made her a good friend too.

Her boyfriend, Flap, on the other hand, was floundering in Potsdam. He had begrudgingly come over there with Jill after receiving a dishonorable discharge from the Navy for almost killing someone in a bar fight. It wasn't his first time in Europe, but he still didn't feel like he fit in there.

"There was something so off about him. I hated when she used to bring him to parties," Chloe said.

"Yeah, he would just stand there with all those tattoos, looking so bored. If you tried to strike up a conversation with him, he'd look really uncomfortable. Why would she bring him in the first place if he was just going to stand there like a statue?" asked Jay.

But Jill liked Flap. She thought his tattoos were cool, even though to us they were too obtrusive. He had stars tattooed on his face around his eyes. It was trashy.

"Was he in a gang? I mean, what was that look?" asked Lucy.

Flap was a recovering alcoholic too. He swore he never touched the stuff anymore, even though Jill was sure he wanted to. Especially when the winter came, blanketing snow over the golf course on the base where he kept the grounds, shutting him out of any work until spring.

"What exactly happened to their relationship?" Lucy asked. "I never quite got that story."

"He started drinking again," said Chloe.

Jill and Flap had decided to go to Estonia for a small holiday. Jill was calling it a "holiday," but it was clear to both of them that it was a last-chance kind of thing to see if they could save their relationship, which, like Flap, was also floundering.

They were in a restaurant in the center of Tallinn, Estonia, having dinner and drinks. That was when things started to go wrong.

"What happened?" Lucy asked.

"Flap said something to her about Mormon girls. How they really know how to fuck or give head or something," said Chloe, not without the requisite tone one affords a friend who's been betrayed.

"Does that mean he was sleeping with someone else?" asked Tandice.

It didn't really matter whether or not it was true. Jill has a natural hair trigger for infidelity, seeing as how her father had been a major womanizer, sleeping around on her mother for years back in Alabama. So she threw a glass of beer in Flap's face in the middle of the restaurant. He pounded his fists and threatened to jump over the table and strangle her. They were quickly asked to leave.

"It was the alcohol," Jay said. "He'd never been like that when he was sober. Just quiet and antisocial."

"They were only drinking beer," Chloe said.

The two stumbled down the street toward the inn where they were staying, both completely wasted. That was when Flap pushed Jill, who then tripped on a curb and fell into a ditch.

"I really hate hearing about this," said Lucy. "I hate violence against women."

"Does anyone *like* violence against women?" asked Tandice.

"We all have a type," Peggy said.

Jill said Flap told her to get up, but she was drunk and couldn't move for some reason, so Flap kicked her.

"This is making me feel very uncomfortable," Lucy said.

"Imagine how Chloe, Jay, and I felt when she was telling us the whole story back in Potsdam. I had to restrain myself from shaking her," Peggy said.

When Flap and Jill got back to the inn, she went into the bathroom. Flap knocked on the door to be let in because he had to pee, but Jill took her sweet time. When she finally came out, Flap was peeing in a glass. Jill took the glass and threw the pee in his face, like she'd done earlier with the beer.

"She certainly knows how to make people mad," said Ryan.

"What happened to her after that? I almost hate to ask," Lucy piped in.

"Let's just say she found her way back to Germany by the skin of her teeth," answered Peggy.

JILL AND MITCH STARTED DATING exclusively after their Halloween together. We thought it was all rather sudden. Jill hadn't been single all that long after she'd left Flap and Germany and the trauma of that relationship. None of us thought she should've jumped into a new thing so quickly.

"What's the deal with Jill and recovering alcoholics anyway?" Tandice asked.

"Who knows. Her taste in men is so shitty. Have you seen pictures of the two of them on Facebook? Mitch is not attractive. Like, at all. I don't get it," Peggy said. "There's something a little Downs-y about his face, quite frankly."

"That's really mean," responded Tandice.

"Well, look at him."

Mitch was a couple of years younger than Jill and didn't have a lot going on in Alaska. He worked in a liquor store, which, to all of us, seemed like a rather unfit job for a recovering alcoholic.

"Why would he put himself in that kind of a situation, where every day is a big struggle against relapsing?" asked Lucy.

"Maybe he thinks it makes him stronger," said Ryan.

"They're certainly taking a lot of pictures together and posting them all over Facebook. I can't say she looks unhappy," Peggy said in a group e-mail. Always sort of boiling it down for us like she had a PhD in Jill Theory. Like we should all defer to her on this subject exclusively.

There was something different about Jill now, though. Those of us who'd known her in Potsdam probably sensed it the most. She appeared to be "nesting" with this Mitch guy. There were no more pictures of cocktails with her and her friends, each of them tagging each other on Facebook as the lime, the chunky ice cubes floating on top; Jill, the long pink straw.

"Staying in tonight with my man…" her status updates now said. "Woke up this morning, and I love my life. Mitch made me French toast!" along with a picture of said French toast served on a bamboo tray and a wilted violet in a red Solo cup. We all "liked" it on Facebook, so she must've thought we approved.

"God, isn't he classy?" said Tandice.

It was Peggy—again—who broke the big news in a group text. "Everyone, check Jill's Facebook right now. Like right the fuck now."

"Mitch and I would like to announce that we are—wait for it—PREGNANT!!!!! We're completely thrilled to be welcoming a baby into this world!" Jill had attached a picture of her First Response pregnancy wand, or whatever they're called, with the little pink line indicating that she was, in fact, pregnant.

"She basically just posted a picture of something she peed on," Tandice replied to all.

"Why is she telling people this early? Aren't you supposed to wait at least three months?" Lucy asked.

"It's Jill," we all replied.

We tracked Jill's pregnancy through her Facebook posts. We saw pictures of baby stuff they were buying: a crib (that looked somewhat used), rainbow pyramids with stackable plastic rings, a bag of diapers.

Peggy asked if she could throw her a shower. Jill replied that she didn't want everyone to have to travel all the way to Alaska to celebrate a baby that was roughly the size of an olive. She did, however, send Peggy a small list of items they needed if anyone should want to send a gift.

Two months into the pregnancy, Jill posted that she was sad to report she and Mitch had lost the baby and were going to try to work through the grief together. And then maybe try for another one.

"That's why you don't put all that stuff out there on the Internet. It's so much worse now than if she and Mitch had privately lost a baby that no one knew about yet," said Jay, who had group-texted Chloe, Ryan, Lucy, and Toby to discuss what had happened.

"Dare I say this might be a blessing in disguise?" suggested Lucy.

ACCORDING TO PEGGY, WHOM JILL was talking to on the phone regularly, Mitch had started drinking again after he and Jill lost the baby.

"Alcoholics use any excuse to start drinking again," Tandice told her, uncharacteristically stating an open dissatisfaction with the way Mitch seemed to be treating Jill.

"All she wants to do is stay home and try to grieve over the loss, and all he wants to do now is go out to the bars and get wasted," Peggy reported back to us.

"This is very worrisome," said Lucy.

"Didn't she say he's just drinking beer?" Chloe asked.

"Yeah, that's always worked out well for her," Jay remarked.

Jill threw herself into her job. She began working on a conservation project for some land outside the Tongass National Forest that was the unprotected habitat of a species of wild fox. She was spearheading a campaign to get the species of wild fox on the protected list, a tall order in Alaska but not an insurmountable one. With Jill on the case, the foxes had found a lifelong ally. Jill was nothing if not fiercely loyal.

Which was why everyone was (happily) stunned when they checked out Jill's Facebook status a month after she and Mitch had lost the baby: "To everyone: I want to let you know I've decided to part ways with Mitch because of reasons that are quite obvious to him."

Peggy called her almost immediately and got the full scoop. Apparently, Mitch had been chatting up an old girlfriend from California via e-mail on Jill's computer. Jill found his open account on her computer and read through the e-mails, some of which had alluded to a tryst they had while he was already together with Jill.

"What an idiot," Tandice said.

"Are you really that surprised?" Peggy said.

After Jill read through the e-mails, she called down to the liquor store where he worked and said he could come by and get his stuff within twenty-four hours or he could find it all on the front lawn. When she was gone the next morning, Mitch stopped by and picked up his clothes. It was her house, and after she kicked him out, he had to go live with his brother ten miles outside of town. He also lost his job at the liquor store because he'd been so drunk one night after drinking practically half a handle of whiskey that he had thrown beer bottles at a couple of women who were shopping for wine.

"He sounds psychotic. I'm glad Jill finally wised up," said Ryan.

"I know. Thank God," Lea said.

When Jill went "dark" on Facebook, we all simply thought she was taking a break. Lucy theorized that perhaps Jill had finally learned her lesson about putting so much out there on social media, especially after the double blows of the miscarried baby and then Mitch's betrayal. Everyone felt better that she'd left that relationship. "Maybe she'll come back East," said those of use who'd ended up in New York after Potsdam. "Maybe she'll move back to Potsdam," said those who were still assigned there. Or Oregon again. We all agreed that this time she wouldn't be panic-leaving but relocating, on her own terms.

Peggy started to get worried, though, when, after a whole week, Jill still hadn't answered her phone or returned any of her messages.

"This isn't like her. I'm definitely starting to get worried," she said in a group e-mail.

"Shouldn't someone call her work?" suggested Jay.

"I don't know the number," Lucy said. "And I don't think Peggy has it either."

When word finally got to us, it came from Jill's mom, who only conveyed the most basic details of what had happened. It sounded horrifying, but according to Peggy, who spoke directly to her about it, Jill was going to be okay.

"I mean, physically," Peggy clarified.

Mitch had gotten drunk and convinced his friends to drop him off at Jill's house. Jill's mom told Peggy he'd managed to talk his way into the house, although Jill wasn't particularly forthcoming with details regarding how that had happened.

"He's obviously able to convince her of multiple things that are patently false, one of which is the fact that he's not hideous," Peggy stated to us.

Once inside, he punched her in the face. Jill said he hit her so hard that she knocked her head on the wooden fireplace mantel, then passed out. When she came to, Mitch was passed out drunk on the couch nearby. When she inched over to the front door, however, he woke up and blocked her way out. He kept her in the house for four days.

"How did she get out? Oh, my God, did he rape her?" asked Tandice.

Peggy didn't answer.

According to Lucy, who had called Jill's mom after Peggy did, Jill told Mitch she was cold and needed to get her slippers from the bedroom. It was mid-afternoon on the fourth day of her captivity. She made her way towards the bedroom and then dashed for the front door. She saw neighbors outside and ran to them for help. They were the ones who called the police.

"What's going to happen to him?" asked Ryan in a text to Peggy.

"He's been charged with second-degree battery and false imprisonment. He's definitely going to get time," she answered.

Lucy mentioned that she saw on Facebook that Jill had moved back home to her mom's house in Alabama. "Panic-leave," Lucy said.

"Does she even have a job anymore?" Chloe asked.

"They let her go after she took so much time off," Peggy told us. "She's not doing well. From her mom's description, she sounded very skittish."

This was never a word we would've used to describe Jill in the past. Skittish. She was the most fearless person we knew.

"Well, she *used* to be fearless," Jay said.

"I feel like I don't even know her anymore," Lucy said.

"I'll pray for her," said Lea.

"She has to go back to Alaska for the trial next month. Someone should be there with her," Peggy said.

"But who?" Lucy asked. Everyone seems to be so busy these days.

Women
of a Certain Age

THE FIFTY-SEVEN-YEAR-OLD AMERICAN ACTRESS, A back-to-back
Daytime Emmy Award winner for Best Lead Actress in a Daytime
Drama ('85 and '86)[1], who was once proclaimed the "Sarah Bern-
hardt of soap operas" by Carolyn Hinsey in *Soap Opera Weekly* in
a 1991 feature article, sits in her dressing room, quietly nursing a
gin rickey—a native D.C. cocktail for the once native daughter—
while her neck is wrapped in cornhusks that have been soaked
in the prepubescent oils of the undocumented young Mexican
women who clean the fifteen bathrooms that are spread throughout her palatial home. Only moderately overweight (she main-
tains a "matronly figure—prison matron," as it was described by
Joan Rivers on E!'s *Fashion Police* once), she's a *real* actress who
was once nominated in the early 1970s for the Tony Award for
Best Actress in a Featured Role in a Play before she began her
thirty-five year (and counting) reign as Lydia Wirthmore on *Falcon Palace*, the matriarch of the Wirthmore family who own and
operate the largest high-end luggage distribution in the fictional
Southwestern city of Silver Platte, Nevada (yes, there is more than
one high-end luggage distributor in the city, she's had to explain

---

[1]A feat matched by only Helen Gallagher in '76 and '77 for *Ryan's Hope*, Judith
Light in '80 and '81 & Erika Slezak in '95 and '96 for *One Life to Live*, and Su-
san Flannery in '02 and '03 & Heather Tom in '12 and '13 for *The Bold and the
Beautiful*.

to several inane daytime talk-show hosts throughout the years who clearly had done no research whatsoever—how else do they think the writers create the familial rivalries, the weekly back-stabbings, the tortured romances that provide years of storylines in which Lydia may inevitably shine?). The Actress is the winner of several "Best of" *Soap Opera Digest* Awards throughout the years including: Best Villainess ('79), Best Couple ('84, an honor she shared with Hayward Griffin, whose character she murdered in self-defense two years later at the climax of a groundbreaking marital-rape storyline that secured her second Daytime Emmy Award in 1986), Best Kiss ('93, shared with Valerie Cortlandt for her later-in-life lesbian storyline, a short-lived dalliance that was over before it even took off and has never been mentioned by any of the other characters ever again, yet has since spawned its own acronym—a "L.i.L.L.y"—memorialized on urbandictionary. com and attributed solely to her storied performance). Now fifty-seven, the Actress, who lounges around between takes in a char-treuse house robe her own sister, a one-time assistant, sewed for her by hand as a birthday present before the two were forced to permanently part ways both professionally and personally, whom *The New York Times* once referred to in response to her perfor-mance in Eugene O'Neill's *A Moon for the Misbegotten* as "the inheritor of the legacy of such stage greats as Eva Le Gallienne, Jessica Tandy, and Geraldine Page," is five foot seven, 168 pounds, with hair colored a "burnt sienna" bimonthly with the aforemen-tioned Third World-oiled cornhusks wrapped around her neck to combat the "turkey neck"—God, how she loathes that term: why not "weathered swan neck" or "crepe-paper skin" or some-thing halfway elegant; why is every day a battle she must fight against her own womanhood?—that has crept into her visage in the last decade or so, resulting in (and she is quite sure of this) a reduction in screen time, a drastic cut in romantic pairings, the acknowledgment by one of these insufferable new teen charac-ters in-scene that she was his great-*grandmother*, the striking of

the Wirthmore office set, a place she considered almost an exten-
sion of her own home after all these years. She looks closer at the
dressing room mirror with light bulbs lit on its periphery like the
ones that hugged the end of a Broadway stage she was on for only
that one 363-performance run of *A Moon for the Misbegotten* at
the Winter Garden Theatre, the one extra light casting a ghoulish
emphasis on the deep wrinkles in her forehead, the unforgiving
lines down the sides of her face from so much yelling on the set,
so much screaming in pain while giving birth to one of her four
screen children, all that desperate calling for help when her iden-
tical cousin Christina (which she herself, of course, played) was
holding her hostage at the bottom of a well while she took over
Lydia's life. She places a camisole up to her cheek to wipe away
the clownish rouge Dana the makeup lady had applied so hurriedly this morning and smears off the coral lipstick chosen for
her by focus groups—the only women who wear coral lipstick
are those who have recently been embalmed—pulls herself out
of the support girdle the wardrobe people shoved her into, and
lets her folds breathe happily against the fabric of her house robe.
Her dressing room is located near the old Wirthmore office set in
Studio B of the NBC-Paramount Studios in Burbank, California,
which is about twenty-five minutes from her house in the Hollywood Hills, which is paid off in full. Now that the set has been
struck, Lydia's office scenes are now filmed in her living room, in
an alcove that only reads "office" by virtue of the presence of a
cubbyhole stuffed with envelopes, a sterling silver letter opener
(which Lydia used once in 1992 to fend off an intruder), and a
desk lamp with a hunter-green shade. The Actress sits waiting for
her call, choosing not to focus on the round of bells and whistles
from the game show taping across the way, one of the many pro-
grams supplanting the entire soap opera genre because they're so
cheap to produce, cheaper than keeping up the appearance that
Lydia Wirthmore's fortune is somehow untouched by the outside
economic calamities of the real world, the 2008 housing crisis

and bank bailout, the election of the nation's first black president (the "president" in *Falcon Palace* is a nameless white man forever modeled on Ronald Reagan), years of sexual revolution having passed by most of the women in the cast like clouds that have morphed from a dragon to a bunny when you look away for a second, thinking that if she could have just one more epic storyline—the revelation that she is actually Serbian royalty, a final triumph over Wirthmore's main rival DiSanto Leather, Inc., with her, Lydia Wirthmore, at the center of a coup d'état, a cougaresque affair with her stepson Derrick—she wouldn't be sitting here pondering what Ionesco might have thought of all this love in the afternoon or if O'Neill or Albee or even Ibsen might've found the lick of courage deep down inside the character of Lydia Wirthmore that the Actress has had to find or if any of these playwrights whose immortal words she should be performing as a woman of a certain age[2] would've dared pare down her scenes, diminish her character, strike her rooms.

---

[2] The Actress is not fifty-seven. She hasn't been that age in more than five years.

Why Burden a Baby with a Body?

IN HER DREAM, HIROMI HEARD the screaming. Terrifying, high-pitched screams that felt, at one moment, as if they were right beside her, but then when she reached in front of her—with her hands grasping at the empty air—they were impossibly far away, like they were coming from the bottom of a deep well. Punctuating the screams were breathless gasps, searching for more air to fuel yet another scream, as babies do. It was in those little moments in between when it appeared Anima had finally calmed down. But then there was a manic reignition of purpose, a steady rise in intensity, then more unquenchable wailing. Her baby was looking for her.

In her nightgown, Hiromi made her way through a dark, wet cellar, her bare feet scraping the slick set of steep, cramped stairs. She struggled to move forward but was arrested, as if she were walking through a thick paste like brown beet molasses. Her baby's cries—Anima's screams—had become more desperate, angry even, as if the original need, still unattended, had been compounded by the child's resentment at the lack of human touch. "Where are you?" the baby's cries seemed to imply. Anima needed to be found; she had turned vengeful.

Groping her way farther up the stairs, Hiromi reached for the wall to steady herself. As she ascended the staircase, it became wider. With each step she landed on firmer, more navigable ground. She noticed something at the top of the stairs. She moved closer and realized it was a bassinet, just like the one they'd wanted to buy for Kimi but couldn't afford, made of birch with a tatami base and pieces of turquoise and magenta ribbon woven alternately along the bars, shellacked. The screaming was only for show now, as Hiromi knew Anima could sense her presence even though she still hadn't seen her mother. She felt the cries had lessened in intensity and purpose, decreasing, it seemed, almost in step with the cadence of Hiromi's movement toward the bassinet.

The light in the staircase had changed as well. A thin pink beam of light, dense and straight, led right into the bassinet, pointing the way. She climbed the final steps and came up to the bassinet. It was shaking. As she reached inside, her hands broke through a layer of cold air before they finally met Anima's outstretched arms—her electronic arms. Hiromi grabbed hold of Anima's tiny wrists, but they burned her fingertips, cold but sharply hot, like dry ice. Then the screaming finally stopped.

With a start, Hiromi woke up from the dream and immediately felt for Takahiko beside her, but he was gone. *Prius,* she instantly thought. He was already at the café playing *Prius* without her again. A bit of a panic rose in her as she tried to adjust her eyes to the darkness of their bedroom. He could be with their new baby, Anima, right at that moment while Hiromi was sitting up in bed, wasting time only thinking about her. She had to get to the café in Akihabara and quickly.

A shaft of pink light from the all-night pachinko parlor across the street came through a ripped hole in a paper square of the shoji screen, and she used it to grope her way to the large walk-in closet, the only other "room" in their apartment besides the bathroom. This apartment was the best they could afford with the money from the public assistance program she and Takahiko had been on for more than a year and a half. While Motoha-sunuma wasn't an ideal neighborhood, it was only a few stops on the Mita line to the Yamanote line, which was that much closer to Prius.

The tan jumpsuit Hiromi preferred to wear while gaming hung from a crooked hook another tenant had installed on the door. She pulled her nightgown over her head and slipped into the outfit, zipping it all the way to the top. She put on a pair of white canvas shoes, scuffed with black marks from the rude, clumsy steppings of her fellow passengers on the train.

Through the jumpsuit, she grabbed at the misshapen bulge of her stomach, squeezing the flabby skin left over from Kimi's difficult birth. She was still disgusted by the state of her body. Her daughter had been born premature. Arriving too late to the hospital, Hiromi was forced to forego an epidural and deliver her with minimal pain medication. When she was ready to finally expel the child, a sick river of bile rose in her, and she vomited at the moment Kimi crowned. She felt as if the baby had swum out of her womb to safety on a raft of thick blood and brine, escaping the cage of her ribs and haphazardly pushing aside her vital organs. When the nurse handed her the wrinkled little thing, its skin so much darker than hers and Takahiko's, the baby opened its mouth and emitted a horrible shriek like a preening beastling, its eyes stapled shut with lines of mucus.

Hiromi found a half-full bottle of formula on the kitchenette counter and tossed it into the crib at the back of the closet. It landed next to the stuffed Pikuro doll her voiceover director had given them before Kimi was born. The doll had a huge mouth that opened into a wide, toothy smile. Its arms were outstretched on either side, curling at the fingertips, as if its default were to hug indiscriminately. She saw the Pikuro doll move a bit, then noticed Kimi creep from behind it. The doll somehow had gotten bigger than Kimi, or Kimi had gotten smaller; Hiromi wasn't sure. Kimi grabbed the bottle with greediness, Hiromi thought, and sucked on it venomously, her spare paws rattling the bars of the crib in vain. Hiromi looked into Kimi's eyes.

She couldn't stand looking at Kimi, that blank, sad stare pleading with her for something. *What? What do you want from me?* she felt like screaming. Anima never looked at her like that. Anima, with her round, blue eyes that were dewy and soft, her long lashes flicking back and forth so delicately, like an elegant spider perched on top of her eyelids, bending their eight black legs. Without speaking, Anima was able to let Hiromi know she was there to help guide her through Prius and all the wonders of that world—not that Anima couldn't talk, of course. On the rare occasion Anima needed something from Hiromi, she was fully capable of communicating her needs in a tiny, lovable voice that was comforting and familiar to Hiromi.

Anima didn't need anything from Hiromi. She was there to help her mother, protect her even with warnings of town invaders and town dissent (not everyone in Prius proper could be trusted). She didn't demand things from her; she didn't require thing after thing after thing from her with the desperate clinginess that Kimi's urgent, manic moans lately had embodied.

Months before Kimi was born, Hiromi had stumbled upon a link to a voiceover audition while surfing the web at an Internet café in Akihabara, Tokyo's "electric district." The *tekki* card she'd been able to wrangle out of her last temp job was set to expire at the end of the month, so she'd no longer have access to all the stops along the Yamanote line. With the entire subway line at her disposal, she more often than not chose Akihabara, mainly for its free twenty-four-hour Internet café located on the third floor of Laox, a discount electronics store.

But she also could disappear in Akihabara. Comforted on all sides by the never-ending lights that illuminated the discount electronics storefronts, she luxuriated in the pointed lack of interest shown by passersby. There was so much else to grab one's attention—vacuum cleaners shaped like people that cleaned the floor of their own accord when they detected dirt from fine sensors at their base; cell phones thin enough to fit in the credit card holder of a wallet, and facial-recognition robots that could greet you at the door because they knew who you were.

Never having done any voiceover work at the time of her recruitment, Hiromi had been unsure whether she had what it took to pull off a child's voice, in this case a mystical helper baby in an alterna-world game called *Prius*. Hiromi, whose only exposure to gaming culture had been a requisite dip into childhood video games, found the idea of Prius very soothing. The director of the voice audition, a portly woman with a traditional Edo look, had explained the landscape of the game to her.

The world of Prius was not unlike the large temple gardens Hiromi had visited in Kamakura in her youth. Dense pockets of forest appeared in the game as well as more manicured areas of play where players could set up lodging and businesses according to an earned-points system. Inhabiting Prius was like living in a village that looked like Kamakura but with neighbors and your own residence. New players were each assigned a job as well as a set amount of coins to purchase necessities. Players could earn additional credits through different tasks and accomplishments, such as defeating invaders of Prius. According to Hiromi's director, border people were always trying to find their way into the village. Players who were equipped with the appropriate weaponry and earned knowledge of secret passageways through the intricate maze of the forests could extinguish these invaders and therefore gain access to more of the town's amenities and eventually receive their own dwelling. After being assigned "careers," players came together for tribe meetings to discuss village issues and ordinances and compare point totals. Hiromi would eventually became the proprietor of an apothecary at the center of Prius. Anima was a flaxen-haired little girl whom high-ranking players could earn after a set number of good works and credits.

Hiromi recorded several sentences for the Edo woman that could be used to construct any number of voice cues for the Anima character. Years spent working at 7-Eleven, before she'd met

Takahiko and gotten pregnant, had prepared her to dip into the highest registers of her voice. "*Irrashaimaise!*" the attendants on duty would say, one after the other, like a chorus of robots to welcome each new customer into the store. Her supervisor told her that it was important to go into a high head voice. The men at 7-Eleven went almost as high as the women. Rather than have Hiromi collect royalties on the voice work, Takahiko had insisted she let Second Life, the company that created *Prius*, pay her in one lump sum, which would release all her rights to the voice. The money, though, had gone quickly, and now they were on the dole.

Kimi's elbow hit the side of the crib jerkily, a shudder running through her as if she were seizing. Hiromi hadn't noticed this the last time she had seen her, which, she only now realized, must have been some fifteen hours before but could have been longer, as she had lost track of when she'd come home from the Internet café at Laox. She remembered being exhausted when she had returned from the café the night before, so tired yet still exhilarated by her time in Prius; it had been thrilling being that close to Anima. After all these months of playing to earn the child, it felt natural to Hiromi to finally be able to enjoy Anima's companionship and trust in her abilities. She simply had looked past Kimi's crib on her way to bed with only a quick dart in its direction where it sat in the back of the closet. Kimi wasn't making a sound, and her blanket was pulled almost all the way over her head, as if she were a sack of potatoes with one blackened spud peeping out of the top for air. Hiromi hadn't had the energy or the desire to pick her up or even touch her. She had quickly put on her nightgown, then fallen onto the unmade futon on the floor.

Something clenched the pit of her stomach at the thought of touching the thing, Kimi, this whining sack of flesh, who, if she thought long and hard enough about, neither looked nor sounded like her. Kimi smelled foul even though Hiromi was sure Takahiko must've changed her before he'd headed back to the café. Anima wasn't like that; she didn't need to be fed and changed on a constant schedule. A couple of days before, while rearranging the bedding, Hiromi had brushed her hand against Kimi. The touch seemed to awaken the child from some kind of deep, troubled sleep. Kimi's eyes were weak but still bore into Hiromi with the desperately unfocused stare of a blind person. The infant searched for the source of the disruption and had reached out to Hiromi for something (for what, Hiromi didn't know, which made her angrier, this lack of clarity in Kimi's constant desires and needs); Kimi grabbed at Hiromi's wrist from a corner of the crib like a spastic roach. Hiromi had pulled her hand out of the crib, then hastily turned out the light.

The sun was coming up when she finally hit the streets. She was thankful, on the one hand, that she was up early enough to catch the first train downtown. It annoyed her, however, that the Yamanote line adhered to such a ridiculous schedule, strictly closing the gates each night at 12:30 a.m. sharp. Even if Hiromi were running toward the station entrance to catch it, her shoes untied, breathing in the dragon-like up-rush of air that came from underground, she would often find the gates at the bottom of the stairs closed and locked. She was thankful she could now get back to Akihabara, back to the Internet café at Laox, back to the safety of Prius, where Anima, she hoped, was waiting for her.

She was also worried, though. Takahiko must have taken the last train of the night only six hours before her. Only she wasn't sure when he had left their bed or even whether he'd come home at all. Could he still be at the café in front of the game since they'd last gone together the morning before? She was concerned that he might be cross with her when she found him. When he was awake more than twenty-four hours, she had a difficult time gauging what kind of a mood he might be in.

If they didn't start out playing together, Hiromi often found it was harder to connect with Takahiko. Losing oneself inside Prius was disorienting at first. Players had to let go of themselves in the "real" world so they could belong to themselves in the fantasy. When Hiromi and Takahiko entered the forest together, they did it as a unit. They were a team, which was how they'd always envisioned themselves when they'd first started to play *Prius*. Advancing in the world of Prius had been a way to achieve something together they'd been unable to pull off outside of the game. As they walked together into the dense, thick brush of the entrance to Prius, they were confronted with the tallest trees imaginable— taller even than the monstrous firs in Yoyogi Park. A warmth glowed from within the center of the collection of trees. Hiromi even saw a kind of misty halo over her character's head as she glided through the forest entrance. Holding hands, they'd step in unison over ancient logs that were filled with peonies that grew out of small cracks, just like the ones Hiromi used to see growing along the banks of the Arakawa River. Strong shafts of yellow light from an unseen sun broke through the leafy canopy, leaving a path of light pockets for them to hop farther along together, so swiftly, so effortlessly that their ankles felt winged.

If she found Takahiko at the café *after* he'd already entered Prius, it was like entering that same forest, but it would be dark and quiet because she was alone. With no one to help guide her through the initial thickness of the foliage, she was pricked and poked with jagged brambles. The forest floor would shift below her, unstable and prone to sudden holes that, if she fell into them, would subtract credits from her bank. Lose too many credits, and there went the house, her alliances with neighbors (fellow players); even her hard-won child could be stripped from her. The prospect was frightening to ponder. Takahiko was almost impossible to connect with once he'd already entered Prius.

Several bunches of white, blue, and orange balloons blocked the entrance to Laox. It appeared that the store was having some type of sale. Hiromi pushed through the balloons and headed toward the escalators that would take her to the café. When she made it to the top of the escalator, she spied Takahiko at their usual station, at the end of a long row next to the aisle. She sat down at the terminal beside him.

"Have you left at all?" she asked him. He looked at her briefly then went back to the game.

"Huh? What? No," he grunted at her.

"Have you eaten anything?"

"I'm eating now."

She looked at his screen, and sure enough, Takahiko was wolfing down virtual kimchi at the dining table of their thatched-roof home in Prius. The clock on his screen indicated that he was going on his eighteenth hour of play. A small pop-up message appeared in the corner of the screen and asked, "Maybe you should go outside?"

"Have you seen Anima?" she asked cautiously.

"She's around."

Has he gotten bored of her this quickly? she asked herself. He didn't know how to talk to Anima like she did.

"I saw her talking to someone," he said.

Only recently had Hiromi finally won them their child. She had mixed a potion in the apothecary that had saved a member of the royal family, a princess who had been poisoned by an outsider posing as entertainment for the castle. Anima had descended into the forest in a globe, like a weather balloon. She was an amnesiac and didn't know where she had come from. A blank slate, she brought no baggage to her relationship with Hiromi. But her missing knowledge held several clues to the secrets of the town. And the closer Hiromi could get to her, the closer she would be to unlocking the secrets of Prius.

Hiromi donned the headgear that allowed her to enter the virtual chamber of the game. She positioned her hand on the computer's mouse, which featured a red sensor that lit up when it was in use. Then she entered Prius. Just as she thought, uncertainty plagued her initial descent into the forest opening. Black vines hung in front of her face, and the small rays of light that made their way down from the canopy forest weren't strong enough for her to make out. Anima popped out from behind the trunk of a large cryptomeria tree and walked alongside Hiromi as she went through the forest toward the village center.

Anima tagged behind Hiromi with a friendly gait, those wide eyes of hers brimming with beauty. But she wasn't someone to be messed with. Because she walked behind Hiromi, she could be on alert to attacks from behind. The alterna-world helper babies looked cute and friendly, but they possessed powers and abilities that were hidden even from their parents. Hiromi hoped the longer she had Anima, the more she could use the child's knowledge and abilities to advance further in the game. Being the apothecary of the town was an honor, of course, but she was certain she could climb further.

"Mochi, mochi, Mama!" Anima said to Hiromi, who reached into her satchel to give the blond baby girl several pieces of hard candy. Anima's skin tone was a closer match to her own than Kimi's, and it was like hearing her own voice when Anima spoke, which, of course, it was. She could hear the high note of accommodation in the voice, the same one she had used at the 7-Eleven. Patient, kind, inviting.

On their way to the apothecary, Hiromi and Anima crossed paths with Takahiko, who was heading back from the orchard where he had been picking apples to sell at the open market.

"Hello," she typed into the message panel.

"I have to sort these apples back at our hut," Takahiko answered.

"Can Anima and I help?" Hiromi asked.

Anima circled over to where Takahiko was leaning against a tree. She had taken the full weight of the basket of apples and was placing it on her back. "I'll take these home for you," she told him.

"Thank you, Anima," said Takahiko.

They watched together as Anima traveled farther down the path toward the village. Anima turned her head back several times to look at them.

Takahiko sat down against the tree. Anima looked back once more before disappearing around the corner.

Hiromi saw a rare opportunity to initiate sex. Taking herself out of the game for a moment, she pulled down on her jumpsuit to make her stomach look less lumpy. She had gotten a warm fluttery feeling when she'd accidentally rubbed up against a man when taking a seat on the train that morning. It had surprised her, this feeling, the sudden rush to her cheeks, its strangeness. It had been so long since she'd felt any human contact that the sensation had felt foreign to her. Before she'd become pregnant with Kimi—before they'd discovered Prius—Takahiko had wanted to spoon with her from behind on their futon. He'd hold on to her stomach as if it made his hands warm to touch her there.

She placed one of her hands down the front of her pants, waving a finger or two delicately over her vagina just to tease herself at first. She scanned the café and spotted only a few people on the other side of the room, all of them deeply fixated on their screens with blank expressions. She glanced over at Takahiko, who sat at the computer station beside her. He also was staring straight ahead in a similarly rapt fashion, but he seemed to indicate that he understood her intentions. His dry tongue hung out of his mouth in a parched and desperate way, then it ran over his lips like an invitation to her. She realized he wanted to have sex too but that it had to happen inside the game. So Hiromi went back into Prius. She sent an instant message to Anima to wait for her at the apothecary.

Hiromi pulled Takahiko aside, behind one of the thatched-roof homes, and took off his weapons—the quiver full of arrows first, then the gun at his side, and finally the bow. The rest of his armor came off in one slick move, and his massive torso was revealed. Hiromi slipped out of her bodice and grabbed the sill of a window so Takahiko could enter her from behind.

As their bodies undulated under the straw thatch of the roof, hidden from the sight of passersby, Hiromi saw through the window into the house. Anima had stayed at the apothecary as she had been told but was talking to a woman who lived in this house. Using points in her cache, Hiromi gave herself the ability to hear the conversation inside.

"We can make it look like she did it. Who else in this town has access to poisons?" Anima told the woman.

It was inconceivable. Was her own child plotting against her with another player, setting her up as the patsy, wanting her to take the fall for what—a murder? There was no mistaking what she had heard. After all, it was her own voice she had just listened to.

"Stop, Takahiko," she said, trying to push him off her and get back into her bodice so she could get into the house.

"I'm almost done. Just wait."

"I have to get over there! Now! Get off me!"

He kept thrusting and had grabbed her neck, pulling it back so far she was sure he would break it.

"Get off me, you fucking bastard!" She exited the game and pushed him out of his chair.

"Stupid cunt," he muttered, looking up at her as he lay on his back. He was glassy eyed, and sweat ballooned under his arms, emanating a stale body odor from his hours of listless, stationary play. Hiromi left him stinking on the floor of the café.

She ran down the long set of stairs into the dark underground of the train station at Akihabara. A man was urinating near the entrance. When she swerved to avoid walking through his stream, she lost her balance and fell against a support beam, but she recovered quickly and continued down the stairs. The hot, stale air blew through her as she made her way farther, dodging through what felt like an army of young men in suits flanking her sides but also rushing toward her from the bowels of the station. Most were heading to meetings, but several were probably en route to electronics shops, the gaming center, or the capsule hotels where a man could stay in what barely amounted to a coffin for the night or an afternoon if he was too far from home or too drunk—an overnight tomb.

Hiromi pulled a five-hundred-yen coin out of her wallet and slipped it into the slot to obtain her ticket. Once through the turnstile, she found herself pressed against a throng of people, salarymen mostly. She felt her grasp of something as orderly and concrete as time had vanished, and she couldn't be sure what time it was. In Prius the sun never went down, so there was never any night. The forest may have been a bit dark when players first entered, but only the dense nature of the trees shielded them from the sun.

Three drunk men were laughing at something, punching one another in the arms. One of them noticed Hiromi and motioned to the others to look at her as well. They stopped laughing and moved away from her to join another line forming along the yellow-painted subway platform. Hiromi didn't know what they had seen in her to make them look away. Was what they had witnessed the same thing Kimi saw when she watched her through the bars of her crib tucked in the back of the closet?

As the train approached, the single-file lines that led to each available train-car door tightened like accordions. Hiromi felt a man behind her breathing against her neck, his briefcase jabbing hard into the small of her back, as if it were trying to turn on a switch attached to her spine. The train stopped, and when the doors opened, the lines of passengers streamed into the car. Hiromi barely lifted her feet, but she felt herself carried along toward the center of the car. She grabbed a metal bar attached to a seat so she could steady herself, but two more people came to either side of her, pressing against her chest. She barely could expand her lungs to take a breath. Trying to swallow, she also realized she was almost unbearably parched. How long had it been since she'd had something to drink? To eat?

A schoolgirl stood next to her, texting on a pink flip phone, with a Hello Kitty charm dangling from a metal loop in the corner near the hinge. She wore a plaid, pleated skirt with long white socks that bunched up along her shins. Her backpack, hot pink intermixed with black-and-white stripes, featured Pikuro, the doll in Kimi's crib.

Hiromi wondered about Kimi. It was one of the only times she had thought of her without the child actually being in front of her in what felt like days, maybe a week. Without Anima now, she felt as if there were more space inside her to fit Kimi—Kimi, with her little Pikuro doll that watched over her because Hiromi and Takahiko could not. Wasn't that all right? What else did she really need besides her toy, this character, that bottle? Hiromi was sure there'd been formula in it—a white vanilla-tasting powder that came in large tin canisters she got from the grocery near their building. But then she remembered the formula had run out, and neither of them had gotten more, and how long could you simply add more water to fill up the bottle before it was just water? The train stopped, and she fell out into Sugamo station and went down more stairs, farther underground, to switch to the Mita line, which would take her to the station at Motohasunuma and then home.

The Mita line wasn't as crowded as the Yamanote, but the harsh lighting inside the train made Hiromi feel exposed. She looked down at the tan jumpsuit, the one she always wore, and noticed various stains on the pant legs. Under the arms the fabric had become discolored and rough. Her reflection in the train-car window shocked her; her face was gaunt, her cheeks sunken. Her hair was ragged and oily. She put her hand up to her mouth to hide a gasp. After five stops, she arrived at Motohasunuma station.

It was raining, and the steps that weren't covered by the awning leading out of the station were wet and slippery. Hiromi grabbed the handrail and pulled herself up the steps two, three at a time. When she hit the sidewalk, a rumbling of thunder in the distance propelled her along the way. She remembered how scared of the thunder she had been as a child in the small fishing village in Kunisaki Prefecture, where she had lived with her grandmother; she'd hide under her bed as it crashed down. *Is Kimi afraid?* she wondered. How could she be afraid? Hiromi didn't know. She knew nothing about Kimi.

Her stride had become faster, then morphed into a sprint. She bolted down the sidewalk, sloshing through puddles on the ground, avoiding placards set up along the sidewalk to promote dinner specials at the noodle shops along the street. Then she heard the screaming again; it wasn't as high-pitched as in her dream, but a deep, burning moan that cut through the sound of the taxis rushing down the street. It was right beside her, in her ears, in her head. Hiromi looked to either side, but no one was there, so she ran faster to escape it but she could still hear it. When she dashed past a wall with a rectangular mirror reflecting the passing traffic, she saw her hair plastered across her forehead and her mouth wide open. She was the one who was screaming.

Hiromi ran up the stairs to the second level of their complex and fumbled through her pockets to retrieve her keys, but they fell from her fingers when she brought them up to the locked door. Snatching them up quickly, she finally opened the door, and the wind and the rain sucked it shut behind her like the crash of the gate at the station. She crept through the dark room, feeling along the wall by the pink light of the pachinko parlor across the street. A faint jingling noise whispered to her through a crack in the window that sounded like a faraway jackpot, men making fortunes on the other side of the street. She thrust her hands in front of her until she felt the molding around the closet door. She approached Kimi's crib. It was silent. She reached inside and grabbed one of Kimi's tiny arms.

Verisimilitude

DEIRDRE CROSSED OUT THE SENTENCE several times, stabbing her pen through the pages behind it as if she could gut the very words out of existence:

> Even in her best of moods, Molly had always found it hard to work up the enthusiasm that seemed to be required of her to give good oral sex and with no arms now, she was clearly at a logistical disadvantage as well.

Two hours before, when she'd first written the sentence down, right after coming home from Jim's house following a marathon of sexual calisthenics while his wife was in Burlington getting chemotherapy, she had thought it was some good, clear prose. Ironic, without being sarcastic (a known crutch of hers). A touch of her trademark humor without her outright laughing at the character. Empathy: a quality she'd been accused of lacking in the past.

She even liked what the sentence said about her main character, Molly, a recent double-arm amputee, depressed, and near suicidal. A woman being given a second chance at love with a fellow patient in a remote recovery center in the Catskills. Deirdre's impulse had been to grant Molly more agency in her life right at the moment it seemed she had lost all control. The woman, after all, had no arms: there were literally hundreds of ways in which a writer could push her through the world.

But when she read the sentence again, this time with a more critical eye, the entire conceit of the story seemed up for debate. Who was Molly *before* the accident? Was she even someone who wanted to give blowjobs? What did her willingness, her eagerness even, to give them say about her as a character? As a person? As a *woman*?

These were questions that Raquel, another professor in the creative writing department at Middlebury College, had raised with Deirdre while fleshing out the story with her over coffee a couple of weeks before. Raquel's albino-looking daughter, Starla, had been crawling underneath the wicker table at the café in Frog Hollow like a monkey, grabbing hold of Deirdre's ankles with a vice-like grip she'd found frightening coming from such a small child.

"Why exactly is Molly so enamored of this man? Shouldn't she be more focused on her own recovery? I mean, where is *Molly* in this story?" Raquel had asked.

Deirdre felt annoyed having to answer to a colleague, not that Raquel had even left an appropriate space after any of her questions for her *to* provide an answer. She'd simply rattled them off as Deirdre imagined she must do in her own workshops, with a sort of rhetorical flourish Deirdre would feel pompous and fake if she were to attempt it in her own classroom.

But, really, what favors *was* she doing for herself, giving her reader the image of an armless woman giving a blowjob—in sterile, mesh, standard-issue hospital scrubs no less—to a man with only half a face, the beige ligaments that crisscrossed his cheekbones in a horror-show fashion that in no way could be called human?

"And, honestly, Deirdre..." Raquel had trailed off.

"What?"

"Haven't you kind of written this story before?"

Deirdre ripped the page off of her legal pad and threw it in the trash can by her desk.

These were mistakes she would've chided her own students for making: oversexualizing characters for shock value; setting scenes in remote places she'd never visited or even researched and, therefore, had zero authority in describing; giving in to what she often called in her class the "last chance for happiness" impulse, a trope where a character down on their luck encounters the one thing or person that will save them. It was all just so trite. Raquel was unfortunately right: it was also only a cheap variation on a story she'd definitely already written.

When the college had hired her as a visiting professor at the tail end of the summer, this was not the kind of paint-by-numbers fiction for which she had been known. In fact, only four years before, she had been singled out by *The New Yorker* as one of their "20 Under 40" writers based almost solely on a short story she had published in *The Atlantic Monthly* entitled "My Sometimes Sister." The main character of the story was a paraplegic woman living in the 1970s confined to a remote country house. She is hopelessly in love with her own brother (from whose viewpoint the story is told), who is her sole caregiver and also the person directly responsible for the accident that caused her condition. It was such a heavy premise, but somehow she had managed to pull it off, mainly because of the affinity she had felt for the woman, paralyzed not only in her own body, but by the fear of the feelings she had for her own sibling. After a tender seduction scene Deirdre had somehow crossed a very precarious tightrope in writing successfully, the sister ends up hitching a ride with a young female farmhand, lighting out for a destination unknown. Andrew Wyeth's "Christina's World" had appeared on the opposite page in the issue. Donna Tartt was overheard at a party stating that the story "could be instantly anthologized." T.C. Boyle sent her a note telling her that it was "canon fodder, the American Canon." One reviewer for *Publishers Weekly* had gone so far as to compare her to Flannery O'Connor, which she thought was a bit generous if not, she had privately acknowledged, close to the mark. Her thesis advisor from grad school told her that she had finally "arrived." When her collection came out, in which "My Sometimes Sister" was prominently positioned as the final story, Michiko Kakutani stated in her *New York Times* review that "Deirdre Kirkendoll manages to elevate her mangled women to near beatific heights, limning entire lives in just a handful of pages. This collection soars."

But now there was always this question of what she was working on now. "What are you working on now, Deirdre?" "How are you going to follow up 'My Sometimes Sister'?" "Can I hear a little bit of your newest piece, Deirdre?" For several weeks, she had deconstructed, rewritten, revised, and obsessed over this new Molly story. She'd replace a verb for another here, switch pronouns there, eliminate the passive voice, then suddenly decide that it brought just the right tone and needed to be reinstated. And those pages, now marked up in red and pink ink like a weave of never-ending capillaries running through a heart on life support didn't qualify her for even the position she had at Middlebury. It wasn't just a writer's block; it was a writer's paralysis.

Deirdre looked at her clock radio. It was almost past three. She'd be late to meet her thesis advisee, Ian, if she didn't hurry. After leaving Jim's house, she'd been so driven to write that she hadn't even taken the time to shower.

She looked at the crumpled page in the trash can. The curling edges of the rest of the Molly story sat on her desk underneath a paperweight Jim had given her after offering her the visiting professorship. It was a mermaid perched on a rock in shiny pewter, her cold vacant eyes staring off into the distance at some sailor she imagined would rescue her from the confines of the sea. Or whom she might drag down to his watery death with song.

Although she hadn't thought much of the paperweight, she felt it looking at her now with judging eyes. It had been enclosed with the college's official offer letter to join the staff of the creative writing department as a visiting "writer-in-residence." She had packed the mermaid paperweight alongside her dog-eared copies of *Beloved* and *Bad Behavior*, nestling it in a spot near the corner of one of her many boxes of books.

At the fall faculty mixer, when she'd had more time to observe Jim in action, his intentions towards her felt more dangerously obvious. She had arrived early and parked her beat-up Le Car next to a couple of similarly used vehicles in a turnaround at the foot of the large hill upon which his house stood, an old Victorian that had once housed part of the women's college. Once inside, she noticed that only a few professors were there, including Raquel who she'd met briefly when Raquel had popped into her small office down the hall. Raquel was wearing a silk blouse that revealed a large motherly bosom and was downing what looked to Deirdre like her second or possibly third drink judging from the splotchy flush that spotted her exposed chest.

No one else had thought to bring children, yet there was Raquel's small daughter, Starla, running around in circles, darting through the groups of conversational hives that had begun to formulate around an area of the kitchen that had been fashioned into a makeshift bar. Card tables set up in the living room held an array of New England-style appetizers. Deirdre quickly accepted a cocktail from one of the students, Ian, an ice hockey player who was studying American Literature and creative writing on a hockey scholarship. A sweet, bland, and bovine-looking girl with one eye that seemed larger than the other was also serving at the party.

"They're...Vermonters," Raquel said, nodding towards Ian and his girlfriend who were both wearing white button-down shirts and black pants, passing around drinks and working the bar. Deirdre would say that the girl was improperly matched with the strapping Ian.

"He's from Montpelier and she's from Barre," Raquel continued. "Even in a school this good, there's a certain hierarchy. The Vermonters think they have to try harder than the kids from out of state. To prove themselves."

"Deirdre, I'm glad you could make it," Jim said as he came over to the two women. He wore a vest over his flannel shirt, reminding Deirdre of her middle school woodshop teacher. "I hope you're meeting people." His eyes lingered on her chest.

"Yes, I am. I've mostly been chatting with Raquel here," she answered.

"Excuse me, please. I see Starla has gotten into your bookshelf again!" Raquel said.

As she hurried over to her daughter, Deirdre could see the little girl was already paging through *The Collected Works of Dorothy Parker* before she then tossed it into a pile of other books. It looked like she was planning to burn them all in a toddler bonfire.

"I've said this to you already, Deirdre, but it really does bear repeating. I was enraptured by 'My Sometimes Sister.' There was a certain…hunger you captured so magnificently. I would venture to say it's one of the more important stories to have come out in the last decade. And it almost single-handedly put you on *our* radar." Jim took another sip from his drink.

"Thank you, Professor McNulty."

"Jim. Please. Call me Jim."

"Jim."

"Tell me. What are you working on at the moment?"

And there it was, Deirdre thought. The Question.

"A new piece, something I've been thinking about for a while."

"Well, I hope you end up sharing it at the faculty reading later this semester," he said, placing his hand on the small of her back. "If I had rested on the laurels of that first Skipper book, I would never have been shortlisted for the PEN/Faulkner for *Skipper at Sea*, now would I have?"

As the evening progressed, Deirdre kept noticing a pale woman in a silk head-scarf who kind of floated along the periphery of
the groups of professors. She'd be listening in on whatever story
was being told and then, if there was a punch line or a clever quip,
she'd look to Jim's reaction before offering a muted facsimile.

"That's Jim's wife," Raquel whispered in her ear as if she were a
stage manager, darting from the wings as if to impart some crucial knowledge to a leading lady suddenly stricken with amnesia.
"She has breast cancer. Already a double mastectomy and now
chemo. Poor thing. She's not even fifty yet. It's just awful."

She could see Jim laughing, surrounded by a group of professors. He leaned his head back to let out a bellow, the sparse beard
covering half of his neck. When he took a sip from his drink, he
caught Deirdre's eye from across the room and smiled at her.

"What's her name? The wife?" Deirdre asked Raquel.

"Nan."

Deirdre thought Nan looked like a ghost, like half a woman
in her flat shift dress, wandering in and out of rooms, quietly
haunting the guests. Not a thing to say, really, just a woman hov-
ering at the edges of conversations. She was the physical embodi-
ment of those brief bursts of cold air that sometimes appear out
of nowhere in these old New England houses and then, just as
quickly, are gone.

"Well, when is it?" Raquel asked her. She realized that she had
completely checked out of what Raquel was saying, so utterly
transfixed was she by Nan's ghostliness.

"When is what?" she asked, switching her plate of food to the
other hand so that she could take a quick sip of wine.

"Your deadline for the short story you were working on? I
heard you mention something about it earlier."

"Oh, well, the editor wanted it sometime before Thanksgiving.
I'm not really worrying about it at the moment," she said, trying
to deflect Raquel's attention. She was not one of those writers
who can't get enough talking about their own work at cocktail

parties. She hated those kinds of people. No one cares. Seriously, no one. Although, she was the first to admit that she naturally liked people more if they complimented her on her writing.

"To be directly approached though to submit, that's pretty fantastic. No pressure, I hope," said Raquel.

"No pressure," Deirdre said, turning her attention back to tracking Nan, who had disappeared once again, perhaps into the kitchen to retrieve another plate of hors d'oeuvres.

"I mean, I'm trying my hand at fiction for the first time and I've already landed a book deal based on a couple chapters, one of which was published in *The New Yorker*. You never can tell who's getting what out there among us all," Raquel said. Deirdre was baffled as to how this related at all to what they had been speaking about. It was a ham-handed segue. It was amazing how Raquel was able to bring conversations back around to herself with such ease. "After you're published in *The New Yorker*, well, no one really gives a shit about any of the other piddling little journals you were in before that," Raquel said. "Being published in *The New Yorker* is like when Jesus was crucified: there is only before and after the event."

"Yes, well, I'm sure it's great," Deirdre answered, half-heartedly. Until she'd actually read any of Raquel's work, she'd assume it was as simple and boring as Raquel herself. Raquel regularly spoke to people about her first book—a non-fiction exposé that had become a moderate *New York Times* bestseller for a few weeks—in this way, as if they'd already read it and were now poised and ready to discuss it with the author.

Raquel embodied everything Deirdre truly loathed about fellow writers: the narcissistic belief that they were writing anything that hadn't already been written, the laborious self-promotion that now seemed to go with being surrounded by others who practice the same craft, the constant one-upmanship, and need to find fault. The joke was really on her though—no one took her seriously. Even her own daughter, as young as she was, seemed to always be looking at her with suspicious eyes and an inimitable scowl, the knowledge of which Deirdre secretly found thrilling.

After that faculty party, Deirdre began running into Jim around campus with an alarming frequency. He took her out to lunch at the Crest Room on campus, introduced her to professors in other departments and offered to read anything that she was working on. Even though she had very little to show him, she appreciated the offer. The affair that commenced soon afterwards wasn't just about getting closer to Nan, not at first. Nan came later.

The first time that Deirdre and Jim had sex in his office, she hadn't really thought much of it at all. She'd focused on the books on his bookshelf, the large Brown University pennant he had hanging over his desk, the first edition collection of his "Skipper" series which sat on display on a mantle over an unused fireplace like a shrine. He was definitely on the larger side, but had a thick penis which Deirdre would always be the first to say mattered much more than most women let on.

There was a picture of Nan on the mantelpiece as well. Deirdre noticed it when she'd first been in the office, but had only made the connection that it was actually Nan once they were in the middle of sex. The woman in the photograph could have been Nan's younger, more buxom sister, the difference between the two of them was that stark. As they were getting dressed, Deirdre asked about her lover's spouse.

"Do you have sex with your wife anymore?" she asked.

"No. I'm not attracted to her. And I doubt she'd want to anyway," he said.

"All women need love. Even the sick ones."

"I wouldn't know how to love her, in that way, anymore. I don't think I'd even be able to get aroused. I used to love my wife's breasts. I'm a tits guy."

She could see the story evolving almost instantly. But she did away with missing breasts and turned them into missing arms.

She wanted more, though. She needed to be as close to Nan as she could get. She wanted the authentic Nan, missing limbs and all. There was something so much more gruesome about the image of her this way. Like she was a bowling pin that one could knock over. Deirdre was reminded of Barbies in the basement of her friend Janice's house growing up and how many of the dolls had their arms missing. But they'd still dress them up and make-believe they were going to a ball, waddling about like little Oscars.

"Can a woman with cancer still come? Even with all the chemotherapy?" she asked.

DEIRDRE MADE HER WAY PAST Voter Hall, the computer center, and then shuffled along the walkway that led to Monroe Hall where her office was located. A cast-iron statue of a dog catching a Frisbee in its mouth in mid-air stood several feet from the path. Legend had it that the Frisbee had been invented at Middlebury. Of course they'd try to claim credit for that; as if owning Robert Frost weren't enough, she thought.

Ian was waiting outside her office when she finally made her way up the three flights of stairs.

"Have you been waiting long?"

"No. I just got here."

"Good. Come on inside," she said as she held the door open for him. She'd read several of the stories that made up his thesis throughout the semester. A couple of them were quite good. Maybe in need of a little bit of polish, but for an undergraduate they were intriguing enough for her to want to read more.

"I've been working on a new story that's kind of a departure for me. I was hoping to get your input so I could begin tinkering with it for the collection," said Ian pulling out a white folder from his knapsack.

"Tell me about it," she said.

He told her about a laundromat in his hometown that used to be a department store and how it had turned into a meeting place for the women of Montpelier. The display window of the store was now the waiting room. There was a girl Ian had seen sitting in there smoking a cigarette and flipping through a magazine one day when he'd been walking by. She was about the same age as him, but was unkempt and "darty" (he liked the word even if he didn't think it was one), her eyes never really on the magazine and always shifting about like she was looking for someone. She had been wearing a hoodie and tight black pants, hair streaked in several different shades of blonde like she couldn't decide which kind of a blonde she thought she should be. She'd been sitting in that waiting room like a chipped mannequin left over from the days when the laundromat had still been a department store. She was the kind of mannequin that was too scuffed up to use anymore and is sent to the back of the store before being tossed into the garbage. He said that just watching her, the entire story had fallen into place. She was a teen runaway, a prostitute. At the laundromat, she crossed paths with a cleaning woman in town who had her own sad, pathetic story. The two began seeing each other romantically.

"I used to walk by that laundromat everyday on my way to the gym, since it's near the Grand Union where my mom shops. I never gave it much thought, but when I saw Mary sitting there— that's what I started calling her to myself, Mary—I couldn't stop thinking about her. The story just began to evolve from there."

As he described the story to her, Deirdre couldn't help but be drawn into it through the authenticity of his voice, the unaffected way he had of describing this woman, her makeshift dwelling, the incredible richness of this laundromat. She usually found stories based on someone's hometown to be painfully derivative and uninspiring. Stop trying to make me care about Smalltown USA and the simple people who live there. She remembered thinking this when she'd read one MFA application after another at Boston University for a few months a couple years ago, a short-term gig she'd been coaxed into by one of her old professors. Each story came with so much built-in esoteric baggage: that special road we all used to drive down, the high school parking lot where we got our cheap thrills and dropped acid for the first time together, those woods where Mr. So-and-So kept his fighting dogs that Stevie Such-and-Such went and freed once (the last page of a student's story who she'd actually ended up recommending for the program because she just couldn't reject them all). It was always a good impulse to write about what you know, but so often she felt like that statement needed the addendum of "but make sure that others will fucking care."

He handed her the folder. "I'm sorry that I won't be at your reading next week. I have an away game that night at Amherst."

"I'll be sure to read this and get back to you with comments, Ian."

"Thanks, Deirdre."

She reached out her hand to accept his new story about the laundromat, "Because We Care."

> Women lived in there.
> They didn't just clean clothes there; they cleaned their souls there. They escaped their tired, dark dens cracked with ceiling, molded with walls. The women set up shop. They pinochled and trashy paperbacked. They crocheted while spitting venomously at daytime's villainesses—those women they loved to hate. They traded miseries and detergent powder. If it weren't for the Laundromat, they would be left alone with their sad-shellacked stories. At least in here, the dirty laundry was visible.
> Even half past seven was early enough for the women to already have moved in for the day. Those who'd been lurking around during the dark hours of the morning slowly filtered out. They were moving onto darker places for the coming of day. Mary ushered into the wide, open space where walls of rotating windows

cleaned the laundry of the week. She was surrounded
by all sorts of women in all stages of disorder. And she
was one of them.

It had once been a department store. Old racks
jutted out of the walls, above the dryers illuminated
by fluorescent lights, yet offered no merchandise. Only
hair bands, watches to tell how long the cycles, a
child's balloon. Once a leash. Wood-paneled awnings
fixed with bare bulbs lit the areas underneath the
dryers, like track lighting on a plane, only pointing
deeper into the place. Homeless wired pushcarts lined
in plaid and filled with old clothes stood against the
aisles like display bins of marked-down goods. Fake
potted plants that were perched upon mannequin
pedestals separated back-to-back washers. The women
peered at each other through a Formica jungle. Clothes
left behind littered the floor underneath the folding
counters. Balls of lint and dust bunnies hid behind
them for cover.

A coin-operated machine dispensing Laundry Aids
stood against a wall. *Move selector lever under desired
brand. Press handle.* There were change machines.

Some people called it the *Wash-Dry & Fold*. Others
simply called it the Laundromat.

*Because We Care...We Ask You Not to Put your
Children in the Carts or on the Folding Tables. Thank
you.* Next to the sign a woman had her baby in a cart.
It looked like she might be shopping for children on
sale.

The front of the Laundromat had once been a
glassed-in showcase for the fashionable wares of
its department store era. It now functioned as a
vitreous cage littered with month-old circulars, beauty
magazines, and the stale, dried butts of the chain-
smoking mothers. Slowly rotating fans hovered over
the smoke clouds, moving them nowhere. Mary sat in
a black metal chair, facing the passers-by, with one
leg stuck underneath her. She was a chipped and
discarded mannequin, unfit for the display of any new
merchandise.

Her hair was greasy from not showering the night before—a long string of nights before—but the blonde part outweighed her dark roots. Blondes can always pull off a bad hair day, she thought. Her hair was tied in the back by a pink ribbon she'd found on the floor, something someone had probably used once for gift wrapping. She wore stonewashed jeans and a knee-length white pullover that, despite her sitting in the middle of a Laundromat, was unwashed. She actually believed she could solicit this way.

After reading the first couple of pages, Deirdre immediately latched onto several images and phrases. The entire opening section, in fact, seemed to evoke so much more than just one singular downtrodden character's sadness. She felt like Ian had reached deeper to capture the small, dry death of small-town New England life in all its utter starkness and chill. She admired how the story was, at once a throwback to a simpler time, yet also painfully relevant in a way, like everyone inside of his fabled laundromat. He made everything immediate and important. She appreciated his inventive use of nouns as action verbs (pinochle, trashy paperback). It displayed a boldness with language she liked to reward. There were still certainly revisions to be done (he had used the word "usher" without a direct object which the transitive verb required), but for a first draft from an underclassman, this showed more promise than she'd seen in a long time. There was even something about it that made her think of her own work.

Ian's women seemed damaged in a far less obvious way than Deirdre's were. Deirdre had always been drawn to visibly broken women as characters in her stories: women with missing limbs, strange body parts, preternaturally ugly faces. She remembered watching *Dead Ringers* in college and being enthralled by the tortuous—downright medieval—gynecological instruments Jeremy Irons used on Geneviève Bujold's freakishly distorted vagina in the film. The friends she had gone to the film with at the time had claimed that David Cronenberg, the director, was a misogynist, a pig—claims that Deirdre found to be baseless and somewhat alarmist.

She came home that night thinking how there was something inherently beautiful about the calm serenity lying beneath the most tortured of bodies. She imagined the possibility of transcending trauma, of positioning oneself above the mangled limbs and the twisted vaginas to actually see the full and complete woman behind them—imperfection worn on the outside as a kind of sad mask for the calm, imperceptible beauty underneath the skin. In a way, these women got to wear on the outside what Deirdre considered her own internal deficiencies, deeply hidden, exposed only briefly on the page under the guise of fiction, if ever exposed at all.

Years later after college, while driving down I-95 on her way from New York back to Boston University, Deirdre had caught an unforgettable glimpse of a woman who had flown through the passenger-side windshield of a car involved in a three-car pileup. Before the car had been cleared off the road, or at least hidden from rubberneckers and other looky-lo's, she'd been able to see that the woman's head had gone through the glass, but had been stopped at the base of the neck, so that she appeared almost as a ceremonial bust. Her head was turned slightly toward traffic and her blonde hair tuffeted around her. Deirdre had been too far away to see any blood, so that she was able to almost immediately remove herself from the gruesome nature of the tragedy to see the dead woman as someone whose beauty had been permanently arrested, captured in the crumpled blanket of cracked glass surrounding her like a large royal robe.

IT WAS A TUESDAY AND she was finished with her morning classes. She got into her Le Car and drove past several inns and small shops along Main Street that led out of town. She was looking around, wary of who might be walking down the sidewalks. A college town is like a regular small town, only more striated. Not only did everyone want to know everyone else's business, they were immediately distrustful of interlopers and transients. She heard a professor who'd lived there for over two decades still being referred to as "that woman from Atlanta" as if one's ancestors had to have been shuttled directly from the Mayflower to the town square four hundred years ago to ever be fully accepted. Deirdre didn't feel the need to try and ingratiate herself with the townspeople. She viewed them much like background, a great sea of faces that made up her current milieu. They were secondary characters not worth much more than a passing hello.

Deirdre didn't want to see anyone while she was making her way out of town for the afternoon. Not any of her students, not Jim or his ghostly wife. Or nosy Raquel. Or Ian, especially not Ian.

She decided on Route 7 through Burlington and then the straight line down Interstate-189 into Barre-Montpelier, a straight shot past the miles of farmland, cows and red barns that gave subject to Vermont postcards. When she finally rolled into town about an hour later, she passed Montpelier High School and then made a left-hand turn at the bridge and then a right onto State Street, a long, wide avenue that flowed right into the small town, America's tiniest capital city. She figured if she continued down State Street, she'd eventually hit a Main Street (wasn't this just the kind of town for a State and Main intersection?), and then once she could find the Grand Union where Ian's mother shopped, the laundromat couldn't be too far away. Ian didn't have the copyright on laundromats. He didn't own them in fiction. And he didn't own Montpelier either. Or this woman Mary, if she was still lurking around.

Main Street was empty, except for a few slow-moving vehicles and a school bus up ahead that had stopped to pick up a child from a gray clapboard house. As Deirdre continued along past an Irish bar, what looked like the town hall, and then a firehouse on her right she spotted the Grand Union. There were several spaces open in the parking lot, so she pulled the Le Car into one of them and began walking around the block.

She saw it almost instantly, catty-corner to Main Street on a street with no name. The words "Wash-Dry & Fold" blinked in blue neon on what looked like a Hollywood marquee. It was almost exactly as Ian had described, even paling in comparison to what he'd written, actually. He'd given it this discarded, ominous quality that she knew must've reflected the way he felt about the town.

As she got closer, she could see the makeshift waiting room he had described so evocatively. Fashioned out of what was once the display window of the department store, the women who sat there were these kind of hideous versions of real people, frozen in a way. They reminded her of the artist Duane Hanson, who did those life-size, three-dimensional model installations of regular people doing mundane things. The piece that had stuck out to her when she'd seen it at MoMA was a woman pushing a shopping cart filled with 1970s era products, wearing a floral muumuu, her hair in rollers. The artist had gone so far as to paint her teeth as if they were stained with coffee and nicotine, a perfect scowl on her face. Those were the women sitting in there. Like something out of a movie, she thought. What fabulously hideous women. She walked inside, feeling for the small notebook and pen in her back pocket.

She began to imagine that one of the women was the proprietress of the Laundromat. A gassy old crone who, in her younger years, had modeled fashions there, back when the space had still been a department store and before the town had suffered from the brain drain that seemed to have afflicted many sections of the state. They'd had normal mannequins, but she had marketed herself as a kind of living mannequin, one who would stand in a freeze position in the display window and then walk around the store to demonstrate how the clothing moved through the space.

Her name was Undine. Deirdre sat down in the waiting room, just like Ian's character Mary, and began to write.

When she finally stopped, she looked up and it was already dark. She wasn't sure how long she'd been there. The washers around her were all rumbling loudly. Several of them were the older models that shuddered in place from side to side like angry machines that have come alive having detaching themselves from the wall. There was a curious smell of floral laundry sheets mixed with cigarette smoke that lingered in the air and the musty scent of grimy flooring and old, dirty clothes. Just as Ian had described in his story, another set of women (along with a couple men, it looked like) had moved into the laundromat to populate a kind of night shift. Under the fluorescent lighting, she could see that several of them had that dark, haunted look like they were unemployed or indigent. Or simply depressed. Deirdre got up, closed her notebook, and left.

THE PROFESSORS WERE SEATED AT a long table in front of the amassed group of students for the faculty reading. Jim read first from one of his Skipper books (*Skipper's Spare*, the third book in the series that Deirdre had mistakenly read first while in college). He had asked all the professors to read new work for the faculty reading, so Deirdre found it surprising that he himself was reading from a book that had been published over twenty years ago. There had even been a film made condensing the first two of the Skipper books, bringing the character to a whole legion of new audiences. He had already been recognized by some of the greatest contemporary writers as one of their own and had the awards on his wall and mantle to prove it. Yet Deirdre felt sad thinking of him resting on the laurels of these ridiculous Skipper books. She realized that he too might be blocked, without even knowing it himself.

While he was reading, she noticed that Nan was sitting in the back of the room. She was wearing a silk turban and a knit shawl and looked rather glamorous for the small-time event. While Jim was reading, she nodded and pursed her lips at several points. There wasn't anyone in the room who knew him as well as Nan did, Deirdre thought. Who knew Skipper. She remembered that in *Skipper's Spare*, the main character Skipper Muldoon has an affair with the wife of a couple with whom he and his wife play tennis. Everything about writers is an endless act of recycling.

Raquel read from a non-fiction piece she'd written about a recent trip she had taken with her husband to Cambodia, researching the sex-slave industry for a book she was writing on the subject. She had spoken about it with Deirdre non-stop, to the point where Deirdre felt like she had not only read the entire book already, but had also suffered through the writing of it as well. Raquel's husband sat in the back of the room holding a squirming Starla, who was trying to wriggle her way out of his arms, exposing pink panties underneath her skirt, decorated with watermelons.

"And now, I'd like to introduce our newest member to the department. I've admired her from afar for a few years now since I read her story in *The Atlantic Monthly*, 'My Sometimes Sister.' Since then, I've had the deep pleasure of getting to know the woman behind those beautiful words. Please put your hands together for a writer who adds a touch of literary allure to this fine institution—Ms. Deirdre Kirkendoll." Jim stepped aside. The audience clapped. She looked up.

She opened the folder she had taken up with her to the table along with a bottle of water. Inside were the handwritten sheets of the Molly story, rescued from the trash can, the armless woman in the Catskills who, last time Deirdre had left her, had her lips wrapped around the flaccid member of a man who suffered a mortar attack in Baghdad and had had half his face blown off. It certainly wasn't something she was going to scrap entirely. She hated just throwing away work because of a moment of worthlessness. She looked over at Raquel who'd just received a huge round of applause for her Cambodia piece. Deirdre had to admit it actually sounded quite intriguing and almost prematurely polished in a way she felt could not have been a first draft. That image she left the audience with of the young twelve-year-old girl helping other children in the orphanage even though she was missing an eye that her pimp had stabbed out when she cried as, day after day, men had stood in a line to rape her. What a global market to have cornered, this genre. Deirdre suddenly hated her for it.

She looked out into the audience at the eager looks on the students' faces. Some of them hopeful and interested, looking up to her, not just at her. She recognized several students from her freshman creative writing workshop and was glad that they had come to hear her. Being the youngest professor there, she liked to think they viewed her almost like a friend, rather than a superior who could fail them. She felt that she had her finger on the pulse of what her generation was writing about. It was something they must've admired about her.

"The Last Living Mannequin" peeked out from under the pages of her other story. Even though it usually took her weeks to actually finish a story, she'd been able to write it in less than ten days and she thought it now needed only minimal editing. It was, in her mind, the best piece she had written in years. Maybe even since "My Sometimes Sister." Undine might certainly be viewed as another one of her "mangled women." But, for the first time, Deirdre had envisioned one of her characters as an actual real person, in the flesh. She had seen this woman in that Laundromat. She knew her entire backstory from just a single look. She thought about Undine constantly. That was why she had accelerated her writing of her story, because she couldn't bear the thought of leaving her in any precarious situation, dangling at the end of her rope in that small town and waiting for Deirdre to come rescue her. It was a feeling she'd never had before. Accountability to character. It was exhilarating.

So she began reading. It wasn't just a reading; it was a dramatic interpretation. She looked around the room and people seemed transfixed by her. Her students were poised literally on the edges of their seats, watching her, hanging on every word. The Laundromat came alive right in front of her, it seemed. She could feel it again just from the words on the page. Could smell it even. And she could tell that they could see it, too. But there was a young woman who was not smiling, not perched on the edge of her seat. In fact, she was slunk back in her chair, scowling at Deirdre it looked like. Who was she? Deirdre kept reading, and then she realized who the girl was. She hadn't seen her since the fall mixer and, for her blandness and unremarkability, had all but forgotten she existed. She was Ian's plain girlfriend and she was making her way out of the room at a clip that was making the other students take notice, climbing over them the way she had to in order to get out of the corner of the row. Deirdre watched her make her way to the exit door and then heard the crash of it as it closed behind her. Raquel nodded at her animatedly as if to say, "Go on."

IAN WAS WAITING OUTSIDE HER office when she arrived the following Monday morning. He had startled her when she'd reached the top of the stairs and had come closer towards her.

"I hope you don't mind me being here, Deirdre," he said to her in a tone that sounded normal, although she was unsure. Everything had taken on a possibility of malevolence. Even she herself was capable of horrible things, she thought.

"No, no, not at all. Please, come in."

She hadn't really expected to get away with it, but she wasn't aware that he'd act so quickly and so, well, decisively given what his girlfriend must've shared with him. Again, though, what lines had she really crossed? There were a couple shared phrases between their two stories, but how else would you describe a bunch of dryers in a wall other than "a wall of windows like on a steamer ship"? It wasn't completely impossible that the two of them might have arrived at a similar turn of phrase.

"So, what did you think of my story?" he asked.

"What?"

"My story, 'Because We Care.' I thought you could go over some of the critique you might've had on it."

"I've made some notes, of course, on the copy you gave me." She began searching through her knapsack

"Great, Deirdre. Hey, I was also wondering if you wouldn't mind writing a recommendation for me. For graduate school. I've decided to pursue an MFA in creative writing. I'm sure a good word from a published writer would go a long way." The tone of his voice. There was something about it that was different.

"Yes, Ian. Of course. I would love to. You're incredibly talented."

"You think so." It wasn't a question.

Later that afternoon, while picking up a sub at Noonie's, the sandwich shop in the Marble Works, Deirdre spied Nan getting out of her car. Nan was wearing a wig she must've worn when she went out in public without a scarf. It was too curly and in a garish reddish color that didn't match her skin tone. In fact, coupled with an ill-fitting navy blue overcoat, it made her look like she was disguised in order to rob a bank. Deirdre saw her tired eyes, the attempt at a quick dusting of blush over her sunken cheeks. Before she was able to duck away back into the sandwich shop, Nan spotted her and her mouth opened just a little bit, involuntarily perhaps, to say something to Deirdre. Instead of speaking though, her eyes narrowed and she dropped her purse to her side, her arms slapping against her thighs. "Well, what? What do you have to say for yourself?" her posture seemed to defiantly state.

So, Deirdre began to approach Nan's car. Nan watched as Deirdre made her way closer. She readjusted her wig and patted down the wrinkles on the sides of her coat.

"I'm not sure that we've ever officially met. I saw you at the faculty party this past fall. I'm Deirdre Kirkendoll," she said extending her hand.

"Yes, I know who you are. You're the one my husband was so excited about. You wrote the story about the crippled girl."

"Yes, that's me." Nan reached into her purse and fished out a tissue to dab at her eyes that had watered a bit.

"I was at your reading the other night. I always go to hear Jim read," Nan said.

"Yes, I saw you," Deirdre said.

"I'm just coming from Burlington and thought that I'd stop for a sandwich. I'm having a strange sort of reaction to some of the medication I'm on. Excuse me." She briefly rubbed the palm of her right hand in a circular motion over chest and made like she was about to open the car door.

"What did you think? Of the reading?"

"It was fine," she answered, curtly.

"Just fine?" Deirdre asked.

Nan paused, her hand on the door handle of the car. "There've been several young professors who've passed through this town. Some of them lasted and became older professors. Some even had modest successes with their novels. Jim has mentored several of them. And, yes, of course, small bits of the town or the college and the people at the college have appeared on the pages in some, usually hastily disguised, fashion." She paused to look down, but then looked right at Deirdre in the eyes.

"There is life lived here. There was life lived here before you got here and there will be life lived here after you've gone. We are not 'material' for you," Nan said.

"I don't think I know what you're talking about," Deirdre said.

"My husband left one of your stories in his office at home and I read it. The woman with no arms? You writers—you're all such vultures. My husband especially. You know that Jim puts me in his novels. He didn't even bother to really change my name. The character's name is 'Nancy.' She's the supposedly clueless wife who gets cheated on by her husband, Skipper, that everyone thinks is such a staple of contemporary fiction. The difference between you and my husband is that he's used up and he knows it. You don't. You think you're writing something new? You're not. You've got one story. You're just writing it over and over and over again. You're used up and you don't even know it."

"If this is because Jim and I—" Deirdre began.

"Just stop. Don't even finish that sentence. There's nothing I don't know about, believe me. And I long ago stopped caring." Deirdre snickered and Nan continued. "There was nothing authentic about the story you read the other day. Nothing. Honestly, it didn't even seem like your story. It was cheap. It was impractical. And what's worse, it was boring. You've committed the worst sin a writer can commit: you've bored your reader."

"Who are you to judge me?" Deirdre yelled at her.

Nan opened the door and got inside her car. She started the car and rolled down the window. Then she looked at Deirdre and seemed to decide in that moment that Deirdre was not worth anything further. Deirdre watched as she backed out of the space and pulled out onto the road.

Caravan

THEY CLOSED DOWN THE BARS first. One by one. Captain Jack's, Renegade, Follies, Masters of the Universe, The Lanai, Butterfield's. Even Indigo. That was where we met, after all. On a Saturday night you could find every one of us there. In the beginning they said it was because of an expired liquor license or the violation of some heretofore-unknown noise ordinance or a zoning law or a safety code—reasons that could be explained and supported by law. No one paid any real attention to it. These things happen. If you live in a city, you have to get used to this kind of change, this kind of churn. If you don't, you're fooling yourself and probably should live in the suburbs. Neighborhoods erode overnight. Then new ones pop up in their place. What's in is now out. And vice versa. It's city living.

So we migrated to other bars, ones we might not have been to quite as often for one reason or another but ones where the liquor still flowed and those beautiful men danced with their apple-shaped butts, an electric current running through our veins, like vodka mixed with 5-Hour Energy spiked with adrenaline and a just-short-of-lethal dash of mercury. And it was fun trying out new places.

But soon thereafter, there were only three bars left in the entire city where we could go. Then two of the last three closed down—both wiped out in a single week, as if from a hurricane.

"It's just temporary," we heard at Barstool, the last bar, to which we had retreated.

"We'll just move somewhere else. We always do," another added.

"It'll get better. Besides, I heard Butterfield's is going to reopen at a new location soon. Lines out the door and around the block, just as it always was. Just you wait. Things'll turn around."

It was true. Things had turned around before. There was a time when we hadn't all lived near one another or run our own shops or frequented our own bars. It was something of a luxury that we'd been able to operate in the space so freely at all. It always had gotten better.

So we gathered at Barstool, in droves most nights. We came early enough so we didn't have to wait in line too long. The doormen—muscular guys wearing armbands around their mammoth biceps—clicked little silver instruments in their hands after we showed them our IDs. A woman affixed metal bracelets to our wrists. Huge crowds of men packed into the small, rather cubbyholed, labyrinthine space of an establishment few of us had visited in the past. (There was word, in fact, that it had only just been erected, almost overnight; none of us could corroborate this though, since we'd never been there before.) Its decrepit, tattered awning from its days as a discount furniture emporium crackled ominously on windy nights like whiplashes, dripping on us while we smoked when it rained. The shellac on the titular barstools, applied so hurriedly during their construction, had crystallized into small stalagmites that stuck us through our jeans as we sat on them. There were bartenders at Barstool we'd never seen before, extremely attractive ones, who, behind their capable pouring hands and accommodating eyes, seemed to be judging us. *Counting* us, one said he thought he might've seen one night.

Inside Barstool, the clash of different strata did make for the occasional scuffle—twinks getting knocked around by leather daddies, the druggies and the kinks sneering at the preps and jocks—but we were generally more amiable and tolerant toward one another than we might've been under different circumstances. After all, who else did we have but one another at a time like this?

"At a time like what?" one older man had said, a fossil from a different generation than ours, all yellowing white hair and a tucked-in flannel (in July, no less). "I've never known a time when we had more freedom and choice in life. You can get married now in this city if you want. How dare you be inconvenienced by the closing of a couple of overpriced, vapid watering holes."

His venom took us aback, but we felt a twinge of sympathy for him. Poor thing had probably lost his lover decades ago and been drinking himself into numbness ever since. It was obvious from the wasting away of his cheeks; the hollow, haunted look in his eyes as they bored into us, through us even. It wasn't our fault that we happened to have come of age at a time when guys were more careful about these things, not as risky.

"He's just jealous," we said to one another and ordered another round. "Cheers!"

At the end of that last night, Barstool emptied out into the street. We'd always joked about the way everyone lined themselves up for picking up that one last trick before heading home. Sidewalk Sale. Discounted, sloppy-ass. Everyone was pretty much wasted. The street was so quiet. A long line of yellow school buses was lined up outside the bar. Guys smoking cigarettes laughed at the absurdity of it.

"Are we going on a field trip?" one of them asked no one in particular—a man in a blue-and-gray striped sweater, flouncing from side to side as he tried to stand up straight.

"They're drunk buses is what I heard. So that no one has to drive home drunk."

"But I walked here," someone said.

"Oh, c'mon. They'll keep us safe from bashers." Barstool was, after all, in a sketchy neighborhood. Men had been beaten in its vicinity recently. You could never be too careful.

So we boarded the buses one at a time. It was fun. We felt like we were reliving middle school but now on our own terms. We could sit in the back with the cool kids now. We were the cool kids now.

Once we were packed in, we heard the door close. It sounded different than we remembered from years ago, like a walk-in freezer door shutting, locked from the outside.

Still buzzed, we sang songs and traded gossip. Then one guy said, "Hey, you passed my stop."

The bus driver looked just like the doormen at the bar, and he refused to acknowledge us in the rearview mirror. He kept driving. The air conditioning had been shut off (if it ever had been turned on in the first place, we couldn't remember). The windows were the kind where you have to press down on plastic tabs on either side in order to pull them down. But the tabs were broken off. We looked behind us and saw the grim, unchanging face of another bus driver and the buses behind that, and the ones behind that—a yellow caravan snaking its way through the quiet city where no one else was outside and no one was watching us. It was almost as if we'd never even been there at all.

So we settled back in our seats, suddenly rather silent and tired. It was like the quiet game we used to play in the car with our parents when we were children: the first one to make a sound loses.

Acknowledgments

THIS BOOK HAS MY NAME on the front cover, but so many others had their hands on it at some point along its journey to publication.

THANK YOU:

To the people who first supported several of these stories at the following publications: *Big Lucks*, *Collective Fallout*, *theNewerYork*, *Glitterwolf Magazine*, *Driftwood Press*, *Carbon Culture Review*, *Anak Sastra*, and *Lunch Review*.

To Stephanie Grant, Richard McCann, Elise Levine, and Andrew Holleran—my graduate school mentors at American University. Their guidance during the most formative and important years of my writing career was so invaluable to me as a young writer. Stephanie and Elise, in particular, had a huge hand in this particular collection. I'd like to thank them for letting me take chances but also for reining me in.

To Brett Millier for her mentorship during my undergraduate years at Middlebury College and for her continued support.

To my unofficial cohort for their essential edits, suggestions, and plot-whispering: K Tyler Christensen, Diana Metzger, Diesel Robertson, Kathy Rawson, Jonathan Church, and Emily Voorhees.

To Stephen Zepecki, Patrick Cournoyer, and Charles Lea for their helpful edits.

To the members of the Sophistigay Book Club for reading this book and then discussing it while pretending I wasn't in the room (at my request).

To Adina Silbert and Liz French for their love and support through the years.

To my loving parents, Grover and Maggi Walker, and my sister, Amanda Powell Walker, for their endless support and encouragement.

To Rick Moody and David Foster Wallace. Two of the stories in this collection borrow from the form and structure of two indelible pieces of fiction by these writers. "A Goddess Lying Breathless in Carnage" uses the repetitive form of the prologue of Rick Moody's *Purple America* (1998). "Women of a Certain Age" employs a similar structure to the one David Foster Wallace used in his short story "Death Is Not the End" which is included in his collection, *Brief Interviews with Hideous Men* (2000).

To Alex Jeffers for his editing and to Steve Berman for his guiding hand as well as his patience and commitment to *Read by Strangers*.

About the Author

PHILIP DEAN WALKER holds a B.A. in American Literature from Middlebury College and an M.F.A. in Creative Writing from American University. His first book, *At Danceteria and Other Stories*, was named a *Kirkus Reviews* Best Book of 2017. He lives in Washington, D.C.

philipdeanwalker.com

CPSIA information can be obtained
at www.ICGtesting.com
Printed in the USA
BVOW11s1456300418
514822BV00005B/742/P